She wanted Turner Garrett . . .

. . . and she wanted him now.

His mouth felt wonderful on hers—hot and demanding. His body felt so good against hers—strong and taut.

There were no words between them. There was only the breathtaking experience of two bodies moving as one in perfect harmony, as though they had spent hours in rehearsal. No man had ever excited Jamie like this. Her blood was racing, her heartbeat thundering in her ears. She couldn't seem to get enough of him.

Then it hit her: she was making love with a man whom she knew nothing about. A man who was hiding a secret. Did she have the willpower to resist him . . . ? Did she want to . . . ?

ABOUT THE AUTHOR

Margaret Chittenden is a multitalented author who started writing children's books in 1972. Since then she has published countless books and more than one hundred short stories and articles. When this busy author has the time, she loves to relax at the beach. Margaret and her husband make their home in Washington State.

Books by Margaret Chittenden

HARLEQUIN INTRIGUE
183–THE WAINWRIGHT SECRET

HARLEQUIN SUPERROMANCE
123–LOVE ME TOMORROW
175–TO TOUCH THE MOON
214–CLOSE TO HOME
310–THE MOON GATE
366–UNTIL OCTOBER

HARLEQUIN TEMPTATION
 40–LOVESPELL
156–THE MARRYING KIND

Don't miss any of our special offers. Write to us at the following address for information on our newest releases.

Harlequin Reader Service
901 Fuhrmann Blvd., P.O. Box 1397, Buffalo, NY 14240
Canadian address: P.O. Box 603,
Fort Erie, Ont. L2A 5X3

Shadow of a Doubt

Margaret Chittenden

Harlequin Books

TORONTO • NEW YORK • LONDON
AMSTERDAM • PARIS • SYDNEY • HAMBURG
STOCKHOLM • ATHENS • TOKYO • MILAN
MADRID • WARSAW • BUDAPEST • AUCKLAND

For my good friends, Kathleen and Bruce Wolgemuth, with my thanks for the laughter

Author's note: The views, the flora, the fauna, the food and many of the places depicted in this book can be found in Bermuda, but all of the characters, and the Wallbridge Police Department, exist only in the mind of the author.

Harlequin Intrigue edition published September 1993

ISBN 0-373-22242-4

SHADOW OF A DOUBT

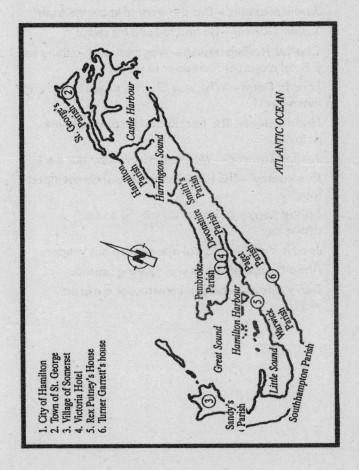

1. City of Hamilton
2. Town of St. George
3. Village of Somerset
4. Victoria Hotel
5. Rex Putney's House
6. Turner Garrett's house

ATLANTIC OCEAN

St. George's Parish
Castle Harbour
Hamilton Parish
Harrington Sound
Smith's Parish
Devonshire Parish
Pembroke Parish
Paget Parish
Hamilton Harbour
Warwick Parish
Great Sound
Little Sound
Southampton Parish
Sandy's Parish

N

CAST OF CHARACTERS

Jamie Maxwell—Did she *want* to know the truth?

Turner Garrett—He had to keep his secret.

Charles Hollingsworth—Was there such a thing as a hotel manager *too* eager to please?

Loretta Dean—Why was Charles's assistant giving him orders?

Linda Belant—The barmaid who said she knew nothing.

Jordan Lathrop—Was he a trustworthy skipper?

Rex Putney—The local philanthropist commanded loyalty.

Bobby Kenyon—He was a witness to the drowning.

Joe Hokins—A tropical diver with a hot temper.

Anna Campbell—She was running scared.

Derry Riley—A bad swimmer . . . or a murder victim?

Chapter One

There was no hint that something terrible was about to happen. The sea breeze wafted through the open casement windows of Bermuda's Tudor Tavern, carrying in the fragrance of the spring flowers blooming outside. Though it was still early in the evening, the sixty or so men and women sitting around the oak tables in the lounge had consumed enough beer and wine to create a convivial atmosphere.

Then someone punched coins into the old jukebox and Bruce Springsteen belted out "Born in the U.S.A.," a song that seemed out of place in such a typical English pub setting. The sudden blast of sound jarred some of the patrons, but most continued their conversations without missing a beat.

A young black waitress, carrying a tray loaded with beer glasses, was the first to see the two men enter the lounge. Both wore trench coats. Both had semiopaque stockings over their heads. The waitress stared blankly at them, thinking how strange they looked, their features flat and unrecognizable, their hair invisible, their ears making odd-shaped bumps at the sides of their heads. Then she saw the guns pointing at her—matte black guns, handguns, two to each man.

The crash of the loaded tray falling to the floor brought every head around. A ripple of paralyzing fear ran through the room as the patrons' eyes followed the woman's fixed gaze. There was a moment's electric silence and then the guns fired and fired again, the two men turning slowly away from each other, so that the bullets seemed to spray into every part of the room. People dived for cover under tables or benches. The bartender disappeared behind the bar as glass exploded all around him. Screams mixed with shouted obscenities as the patrons scrabbled hysterically across the floor. Unfortunately there was nowhere to go.

When the hail of bullets ceased, it was a minute or two before the terrified customers realized it was over. By the time the least cautious among them raised their heads, the two men had vanished. The sobbing of frightened customers, the moans of the injured and "Born in the U.S.A." fading to its final phrases, accompanied the sound of an engine as a vehicle hurtled out of the parking lot and disappeared into the night.

The stunned patrons scrambled to their feet, clasping hands to bloodied faces or legs or grazed arms. The waitress, unhurt, squatting awkwardly, was astonished to find herself scraping together shards of broken glass with a napkin, as though it was important to tidy up right away.

Two men lay on the floor, fairly close to the bar—a black man wearing Bermuda shorts and a short-sleeved shirt, a white man in jeans and a tank top. They didn't move at all.

THE CHIEF SAT with his back to the windows of the cottage. The sun was going down fast and his features were in shadow. As Kyle and his partner reported the shooting, Kyle tried, and failed, to make out the chief's expression. Probably it would have been difficult, anyway— Englishmen seemed able to hide whatever they were thinking, it was one of the things Kyle disliked about them.

"So then we scarpered out of there fast, and I mean fast," Kyle's partner was saying.

"And there were no problems?" the chief asked.

Kyle and his partner exchanged a glance. "Went almost like clockwork," his partner said nervously. Stupid jerk, why couldn't he have said they'd done the job just the way they were supposed to? Which was close enough to the truth.

"Almost?" That was another thing Englishmen could do—make an ordinary word sound full of menace. Kyle shivered. It didn't pay to get on the wrong side of the chief. Witness the two men they'd offed less than an hour ago.

"We were a tad later than planned going in," Kyle said carefully. "Couldn't be helped. And the two suckers waited for us like good little soldiers. I plugged 'em dead center. They're goners—no doubt about that."

"How late were you?" the menacing voice asked.

Kyle muttered a couple of choice words. "Half an hour," his partner admitted.

"Why?"

Kyle took in a breath and let it out. Better if he laid out the scenario himself. "There was this redheaded guy in the parking lot. Taking pictures of the outside of the tavern. Never saw anyone so fired up about taking pictures. Must have used a whole roll of film. Student of architecture, probably. Luckily we saw him before he saw us. We ducked back in the van *muy pronto* and sat there until he took off on his moped."

"You ducked back in the van."

Kyle hated the way the chief repeated his words back to him. It put a whole other spin on them, like Kyle was stupid. "We were halfway across the bloody car park before we saw him," his partner blurted out. "It wasn't a problem, Chief. We were picking up the masks and raincoats *inside*, remember? So what if the bloke did see us, which I'm not saying he did—how's he going to tie us to the shooting? Looked like a tourist, anyway. Had a cap on, something written on it. Probably came off a cruise ship. Day or two, he'll be gone."

"Cheers," Kyle said. "That's what was on the hat. He took it off to put his crash helmet on before he got on the bike, that's how we saw he had red hair." He looked at the chief, who was managing to project disgust without moving a muscle. How the hell did he do that? "He was well out of the parking lot before we made our move."

"Did it occur to either of you Neanderthals that he might have taken a picture of you or the van?"

"Uh-uh. He didn't take a picture of us. We'd have seen him do that."

"And the van?"

Both men squirmed. "Nah," Kyle said.

The chief sighed. He could even make that sound like a threat. "Find him," he said, still without raising his voice.

"Aw, Chief—"

"Find him. Get the film."

When the chief got that snotty tone in his voice there was no arguing with him. "Yes, sir," Kyle and his partner said in unison. "What if he has it on him?" Kyle asked. "What if he catches us getting it?"

Another sigh. The chief leaned back. The meeting was over. "We use our own discretion, right?" Kyle suggested.

There was no answer. *Do what you have to,* Kyle interpreted.

Chapter Two

The young blond Adonis who had accompanied Jamie to the third floor gestured at an open doorway. "That's Inspector Garrett's office, miss."

"Thank you, Sergeant." Though inside she was simmering with fury, Jamie Maxwell managed to keep her voice under control. Glancing into the room, she saw a tall, lean but athletically built man with smooth dark hair taking books from a shelf. He was probably in his mid-thirties, his clean-shaven face somewhat sharp featured. His police uniform was as immaculate as the sergeant's—a short-sleeved blue shirt with epaulets, navy blue Bermuda shorts, knee socks and polished black shoes. His dark tie was very precisely knotted.

Jamie put up both hands to pat down her long, copper-colored hair. Since she'd had the spiral permanent done a month ago her hair had developed a wild life of its own.

Apparently not noticing he had visitors, the inspector squatted to put the books into a cardboard carton on the floor, then took them out again and rearranged them. Closing the lid, he caught sight of the young sergeant and stood up. "What is it, Vance?" he asked.

"Miss Jamie Maxwell from America to see you, sir."

The inspector turned a speculative eye on Jamie. "There must be some mistake."

The sergeant gestured Jamie inside. "Downstairs sent her up, said to ask for you. Isn't that right, miss?"

"Yes," Jamie snapped, no longer trying to hide her irritation. How could the inspector decide a mistake had been made when he didn't even know why she was here?

"Very well, Vance," he said dismissively and the sergeant turned smartly and left the room.

"What might I do for you, Miss Maxwell?" The crisp British accent gave a definite impression of impatience.

"I want some information," Jamie said. "I arrived in Bermuda yesterday and—"

"On holiday?" he interrupted.

"Not exactly."

Raising an eyebrow, the inspector sat down at his desk and gestured Jamie to the opposite chair. He had a stern mouth, Jamie noticed as she seated herself. Plus a jawline that spelled trouble for anyone who opposed him. His eyes were so dark it was impossible to read any expression in them. Her mouth dry, she plunged on. "I'm a meeting planner for a major software company in Boston. One of my colleagues, Derry Riley, came to Bermuda on vacation in April. He took a trip on a glass-bottomed boat to the coral reef and somehow fell overboard and drowned."

"I'm sorry."

Jamie continued doggedly. "The report the police sent to Derry's mother didn't satisfy her. She asked me to find out exactly what happened." This wasn't true. It was Jamie who wasn't satisfied, but she hoped the excuse would cloak her with authority. "The report was signed by a Sergeant Cornell Alexander."

Had his eyelids flickered slightly? "I asked about Sergeant Alexander at the police station in Hamilton this morning," she went on. "They told me to come to Wallbridge. An officer downstairs told me he's not here. Everyone was very polite but very busy. Each one passed me along to somebody else. I ended up here."

She sat very straight on the hard chair, aiming to give an impression of determination—and staying power.

"I fail to see how I can help you," the inspector said, gesturing at the carton. "As you can see, I'm in the process of moving out."

"You're changing offices?"

"Not exactly." There was a wry note in his voice as he repeated the answer she'd given him earlier. "Did you tell Sergeant Murdoch what you wanted?" he asked.

Was he implying someone of a lesser rank should have dealt with her? She shook her head, getting more and more irritated. The superintendent who had sent her up to see Inspector Garrett was the only one who had even listened to her for more than ten seconds. A charismatic, black Bermudian, he'd even gone so far as to check the files to see what they had on Derry, which had raised her hopes, but then, like everyone else, he'd passed her on as if she was a baton in a relay race. "I had a time even finding this place," she complained. "Couldn't someone put up a sign? How can the public find a police station if it isn't even marked?"

"Wallbridge isn't exactly a police station."

"What is it then?"

"Sorry. We prefer to operate on the qt."

She looked at him blankly.

"We keep a low profile, as your countrymen would say."

He sounded so stuffy she couldn't resist hazarding a guess. "Drugs?"

Something that might have been chagrin glimmered in his dark eyes, but he didn't give her a direct answer. "We're a bit of a mixed bag, actually," he said. "I'm rather surprised you were sent up here, all the same. I certainly have no knowledge of the accident you mentioned. Not in my line of work at all, unless..."

"You can forget drugs where Derry was concerned," she interrupted. "There's no way he'd get involved in anything like that."

His expression had taken on a cynical edge, which infuriated her all over again. "The point is, the superintendent sent me to see you and I don't . . ."

"The superintendent? Superintendent Baldwin?"

She had his full attention now. "Why on earth . . ." He drummed the fingers of one hand on the desk's glossy surface. "You told him it was just an accident you were looking into?"

If she was to get anywhere at all, she would have to jump in with both feet. Which was her natural way of doing business, anyway. "I told him I wanted to make sure it *was* an accident."

His hand stilled. "You're suggesting it wasn't?"

"I'm not suggesting anything. It's just that I knew Derry well and he wasn't a swimmer, he could barely float. When he was little some big kids threw him into a swimming pool and he almost drowned. It had an effect on him. Made him nervous around water, phobic even, and very, very cautious."

"If he was so phobic, what was he doing on the boat?"

She bridled at his sarcasm. "You'd have to know Derry to realize that wasn't a contradiction. He used to joke that he might be phobic but he was damn well going to be a functioning phobic." Dammit, she was *not* going to cry.

The inspector regarded her impassively for a moment, then said, "So it wouldn't be unusual for him to go aboard a boat?"

"Not at all. The unusual part would be for him to get too close to the rail. We took a few trips on excursion boats in Boston Harbor and he never got anywhere near the rail. Never."

She studied the planes and angles of his face. Some people's faces seemed modeled from clay, but the sharp-featured inspector could have posed for Mount Rushmore. She leaned forward. "What I want to know is, was the rail broken? Was the deck slippery? Was the weather stormy?"

"That information wasn't in the report?"

"No. The report said he stumbled, lost his footing and fell overboard and hit his head on some coral, which knocked him out. Several people saw him fall, apparently, including a diver who worked with the boat. He dived in after Derry and brought him up, but it was too late. A doctor on board tried to revive Derry, but he wasn't able to. Derry's mother subsequently arranged for his body to be sent home for burial. His belongings were also returned. I unpacked his bag because his mother couldn't face the job. That's it."

His dark eyes studied her face with piercing intensity. "Might he have taken his own life?"

"No way," she snapped.

"Sometimes we don't know people as well as we think…"

"I *knew* Derry. Through and through." She paused. "I feel a responsibility here, Inspector. Derry wanted me to come to Bermuda with him, but I couldn't get away."

Again this wasn't strictly true. The reason she'd turned Derry down was that he'd shown signs of wanting a change in their relationship, a change she couldn't begin to imagine after twenty-seven years of regarding gentle Derry Riley as a bonus brother, a much more sensitive brother than the four she already had. Abruptly her mind flooded with an image of Derry parked in front of his computer, gangling, carrot topped, so skinny she used to joke that if he turned sideways he'd disappear.

She swallowed. "Derry wrote me a cheerful letter three days before he died, telling me what a great time he was having, where he'd been, what he'd seen and done."

"I see." He had a way of lifting one dark eyebrow that seemed to indicate skepticism. "What exactly was your relationship to Mr. Riley?"

"What does that have to—" She took a breath. "He was my friend. We'd known each other since childhood."

"Are you always this loyal to your friends?"

What kind of question was that? "Yes, I am. Always. Is something wrong with that?" She sat forward, lifting her chin in the attitude her brothers called "Jamie taking on the world."

He held up one hand in a peace-making gesture. "It's a good trait, loyalty," he said mildly. "Naturally I can see that you'd find it difficult to—" He broke off. "You don't have any *evidence* of foul play, do you?"

"I don't have any *evidence* of an accident."

Her blunt statement produced an unexpected result that made her blink. Mount Rushmore could smile. It was a very brief smile, like a ray of sunlight piercing through a thundercloud, but for an instant it filled his eyes with light and softened the sharp angles of his face.

"The superintendent checked Derry's file," she said more reasonably. "But he didn't offer me any information."

"He *looked* at the file? And *then* gave you my name?" Once again he was showing some genuine interest. His eyes narrowed. "Precisely when was your friend in Bermuda?"

"He arrived April ninth, he drowned on April eighteenth."

He leaned forward abruptly, seemed about to speak, then sat back again. "Look here, Miss Maxwell, I understand it must be painful for you to accept your friend's death, but if the police report stated it was accidental, then it was accidental. All deaths not due to natural causes are investigated."

Jamie's mouth tightened. "You're saying you won't help me. Okay, tell me where I can find Cornell Alexander and I'll be on my way."

"Unfortunately, Cornell Alexander left the department *and* the country two weeks ago."

A shiver found its way down Jamie's spine.

"It's not an extraordinary thing for him to have done," Garrett continued. "Perhaps I should explain that while Bermuda is a self-governing British colony, not everyone who lives here came from Britain. This country is a rich mixture of Europeans, Africans, Americans, West Indians and Portuguese. Then there are the ex-pats—ex-patriates—foreigners, mainly British, some of whom have been granted status, some who are here on a working vacation."

"What does all that have to do with Cornell Alexander?"

Before answering, he tidied up a stack of papers on his desk, lining up the edges exactly. "Simply this—we have a problem recruiting indigenous Bermudian males to the police force because we have to compete with the higher wages paid by exempted companies. Six out of ten Bermudians are black, so to ensure a balanced racial makeup we recruit in the West Indies and Great Britain. Cornell Alexander was from the Bahamas. He said he was homesick and wanted to go back to the Bahamas."

"Right after Derry's accident."

"Which is probably not at all significant."

"Uh-huh."

"I'm not saying I *won't* help you, Miss Maxwell, I'm saying I *can't* help you. And there's not much point in passing you on to anyone else, nobody's going to reopen an accident case without good reason. You'll admit, I'm sure, that your suspicions rely on women's intuition rather than hard facts."

Jamie's feminist hackles rose. "You have a problem with that, I suppose."

To her surprise, he smiled again, wryly this time. "Actually, I have a healthy respect for women's intuition. I've often seen it in action." He raised an eyebrow. "Men have intuitions, too, you know—we call them gut instincts."

"Then I'm sure you won't object when I say that *my* gut instinct tells me I shouldn't leave until I get some answers."

He looked exasperated, then his expression hardened to granite again and he stood up. Bending down to the carton he'd packed so carefully, he opened it up, reached in and pulled out a folded newspaper, which he handed to her. "Perhaps if you read this, you'll understand my dilemma."

Puzzled, Jamie unfolded the newspaper on the desk and looked at the front page, which was dated a few days earlier. "Police Brutality," the banner headline screamed. "Inspector Turner Garrett accused."

Jamie glanced at the inspector's impassive face, then looked back at the newspaper article. "It says you beat an elderly black man senseless with a nightstick," she said, without attempting to conceal her outrage. "He's in a hospital, in a coma, suffering from possible brain damage."

He nodded. "His name is Walter Seaton. He's one of our regrettably increasing number of street people, a person of interest in a recent murder investigation."

"He was resisting arrest?"

"Vigorously."

She read on. "The reporter says he was much smaller than you and he wasn't resisting."

"Seems one of us must be mistaken, doesn't it?"

Or lying. Thoroughly shaken, she handed the newspaper back, watching as he folded it neatly into the carton and reclosed the flaps. "Why did you show that to me?" she asked.

"So you'll understand why I cannot assist you. In cases of this nature, Miss Maxwell, an internal investigation is required. As of today, I have been suspended for an indefinite period, pending investigation of the charges against me."

Appalled that the aristocratic-looking man seated opposite her could beat a poor old man so ferociously, Jamie stood up and headed for the door. She would go back to the ground floor, insist that Superintendent Baldwin do something, anything....

Hesitating in the doorway, she saw that Sergeant Vance Murdoch, the Adonis look-alike, was standing close by, his back against the wall. Seeing her, he straightened. Obviously he'd waited for her, knowing she would be sent packing.

Turning back, she glared at the inspector. "Superintendent Baldwin must have known this was your last day. Why the hell would he tell me to talk to you?" Before he could answer, she voiced her own conclusion. "I suppose he wanted to get rid of me and my questions."

That had been Turner's first guess, too, though admittedly it was a weak one. He had to confess, however, that he was becoming quite intrigued by this accident, especially as it had Cornell Alexander's name attached to it. The fact that Dunch Baldwin had referred the young woman to him personally was also of great interest.

Actually, he would rather enjoy helping Miss Jamie Maxwell. She wasn't a beauty, but he liked her looks, the "don't give me any nonsense" expression that shone in her intelligent eyes. She had good bones, strong features, a glow to her tanned skin, a vibrancy to the long mane of coppery hair that looked as if it had been curled with a hot corkscrew. Her jeans fitted her well-toned body as though they had been hand tailored. Her short-sleeved blouse was an exact match not only for her green eyes but for the sunlit sea that surrounded the island. He thought it amazing that she would go to all this trouble for a friend. He couldn't think of any woman who might do as much for him, which was a sad commentary on his personal relationships. If he didn't have so much on his plate at the moment, he might even . . .

He leaned forward on his desk, as the realization of a way he might use this young woman and her quest thrust itself to the forefront of his mind. "I suppose I *could* take a look at the file on Derry Riley before I leave," he said. "Depending upon what I find, I'll consider looking into the circumstances surrounding your friend's death. I will, however, have to do it as a private citizen."

"I could pay you for your time," Jamie said, her green eyes blazing with gratitude.

"We can discuss that, when we see how much time is involved," he said shortly. Extracting a business card from his shirt pocket, he wrote on it and handed it to her. "My home telephone number. In case you think of any other information that might be helpful." He shrugged. "Probably I'll find there's nothing out of the way about your friend's death."

It wasn't a very enthusiastic response to her request, Jamie thought, but at least he was willing to do *something*. She had no choice but to accept any crumb that was offered. At the same time, after reading that disturbing newspaper story, she wasn't sure she wanted Turner Garrett's assistance. If he did turn up something in Derry's file, maybe she'd just look into it herself. "Thank you, Inspector," she said, trying not to show the turbulence of her thoughts.

"Not at all." He held out his hand as if to seal a bargain, and she felt obliged to accept the gesture. His handshake was firm. She was suddenly very aware of the strength behind the man's lean but athletic exterior. He could probably batter a man into unconsciousness *without* a nightstick, if he wanted to.

Had Walter Seaton resisted arrest? she wondered, as Sergeant Murdoch escorted her downstairs. What difference did it make? Even if that poor man *had* put up a fight, was there any need to beat him into a coma? The newspaper story had been very graphic. Etched in Jamie's mind was an image of Turner Garrett, nightstick raised, looming darkly over the sprawled body of an old man.

THROUGH THE OPEN cottage window Turner could hear the nightly chorus of the whistling frogs, the splash of waves against the shore. His friend Tom was sitting on the window seat, his lanky body silhouetted against the darkening sky. He had been silent for a while, but now he stirred. "As I understand it, then, you're planning to use this... Jamie Maxwell as some sort of cover?" he asked.

Turner nodded.

"*Was* her friend's death an accident?" Tom asked.

Turner shifted slightly on his chair. "All appearances would seem to indicate that it was."

"But that's not what you're going to tell *her?* Isn't that a fairly despicable thing to do?"

"Results occasionally justify the means," Turner said shortly. "Witness Walter Seaton." He leaned back in his chair. "Look, Tom, all I'm proposing is that I tell her I'm willing to help her look into the circumstances of her friend's death. She's concerned about it. And, actually, Alexander's report *was* a bit sloppy."

"Was that unusual?"

"No."

Tom eyed him. "You didn't like Alexander much, did you?"

"I had reason to complain about him once or twice. As for Miss Maxwell, you must realize I'll be doing her a favor."

Tom laughed shortly. "In my experience, Turner, my lad, women don't always appreciate a favor that isn't quite what they bargained for."

Turner gave an exasperated sigh. "I don't have any choice in the matter, anyway. I have my orders."

Tom raised surprised eyebrows. "From on high? Why didn't you say so?" He was thoughtful for a minute, then he said, "Let me reconstruct, all right? You're going to help this young woman investigate an accident that you're quite sure is an accident, so that you can go round and about with her and ask questions about *our* project?"

"That sums it up, yes."

"I foresee a slight problem. Some people are going to recognize you. Even though you're under suspension they aren't going to want to talk to you."

"I have a plan to get round that," Turner said shortly. "Meanwhile, as well as acting as go-between, I expect you to keep your ear to the ground, poke your nose into whatever looks interesting. Your usual MO."

"Thanks a lot," Tom said with a wry grin. His expression sobered. "I rather think I'd do better to watch you. I'm a bit concerned about the conclusion of this project of ours. You have a personal stake in it, and that worries me."

"There's nothing for you to worry about," Turner said, standing up to indicate the meeting was over.

Tom looked at him for a long moment. "I want to believe that." He sighed, then shrugged and came across the room to shake Turner's hand. "I wish you good luck with Miss Jamie Maxwell." His thin face cracked into a grin. "Just remember, old friend. Hell hath no fury like a woman deceived."

Chapter Three

While she drank the morning coffee she'd made in the wall-hung coffee maker, Jamie scanned the newspaper she'd brought in from outside her hotel room door. There was an article about Bermuda's commitment to stop substance abuse, another about an escalating rivalry between Reggae bands. One page headlined an "appreciation supper" to be held at the Southampton Princess Hotel for a philanthropist named Rex Putney.

The name caught her attention; Putney's was the name of a department store in Boston. In fact, the white shirt she was wearing with her jeans had come from there. It was a great shirt, made of some miracle fabric that looked like Egyptian cotton but never wrinkled, an important consideration for someone who loathed ironing.

Evidently Bermuda's Mr. Putney had recently returned from a trip to the Bahamas, Haiti and Jamaica where he had delivered medical, food and building supplies, some of which had been bought in the U.S. and South America, some donated locally. A man with an extraordinarily charitable bent, obviously.

Tossing the paper onto the coffee table, she decided she was ready to tackle the day. A glance through the room's sliding glass doors showed her a living watercolor painting beyond the wrought-iron balcony: a wash of incredible blue for the sky; pink, green and yellow marshmallow pastels for the nearby buildings; each one topped with a terraced, wedding-cake-frosting roof. Sunlight glinted on the numerous boats plying Hamilton Harbour's waters. The air smelled wonderful—salt scrubbed and flower laden.

Remembering that Derry's letter had mentioned some of the places he'd visited, she pulled it from the zippered side pocket of her duffel and opened it. About to sit down, she was startled by a knock on her door. "Who is it?" she called, wondering if Turner Garrett could be stopping by already.

The answer, muffled by the door's thickness, gave her no clue. A glance through the fish-eye spyhole showed her a tall, thirtyish, fair-haired man—a stranger.

Opening the door cautiously, she peered out. The man's top half was blazered and businesslike, his lower half clad in tailored maroon gabardine Bermuda shorts, along with the obligatory knee socks and polished shoes. He was smooth featured, slender, with hair the color of sunlight. He had great legs, she noticed.

"Charles Hollingsworth, general manager," he said with a genial smile that crinkled the corners of his blue eyes. "I thought perhaps you might wish to discuss our conference facilities," he continued as she gestured him toward the small sitting area. There was an odor of sweet strong tobacco about him that made Jamie's nose twitch—she had an unfortunate allergy to tobacco smell, as well as smoke.

Her mind had gone completely blank. To give herself time to get her brain in gear, she folded Derry's letter, put it carefully back in its envelope and set it down on the coffee table. Luckily light dawned almost immediately. She'd informed the desk clerk she was here to look into meeting possibilities. She'd thought of it as a sort of cover story. Derry had worked for the same company, he had stayed at this hotel, what could be more natural, as long as she was here, anyway, than that she would be curious about his accident? Obviously the desk clerk had passed the word on.

"I'm a meeting planner for a software company in Boston," she said, hoping her pause hadn't been too noticeable. "We're considering a somewhat important executive conference, inviting several CEOs to see a demo of our new software applications."

All true, except that doing it in Bermuda would run the costs higher than even her generous budget would allow. But she was committed to playing the game now. "Besides accommodations for the attendees, we'd need a large executive suite, a conference room, a smaller meeting room . . ."

"Heavens, that's terribly serious stuff for such an early hour," he protested. "I thought perhaps we could breakfast together, get acquainted, break the ice, so to speak."

Again the crinkling eyes. A definite charmer, this one. Golden Boy. Well, she had no objections to breakfasting with a good-looking man. "If I could just let the front desk know where I am?" she suggested. "I'm expecting a message."

Rising gracefully, he picked up the telephone and informed the desk Miss Maxwell would be breakfasting with him in the conservatory. A few minutes later they were seated opposite each other in a glass-walled room that featured lush greenery and small tumbling waterfalls. Damask draped the tables, sunlight gleamed on crystal and silver. On the way in, Jamie's sneakers had sunk an inch into the carpet's luxurious pile.

She felt out of place in such surroundings. Her hair was still damp, she hadn't had a chance to put makeup on, and she should probably have worn the one dress she'd brought with her. No, that wasn't possible—it was only an hour since she'd pulled it out of her duffel and hung it on the back of the bathroom door, hoping the steam from successive showers would remove the creases. Meticulous and organized in her business life, Jamie tended to be relaxed in private. Messy, her mother said.

"This is a lovely hotel," she said awkwardly.

"We think so," Charles Hollingsworth said. "We draw a distinguished clientele. The gentleman over there, for example, is a major European financier. Very, very wealthy. His wife—you may recognize her—is Lucia Ugo, the opera diva. And just beyond them, the Honorable Mr. and Mrs. Warrender, sitting with Mrs. John Rossiter, board chair of the Kleber Museum." Jamie was glad to see her omelet arrive. None of these names meant a thing to her, but she tried her best to look impressed in deference to the respectful tone of Hollingsworth's voice.

Hoping to get him back to practical matters, she steered him into a discussion of the hotel's amenities, which he described in rhapsodic terms. But when she tried to pin him down to facts and figures, he waved a distracted hand. "You'd best discuss all that with Loretta Dean, my assistant," he said. "She's a very capable woman. Has all necessary information at her fingertips. I'll introduce you to her when we're finished here."

Why wasn't she having breakfast with Loretta, Jamie wondered, but decided she was being churlish.

Loretta Dean turned out to be a young, sturdily built, black Bermudian woman with beautiful skin and silky-looking hair that she wore skewered in a loose topknot. Her office was enviably neat, with high-tech furniture, a state-of-the-art computer system and one perfect flower arrangement. She was dressed in a tailored pink silk suit with an impressive cleavage and had a handshake even firmer than Jamie's own. With the precision of an electronic calculator she rattled off all the rates and information Jamie requested. Her speech had a British flavor, with long vowels, but was most impressive for its abrupt delivery, which gave it a hostile effect. "I'll put everything in writing," she said when Jamie ran out of questions. "You'll want to talk to our chef and the catering manager. You have any questions they can't answer, come back and see me."

As she said this last, she gave a slightly hooded glance at Charles Hollingsworth, who had leaned against the doorjamb during this entire interview, looking elegant and rakish and slightly bored. Jamie, who prided herself on her understanding of body language, interpreted the glance to mean, "Don't you bother with him, I'm the one runs things around here."

Confirming this opinion, Hollingsworth murmured, "Loretta's the brains of this establishment," as they left the woman's office. "I'm more or less relegated to the entertainment end of things, you might say," he added with engaging candor. "I make certain our more important guests are comfortable and happy at all times. Take them snorkeling, cruising, that sort of thing. Delightful job. No harm having fun while slaving for one's daily bread, don't you think?"

They had reached the lobby. "Would you like to take a look at the hotel's boat?" he asked. "Your people might like to do a little sight-seeing while they're here, don't you think?"

It occurred to Jamie she should check for any message from Inspector Garrett, but the mention of a boat had reminded her of Derry and her primary purpose here. "I'd like that," she said, and he escorted her to a side door and gracefully indicated the path that led between high hibiscus hedges to the waterfront. She hung back as he pulled a pipe and tobacco pouch from his blazer pocket. She tried to keep her expression noncommittal as he glanced back at her but he evidently guessed there was a problem and replaced the pipe and pouch with an almost inaudible sigh.

"I'm sorry, Mr. Hollingsworth," Jamie murmured. "I'm not prejudiced against smoking, it's just that my eyes swell up. It's not a pretty sight."

"I can certainly forfeit smoking for the pleasure of your company," he said. His engaging smile appeared again. "Do please call me Charles. And I shall call you Jamie, shall I?"

Was he flirting with her? Yes. There was a glint in his blue eyes, and his smile had acquired a sexy edge.

The boat was a fifty-foot power cruiser with a flying bridge. It was named the *Kiskadee*, which Charles informed her was the name of a local, ubiquitous bird. "Easily recognized," he said with a smile. "The little blighter chirps its own name."

The *Kiskadee* was a beautiful vessel, luxuriously appointed. Two crewmen were aboard, working at various tasks. They both smiled at Jamie. So far the Bermudians she'd run into, black or white, were unfailingly friendly.

Standing at the starboard rail, half listening to Charles as he discussed points of interest around the island, Jamie was trying to decide how to introduce the subject of Derry's accident when Charles gave her the opportunity himself by mentioning the coral reefs. "I don't think I want to see them," she said, with a slight shudder that wasn't at all faked. "A friend of mine lost his life there last month. He fell from a glass-bottomed sight-seeing boat and drowned." He was watching her solicitously, his gaze sympathetic. "His name was Derry Riley," she went on. "He stayed at the Victoria. Did you happen to meet him?"

"Unfortunately, no. I was in England visiting my family at the time. Naturally I was informed of the tragedy on my return." He frowned. "I believe I was told that he worked for a computer company. I take it he was a colleague?"

"Yes." Best not to hint at her suspicions, she decided. At least not yet. "I don't suppose you know any details, do you?'' she asked. "I promised Derry's mother I'd find out more about what happened.''

"I wish I had something to add.''

He really did sound sincere, Jamie thought. What a nice man he was. Slightly vacuous, but all in all a kind person.

"I am sorry about your friend, Jamie,'' Charles murmured as they parted at her door. "If there's anything I can do to make your stay more comfortable, don't hesitate to call on me. And perhaps we can do a repeat of breakfast while you're here?''

"Perhaps,'' Jamie said, managing a smile.

In her room she checked with the front desk and discovered there were no messages. Grabbing her purse, she stuck Derry's letter in it and headed out again. When you weren't sure what was the best thing to do, it sometimes helped to just do the first thing that came to mind. Like checking out some of the places in Derry's letter, for example.

She was halfway across the hotel forecourt, heading at an angle toward the driveway, when a man's voice hailed her heartily. "Yo, Jamie. Jamie Maxwell. Wait up.''

The accent was American. Turning too quickly, Jamie almost collided with a muscular, bushy-haired young man. "Hey, I'm sorry,'' she apologized. He grunted and stepped aside. Beyond him another man was waving at her from a pathway that ran around the side of the hotel. He was stoop shouldered, slightly bulgy in the middle, wearing an oversize, extremely loud Hawaiian shirt over baggy beige slacks, a blue cap decorated with gold braid crammed down over his hair, and opaque sunglasses. His ancient sneakers squeaked on the paving stones as he shambled toward her.

Dismayed, Jamie stared at this apparition blankly as he approached her, his right hand extended, all his teeth bared in a wide smile. She had never seen the man before in her life.

Chapter Four

"How's everything in Beantown?" the stranger asked. "Mom and Dad okay?" Taking hold of her limp hand, he shook it vigorously.

People were walking around them. Fortunately Jamie gathered her wits in time to stop the exclamation that shot to the tip of her tongue when she recognized him. Putting an arm around her shoulders, he propelled her toward the side door of the hotel. Several people entered the elevator with them, so Jamie couldn't question him until they reached her room.

As she closed the door, Turner Garrett pulled off his cap and sunglasses and drew himself up to his full, impressive height, instantly eliminating all sags and bulges. Smoothing his dark hair into place, he said without a hint of apology, "It seemed a good way to test the efficacy of the disguise."

His transformation from stern Brit to ebullient Yankee had been so convincing that Jamie felt sure her mouth must be hanging open. Now he looked a little more like yesterday's impassive inspector, in spite of his flamboyant clothing and the fact that he hadn't shaved. She supposed the dark stubble was meant to add to his disguise. It also made him look very sexy.

"Is this what you call operating on the qt?" she asked.

He grimaced down at his disreputable outfit. "Not too discreet, is it?" He shrugged. "It's my experience that if one requires a disguise one should make it as distracting as possible. This way, any bystander is dazzled by the outer semblance and doesn't look too closely at the real person."

"Oh." Jamie sank into one of the chairs in the sitting area. "Are you an actor in your spare time? Your American accent is terrific."

He looked less than thrilled by her admiration. "I played several American roles in college, actually. I spent many hours practicing an American accent. It's amazing how it comes back to one."

"But is all this really necessary? It seems sort of..."

"Cloak-and-dagger?" He sat down opposite her, dark eyebrows slanted. "I told you I'd have to operate as a private citizen, Miss Maxwell. As I also told you, I do operate on the qt, so I'm not as recognizable as all that. All the same, I can't help you openly because of my suspension."

Jamie leaned forward. "You *are* going to help me?"

He nodded. "I managed to look into Derry Riley's file."

A jolt of nervousness shot through her. "And?"

"I discovered the name of the boat—the *Coral Queen*. Other than that I have very little information to add. The pathologist's findings were consistent with the report your friend's mother received."

She stared at him. "You mean it really was an accident?"

Before answering, he tidied up the newspaper she'd left scattered on the coffee table, folding it and setting it in the exact center of the table. "I'm disturbed by this report," he admitted. "There should have been more information. The doctor's name wasn't recorded, nor was the name of the skipper on duty that day. Cornell Alexander, the sergeant who investigated the accident, did not follow proper procedure."

"Nobody noticed?"

"Probably no one else saw the report. Alexander had enough authority to handle an accident case alone. The fact remains that he did not do a thorough job. One wonders why."

Jamie felt the blood drain from her face. Subconsciously, she must have hoped the inspector would tell her Derry's death had definitely been an accident. "What can we do?" she asked.

"Whatever we do, we'll need to proceed cautiously. If there *was* foul play..."

"You think there was?"

His dark gaze met hers. "I intend to consider Derry Riley's death an accident unless and until it is proven to be otherwise." He hesitated. "I believe you mentioned a letter?"

Jamie jumped up and went in search of Derry's letter, scrabbling through the contents of her duffel bag, ending up with most of her stuff piled up on the dresser. No letter.

Vaguely remembering she'd put it in the zippered side pocket of her duffel bag, she felt around in it. Derry's letter wasn't there, but the enameled four-leaf clover she'd given him on his sixteenth birthday was. She'd found it tucked into his camera case, along with his Minolta, when she'd unpacked his luggage for his mother. Mrs. Riley had let her keep it as a memento. The clover leaf's hard edges pressed into her palm as she gripped it and she felt a sense of loss so acute her heart ached. Reclosing the zipper, she took a shaky breath. Then she recalled putting the letter in her purse before going downstairs. Sighing, she shoved everything back into the duffel.

Turner Garrett was watching her. "You haven't had time to unpack?" he asked as Jamie sat down again.

"I unpack as I go," she said distractedly. "If you scatter stuff around in a hotel room, you're bound to lose track of something." Turning her purse upside down and shaking it vigorously, she dumped her makeup kit, hair spray, wallet, change purse full of coins and sundry other useful items onto the coffee table.

Reluctant amusement glimmered in his eyes. He seemed about to comment, but just then Jamie found the letter. "It arrived the day before we heard Derry was dead," she told him as she reloaded her purse.

Garrett picked up the envelope and studied it. "Posted on April fifteenth," he commented. He frowned as though there was something significant about that, then glanced at Jamie enquiringly. "This is Victoria Hotel stationery."

"Derry stayed here. I've already asked Charles Hollingsworth, the manager, if he met him, but he didn't."

His glance was sharp. "I sincerely hope you didn't repeat your suspicions to him."

"I did not. I told him Derry was my friend and he'd been drowned accidentally."

"Good. Stick to that will you? No need to alarm anyone, and it's certainly the truth as we know it." He hesitated. "Did Hollingsworth have anything to say about the accident?"

"He said he was in England when it happened, but he was told about it when he returned. He's a nice man, sincere, but sort of an airhead. And a snob. Do you know him?"

Garrett seemed to be resisting the urge to smile at her description. "We've met," he said.

"Good grief, he's not a friend of yours, is he? I didn't mean to insult..."

He shook his head. "I don't know him well. I'm perfectly willing to accept your assessment of his character."

He gestured at Derry's letter, and she picked it up and began reading it. "He says he was buzzing all over the island on a moped. Liked St. George Island the best. He watched the cruise ships dock in Hamilton, heard a steel band playing on a restaurant balcony and watched a 'bobby' directing traffic on Front Street from something called the bird cage.'' She glanced up. "Is that the thing that looks like a gazebo?''

He nodded impatiently. "Okay, let's see," she continued hastily. "He visited Treasure Cave, which he said was fantastic, then he goes on about the deliciousness of a hibiscus which he discovered on a personal tour of the local taverns." She frowned. "I didn't know a hibiscus was edible."

For some unknown reason, he was suddenly sitting very stiffly. "It's a drink," he said tersely. "Was he a drinker? That might explain . . .''

She shook her head firmly. "Never more than a beer or two, usually. Once in a while he'd try something exotic. But he loved pubs. At home he used to go to the Bull and Finch, the bar that was the model for 'Cheers,' the television series."

Turner Garrett had narrowed his eyes. Probably he wanted her to get on with the letter. "I'm hoping to go out on a glass-bottomed boat to see the coral reef," she read aloud. "Scary stuff for me, but I'm determined to do it."

The inspector was thoughtful for a while, then he seemed to rouse himself. "If we can retrace Riley's footsteps," he said at last, "we might find something that will determine if his death was an accident or not."

"That's what I was planning to do when you showed up. Should we start with the *Coral Queen*?"

He shook his head. "If there was more to Derry's death than a simple accident, something must have led up to it. Something he saw, someone he met—" He seemed to be thinking hard again. "Did you bring a photograph of Derry with you?"

Jamie hesitated. "Why are you suddenly so willing to help me?" she demanded abruptly. "What's in it for you?"

He let out an explosive breath. "Women can be so dam-
nably exasperating," he complained. "You asked me to help
you find out what happened to your friend. I'm trying to do
so. Why can't you be satisfied with that?"

"I just wondered why you'd bother."

That stopped him for a minute. Then he said in a very
reasonable voice, "If I can find anything unusual in this
case, it might stand me in good stead for my own."

That seemed like an awfully weak reason, she thought,
but Turner Garrett's knowledge of the island would speed
things up. Whatever the reason for his deciding to assist her,
she could surely use his help.

What had happened to her decision to go on alone once
he'd checked Derry's file? Was she rationalizing because she
wanted his company?

Nonsense. Granted he was extremely good-looking, bordering on gorgeous on those rare occasions when he smiled.
Granted his arm around her shoulders earlier had activated
a few stray hormones and set off her early warning system.
Still, she wasn't about to forget the newspaper story and the
violence it implied about Garrett's character. A shiver went
through her. She had never in her life associated with anyone who had a violent nature. This man had been kicked off
the police force—at least temporarily. She would take advantage of his assistance, but she would not forget to be on
guard at all times.

Digging her billfold out of her purse, she pulled out a
snapshot and handed it to him. She had taken it herself. It
showed Derry standing in front of Faneuil Hall, grinning
toothily at the camera, wearing his favorite "Cheers" hat.

Garrett glanced approvingly at the photograph. "A good
clear shot. We'll show it about, see if anyone remembers
him." He frowned as he handed the picture back to her.
"The hibiscus he mentions isn't quite as popular as our rum
swizzles and dark-and-stormies, so that should narrow—"

"What the hell is a dark-and-stormy?" she interrupted.

"Black rum and ginger beer. It's really very refreshing," he added when she made a face.

Struck by a thought, Jamie jumped up and rummaged in her duffel bag again, digging out a handful of coasters and matchbooks. "I'm a collector," she said, handing them over. "Derry sent these with his letter. I brought them along so I could check out the places he'd visited."

He shuffled through them, then stopped abruptly. She looked at the coaster that had attracted his attention, reading the words on it upside down—Tudor Tavern. She was conscious of a sudden intensity in Turner Garrett's manner.

"What's wrong?" she asked.

He looked up, obviously startled by her question. Excitement gleamed in his dark eyes, but he quickly averted his gaze. "The hibiscus cocktail is a specialty of the Tudor Tavern," he said smoothly. "Most tourists find their way there sooner or later. Perhaps it would be a good place to start."

"Now?" she asked.

He nodded, then hesitated. "It might be wise for you to disguise yourself a little. That way if we want to appear in public as ourselves at any time it will be difficult for anyone to connect us with our investigation. There's also the fact that we don't quite know what we'll be running into."

Jamie stared at him. "You think it might get dangerous?"

"I merely believe in taking precautions," he said sternly.

Jamie sorted through her duffel again and came up with a pair of dark glasses with large lenses and a denim hat with a floppy brim. She looked uncertainly at the hat. "I'm not sure I can get my hair into this."

He regarded her gravely. "I could give you a haircut."

Was he making a joke? "No way," she said. "This perm may have been a mistake, but it set me back eighty-six bucks—I'm stuck with it until it unravels."

Digging back into the bag, she pulled out a couple of oversize sweatshirts that she rarely wore because they made her look fat. She'd brought them to use as cover-ups for her swimsuit. She held up the mustard-colored one and when the inspector nodded approval, she slipped into the bathroom to change and pin up her hair.

"You'll do," he said when she emerged. Not what she could call a compliment, but then she did look pretty awful. Picking up her purse, scooping the coasters and matchbooks into it, she hesitated. She had a question she wanted to ask but wasn't sure how to frame it without giving him the wrong impression. Just do it, she told herself. "I hope you don't have a wife who's going to object to you trekking around with me."

He raised an eyebrow, and she plunged hastily on. "I only ask because a while back one of our regional managers drove me from Boston to Salt Lake City for a business meeting and later his wife...well, it created an awkward situation."

"I don't have a wife," he said flatly.

"Okay, then. It was just—" Shut up Jamie, she scolded herself. Awkwardly extending her hand, she said, "Thank you, Inspector Garrett. I do appreciate your help."

He folded his hand around hers. "If we're going to be fellow sleuths, I think we'd best use first names only. Not much point to disguising myself as the ugly American if you're going to go round calling me Inspector Garrett. Actually, we should avoid using our real names altogether. If you have to refer to me in public, call me Digby."

He was still holding her hand, and Jamie was experiencing another unexpected surge of sexual awareness. Even disguised, this tall, lean man was intensely masculine, but such a response was hardly appropriate under the circumstances.

"And you?" he asked.

"Excuse me?"

"Do you have a husband?"

"No way." She shuddered involuntarily. "I've seen what happened to too many of my friends who got married. Self-confident, independent women turned into harassed housewives who couldn't wait to get home from work to fix hubby a hot meal. All of a sudden they couldn't attend conferences or stay in town after work for a coffee with the girls, or go shopping when they felt like it, or—" She broke off, conscious that he was regarding her with wry amusement again.

"Besides," she went on, "I've never met a man I was all that wild about. Maybe because I grew up with four brothers. I can never take men seriously when they get romantic, I keep wanting to say 'Come off it.'" His eyes were glinting again. "Why 'Digby'?" she queried, changing the subject.

"My middle name—my mother's maiden name. We should devise a name for you, too. Have you a middle name?"

She made a face. "Rose."

That smile of his showed up again. It really was disconcerting; she never knew when to expect it. "Rose it is," he said. "Rose and Digby." He grimaced. "We sound like a music hall team." He looked at her in the direct way that was apparently characteristic. Whenever he did that, the air buzzed between them. Which was also very disconcerting. "When we're alone, of course, you can call me Turner," he continued. "And I'll call you Jamie, shall I?"

"Okay," she said. Even to her own ears she sounded rather breathless.

SHE HAD EXPECTED, naturally, that he would have a car. But when they emerged at the rear of the hotel, having used the fire stairs for privacy, he led her over to a moped. After stuffing his braid-trimmed cap in his pants pocket, he took two safety helmets from the moped's front wire basket, put one on, then held the other out to her.

Her face must have given away her surprise. "My car might be recognized," he explained as he fastened his chin strap. "I expect you've found out one can't rent a car here—we barely have room for residents' automobiles, and we're limited to one per family. This is the only alternative, I'm afraid."

He had already seated himself on the moped. Sighing, she pulled off her hat and stuck it in her already bulging purse. Handing the purse to him to hold, she took the helmet and rammed it on over her hair, ignoring the mime he was going through to indicate that her purse weighed a ton. Taking the handbag back and slinging the strap across her chest, she climbed on the bike behind him and put her hands tentatively at the sides of his waist.

"You'll have to hold on tighter than that," he said as he started the motor.

She grasped a double handful of his Hawaiian shirt, but by the time they had careened around the parking lot and out onto the street she had her arms clasped tightly around his middle. He had a very nice middle. Flat. Hard as iron.

"I haven't ridden one of these things for a long time," he yelled over his shoulder as he swerved wide around a corner.

"Obviously," Jamie yelled back.

THE TUDOR TAVERN made all American imitations of the style look ludicrous. This was the real thing, and Jamie's fingers itched for a camera. Sturdy dark beams across the ceiling, wainscoting and white plaster on the walls, horse brasses and fox-hunting scenes hanging here and there. The lounge was packed with customers even though it was just after noon.

In spite of the open casement windows, a haze of cigarette smoke hung like smog over people's heads. The customers seemed oblivious. Jamie's eyes twitched as Turner shouldered a path for her through the mob hanging around the bar. By some miracle he managed to snag two bar stools and she slid onto one of them a split second ahead of a large woman in plaid shorts. "Rosie here wants to know what's in your specialty," Turner told the bartender, reprising his American accent.

Gritting her teeth, Jamie managed not to scowl at him. She hated the name Rosie even more than Rose.

The bartender smiled at her, showing two rows of perfect white teeth. "A hibiscus? It's made of rum, miss, plus apricot brandy, grenadine and crème de coconut."

Jamie shuddered. "I'll settle for a tonic water."

"Same here," Turner told the bartender. "I'm not one to drink and drive."

Jamie felt relieved to hear that. The roads in Bermuda were mostly narrow and winding. Some of them were lined with rock walls. Several times on the way over, one of the ubiquitous pink buses had veered frighteningly close. Added to which, riding on the left side of the road felt all wrong. Even though the speed limit island-wide was only 20 mph, Jamie's knees were still shaky.

Turner had replaced his safety helmet with his out-of-work-admiral's hat. His hair stuck out at the sides. She looked no better, she thought, grimacing at her reflection in his dark glasses. Her hat brim was even droopier than she'd thought. She noted that her eyes were beginning to tingle ominously. Thank goodness for the sunglasses. They wouldn't help, but at least they'd hide the damage.

Rummaging in her purse, she retrieved Derry's photograph and laid it on the bar just as the bartender served their drinks. "Have you ever seen this man?" she asked.

He leaned over the photo, one large black thumb rubbing slowly over it. "Get a lot of business here, as you can see," he said, waving a hand at the crowded room.

As he studied the photo, Jamie looked idly around the lounge. Most of the patrons appeared to be tourists. Somebody nearby was speaking German, a couple of Japanese men were examining a camcorder. Beyond them, his back turned, a man was smoking a cigar. No wonder she was having trouble with her eyes. The man had bushy brown hair that looked vaguely familiar. Somewhere she had seen hair like that before.

"What's the deal here?" the bartender asked. "This boy's gone missing?"

"Something like that," Jamie said.

"That's tight."

"He might be connected with a crime," Turner said.

Appalled, Jamie swung her head around and stared at him.

"Chingas!" The bartender's interest had perked up immediately. "You talking about our shooting?"

"That was a bad business," Turner said. He looked around. "Didn't take the owners long to get the place patched up."

"Took care of it soon as the police got through with it," the man said.

"I heard maybe drugs were involved."

The bartender nodded. "That's the rumor." He leaned forward and lowered his voice. "Heard someone big was involved."

"Who?"

"That I didn't hear."

Jamie frowned. What the hell were they talking about?

"You see the shooting go down?" Turner asked.

The bartender shook his head. "I got off early. Had a killer toothache. My guardian angel must have been watching me that day. I left at six ... the shooting started around half past seven." He crossed himself. "One of the waitresses said it happened so fast nobody had a chance to see anything. She doesn't work here now. Had to leave. Nightmares. Jittery. Couldn't face coming back."

"I should think she wouldn't, poor woman," Jamie said warmly. "Did you say she witnessed a shooting? She should have counseling. Was any provision made for—" A quelling glance from Turner cut off the rest of her sentence.

"Nobody seems to know anything about the guys who did it," Turner said. "It's like they disappeared into thin air."

"Probably left the country," the bartender said.

"You hear that they did?"

The bartender shook his head, then squinted at Turner. "You a Yank P.I.? That why you're wearing the mafia darks?"

Turner looked at him steadily. "The people I work for are offering a reward for information. Utmost confidentiality."

The man's eyes narrowed. After glancing furtively around, he hunched forward. "Story going round there's a new man on the island. American. Might have been one of the killers." He returned his gaze to the photo. "Not this here boy, though. Heard the new fella was black. That's all I've got. That enough for some of that reward money?"

"If an arrest is made," Turner said.

What possible reason could he have for implying Derry had something to do with a shooting? Jamie wondered. He'd better have a reason. "*Did* you ever see the man in the photo?" she asked the bartender.

"He was probably in here sometime between April ninth and fifteenth," Turner added.

The day Derry arrived and the day he wrote the letter. That date *had* been significant. "Red hair. Blue eyes. My height," she told the bartender. "Around five-nine. American."

The bartender continued to study the picture, frowning when someone started up the jukebox, as if the music was interfering with his concentration. "You understand I'd be happy to put the hurt to those crooks," he said at last. "I wouldn't want to finger the wrong person, though. But I do remember this hat. Because of the TV show. Some boy wearing a hat like this here was in one day. Could have been that day. Could have been some other time. He told me he'd been to Treasure Cave and thought it was pretty amazing."

"What kind of cave is it?" Jamie queried.

The bartender gave her a kind, Bermuda resident-to-tourist smile. "Stalactites, stalagmites, that sort of thing, miss. Bermuda's all limestone. Underground streams have carved out caves and caverns." He pushed the photo back across the bar.

"Was he alone?" Turner asked.

The bartender shrugged. "Far as I remember."

"Do you remember anything else about his visit, something that might pinpoint the day?"

The man screwed up his face in a frown. "I remember him saying he wanted to try another hibiscus and us talking about St. George's, but I don't—"

A customer called out for a refill on his beer. "Have to get back to work," the bartender said. He started to move away, then swung back. "I just remembered something else."

Turner came alert, his whole body tensing.

"He asked if we had any postcards showing the building from the outside. But we were sold out. Those postcards go fast," he added as he turned away again.

Turner sighed. "Let's go," he said.

Jamie stood silently by, thinking about Derry while Turner wrestled the moped out from between some later arrivals. Taking off her sunglasses she rubbed her smarting eyes. "Are you feeling all right?" Turner asked. The American Digby had vanished. The English accent was back. How easily he switched.

"Allergy to smoke," she said absentmindedly, then frowned at him. "What the hell was all that about in there? The shooting. The people you work for offering a reward. What people? And what was that stuff about drugs? I told you Derry didn't have anything to do with drugs. And he surely didn't have anything to do with any shooting."

Turner set the moped on its kickstand with great care. "I was just fabricating a scenario, hoping it would encourage the barman to talk," he said.

"Sounded to me as if you had some personal business going."

"If we're going to sleuth together, you're going to have to trust me," he said flatly.

"I'll be happy to trust you, as soon as you tell me what all that talk was about shooting."

"No, Jamie." His mouth was stern again. Obviously he wasn't going to budge.

"Okay," she said at last. "I'll trust you for now. I don't have a whole lot of choice."

He had the most skeptical eyebrows. She supposed she hadn't sounded too enthusiastic about trusting him. Well, she wasn't.

"I was excited when the bartender recognized Derry's hat," she said after a moment's awkward silence. "But I guess we didn't really gain much, did we?"

"Detective work can be very frustrating."

"I've been thinking about what the bartender said. Obviously Derry was here before he wrote the letter to me. He mentioned the cave and the hibiscus. Why did you want to know what day it was? What difference would that make?''

"If we knew Derry's itinerary it might be helpful."

"Oh." She supposed he knew best about such things.

He stared at her face again. "Will it clear up?"

She'd almost forgotten her swollen eyes. She nodded, feeling self-conscious. "It'll pass."

Taking off his dark glasses, he stuck them in his shirt pocket, then cupped her face and studied her eyes closely. "I've never seen anything like this," he murmured.

His breath was sweet on her face. She realized she was holding her own breath. Her face felt hot. Her pulse was hammering in her ears. The air between them was shimmering as though the sunshine had magnetized all the little dust motes and set them dancing. "Fussing makes me nervous," she muttered.

His eyes seemed magnified this close up. So dark a brown they appeared black. The whites were pristine. He must live a clean life, she thought, when he isn't bashing indigent street people.

She stiffened and he released her, raising a quizzical eyebrow. "Why would someone's concern for your well-being make you nervous?" he asked.

She attempted a nonchalant shrug. "As I told you, I have four older brothers. Any time I made a fuss as a kid, they accused me of being a girl."

"But you *are* a girl, Jamie." Taking her elbow, he led her to a bench under a magnolia tree. "Wait here," he ordered, then jogged back to the tavern, Hawaiian shirttail flapping.

Now what? Puzzled, Jamie tried to relax, ignoring the section of her brain that had retained the warm impression of Turner's fingers against her cheeks.

It was a good ten minutes before Turner returned. She had just decided to go in and look for him when he showed up and handed her two soggy brown lumps. "Tea bags," he said. "The tannin is supposed to ease inflammation. My wife used to use tea bags on her eyes after a rough night."

She blinked and his mouth tightened as though he wanted to bite back the last sentence. Apparently remembering he'd said he didn't have a wife, he muttered, "My wife died four years ago," but he didn't explain the "rough night" remark.

Giving him a chance to recover his composure, Jamie tipped her head back and placed a cold tea bag on each closed eyelid. It did feel good, refreshing. "I appreciate this, I really do," she murmured.

After a while the tea bags warmed up and didn't seem to be doing much good. Taking them off, Jamie blinked several times, glad she hadn't been wearing mascara. "Better?" Turner asked softly, leaning over her to take a look.

There was surely nothing more devastating than a strong man who knew how to be gentle. If this went on she was going to melt into a puddle at his feet. *He's not to be trusted,* she reminded herself. "Much better," she said, annoyed that a certain huskiness had added itself to her voice.

His gaze met hers and held for a moment. A flow of energy and awareness passed between them. Jamie's heart thumped. Taking the tea bags from her, Turner dropped them in a nearby trash container, then seated himself on the moped. "Shall we go?" His voice was brisk.

Jamie stood up and put on her sunglasses. "Are we going to the cave?"

Turner handed up her safety helmet; his expression had taken on its usual impassiveness now. "Treasure Cave is closed on Saturdays. We'll have to try it another time. We'll head for St. George's if you're quite sure you're well enough."

"Let's go," she said, settling herself on the moped and clinging to Turner again.

Was this how it was going to be? she wondered, as they swerved around the corner and started across some kind of causeway. Were they going to journey on from place to place, getting no useful information at all?

More important, what was this private agenda Turner Digby Garrett was so vigorously pursuing?

Chapter Five

Apparently, St. George town hadn't changed much since the seventeenth century. It featured steep, crooked streets with names like Featherbed Alley and Petticoat Lane. Pastel houses and quaint shops clustered together on the hillside, looking down on the harbor, terraced white roofs shining in the sun.

After making the rounds of taverns and restaurants, guided by Derry's matchbooks and coasters, Turner and Jamie stopped at an historic house and a carriage museum. The caretaker at the museum and one other bartender recognized Derry's cap, but had no memory of anything else connected with him.

Climbing on foot up a steep street to an old fort that now housed a restaurant and bar, Jamie was tired, sweaty and definitely discouraged.

"This is not going well," she said after they had settled themselves on stools at the fairly busy bar and had ordered drinks.

Turner grunted a vague answer. Ever since they'd come into the bar, he'd been glancing around furtively, as if he was looking for something...or someone.

Sipping her mineral water, Jamie looked around at the high ceilings and whitewashed walls. The place was lit by a wagon wheel full of electric light bulbs. There were several flags hanging from the rafters.

A woman entered the bar and Turner glanced at her, then away. "Are you expecting someone?" Jamie asked.

He had just raised his glass to his lips. The clear sparkling liquid sloshed but didn't spill. "I'm just keeping an eye on things," he said. A lame answer if ever she'd heard one.

"Ready for another?" the barmaid asked, smoothing her blond curls as she came down the long bar to them. The pin on the starched white apron she wore over her "tavern wench" dress gave her name as Catherine.

They both shook their heads, then Jamie dug out Derry's photograph and laid it on the bar. "This man might have visited here three to four weeks ago," she said for the umpteenth time today. "Did you see him? Bright red hair. Light blue eyes."

"That's Derry Riley, isn't it?" Catherine said.

Jamie's heart beat a drumroll. "You did see him? You talked to him?"

The pretty barmaid grinned. "I talk to any chap comes in without a wife in tow." She grinned saucily at Turner. "Would have talked to your man, he came in here alone."

Jamie slanted a disbelieving look at the man beside her. She couldn't imagine anyone who hadn't seen him as himself showing interest in him the way he looked now, hunched over, cap pulled low, five-o'clock shadow darkening by the minute, dark glasses glittering in a menacing way.

"I haven't been in Bermuda long," Catherine confided, "but I've found out the male situation's grotty. I have to depend on tourists for my social life."

"You handle this bar by yourself?" Turner asked.

Catherine shook her head. "Linda should be here, but she's late. Her cycle keeps breaking down."

"I guess we will have some more mineral water after all," Turner said without consulting Jamie. Not that she minded, she needed all the cooling off she could get.

"What can you tell us about Derry?" she asked as Catherine served their drinks.

The barmaid shrugged. "Seemed like a nice chap. Shy, but friendly, like all Americans." Her eyebrows quirked over merry brown eyes. "Came in alone around noon one day, stayed an hour or so chatting me up. Seemed interested, if you take my meaning." Her rather wide mouth turned down at the corners. "Said he'd come back, but he never did. That's men for you."

"Did he say where he was going next?"

Catherine tipped her head to one side. "Said he was going to take a boat out to the Sea Gardens. There's one leaves from the wharf. Said he was having a drink to get his courage up because he didn't like the water. I told him if I was him I'd go see the ducking ceremony instead."

"The what?" Jamie asked.

Turner's hand touched her arm as he spoke himself. "Did he say how long he'd been in Bermuda?"

Catherine shook her head.

"Did he say what he'd been doing?"

She frowned thoughtfully. "Said he was comparing taverns. I told him in England we call that pub crawling. He liked that. Said he was sorry he hadn't got up here before."

Turner leaned on the bar. "Did he drink much?" he asked.

"Just the one beer." She gave the photo back to Jamie. "Is he missing or something?"

"There's a possibility he may be mixed up in some criminal activity," Turner said before Jamie could reply.

"Well I never!" Catherine said, her eyes widening. "A nice young chap like that! What ever did he do?"

Jamie had to believe Turner had some reason for making Derry out to be a crook. He'd come up with this same story everywhere they'd gone today. He would start talking about the Tudor Tavern next, if he followed the usual pattern.

As though reading her mind, Turner inclined his head toward her. She caught a warning gleam behind his sunglasses. His mouth was set in a stern line. The pressure of his hand on her arm had increased minutely.

"You hear about the dust-up at the Tudor Tavern?" he asked the barmaid.

"You don't mean this chap was mixed up in that? And I might have gone out with him!"

"Did he mention the shooting?"

She thought for a minute, then shrugged. "He might have. Nobody talked about anything else for days. Not something you expect to happen in Bermuda." Glancing around, she said in a confidential tone. "Some say the two men who did the shooting were hired killers, one of them an ex-convict."

Turner blinked. "Do they say one of them was an American?"

Catherine shook her head.

"Anyone making any bets on who hired them?"

"Not that I've heard."

Turner sighed. "Could Derry have said he was there when it happened?"

She shrugged again. "I don't remember. I'm not even sure if he came in before it happened or after." She grimaced. "You would never believe how many people claim to have been there. That pub must have been jammed, the way people talk."

She leaned over the bar toward Turner. "Linda Belant *was* there," she added in an exaggerated whisper. "The girl who works with me. She was waiting tables there when it happened."

Jamie's stomach tightened. So that was why Turner had insisted they come up here. Jamie had been ready to quit for the day, but he'd suggested they could manage one more stop. And at the Tudor Tavern, the barman had said one of the waitresses who was on duty during the shooting had left. How had Turner known she worked here?

Of course. When he'd gone back into the tavern, on his mercy mission for Jamie, he must have questioned the man again.

Jamie gave him a dirty look, which he noticed and obviously interpreted. He didn't look at all apologetic. "Linda have any idea who did it?" he asked the barmaid.

Belatedly Catherine seemed to think it might be strange for someone to be asking her such questions. "Who are you?" she asked, staring suspiciously at Turner.

"Name's Digby," Turner said hastily, pulling his cap bill down to his eyebrows. "I'm writing a story on the Tudor Tavern shooting. My magazine would pay well for any information."

Catherine looked impressed. "I never met a writer before. Wish I knew something, but I don't and that's a fact."

She glanced up as a group of rowdy tourists entered the bar. "Sorry I couldn't help," she said brightly, then hesitated. "Linda should be here soon. Can't promise she'll tell you anything, though. She doesn't like talking about it."

Annoyed that Turner had shifted the whole focus of this interview, Jamie turned to him when Catherine moved away. "How can you promise reward money?" she demanded. "What if somebody does come up with useful information?"

"There's some reward money available."

"Oh." She felt slightly deflated, but not for long. "What about that stuff about the shooting and this woman called Linda? You asked the bartender at the Tudor Tavern about her when you went back in there, didn't you? Then you came here hoping to see her. You've been acting like a cat on a hot griddle ever since we arrived."

"What a wonderfully colorful expression," he drawled. Once again, he was avoiding a direct answer.

Jamie lifted her chin. "I realize you don't want to talk about this private business of yours, but if you keep maligning Derry, I'm going to start demanding an explanation."

He frowned at her for a moment, then let out a breath. "Please be patient with me, Jamie. You've understood, I'm sure, that a shooting took place at the Tudor Tavern some time ago. I thought I'd try to track down some information while we're investigating Derry's death. It also gives me a reason for asking about him. That's all."

That brilliant smile of his showed up again, this time with a cajoling edge to it. He was deliberately trying to distract her, she felt sure, but there seemed to be some direct connection between that smile and a certain weakness in her knees that had never afflicted her before.

"If I can solve a crime or two while I'm having this enforced holiday," he added, "it would look well on my record. Keep me out of prison, perhaps."

"There's a chance you'll go to jail?"

"A distinct possibility. Especially if Walter dies."

Jamie hadn't even considered that the old man might die. That would make Turner a murderer. Unless he could prove the man had been endangering Turner's safety. Even then, he would have killed a man. A shudder ran through her.

She was distracted by the rowdy tourists who were asking questions about a medieval banquet that was evidently held in the restaurant on a regular basis.

"I'm sorry," Catherine told them. "There's no banquet tonight. I can show you the banquet hall, if you like."

The group decided to settle for that and followed Catherine out, leaving blessed silence in their wake.

An awkwardness had come between Turner and Jamie. He'd probably seen her shudder. "What about this ducking ceremony?" she asked to get on safer ground. "Is that a secret, too?"

Turner shook his head. "You remember the chair on a long plank in King's Square? Once a week, St. George's puts on a show for the tourists, dunking some of the local girls in the water." He frowned. "It always takes place on a Wednesday. That would be either Wednesday the tenth of April or Wednesday the seventeenth, where Derry was concerned."

"The seventeenth probably," Jamie said.

"Why do you say that?"

"Derry told Catherine he was sorry he hadn't come up here before. If it was Wednesday the tenth, he would have just arrived in Bermuda the day before."

"Well done, Jamie," he said. Taking off his dark glasses, he looked at her admiringly.

"It doesn't add up though," she said. "He told Catherine he was going out to the Sea Gardens that day, but it was the eighteenth when he actually went."

"Perhaps he went out both days."

"Maybe." Jamie sighed. "We're not any further ahead, are we?" she said despondently.

"We've found *something* out," Turner said. "That's the most you can expect in detective work. Whatever lead seems remotely promising, you follow it. Derry was probably here on the seventeenth. He intended going from here to the wharf. Maybe he took Catherine's advice and watched the ducking ceremony instead. Next Wednesday we can go to it ourselves, unless a better clue turns up in the meantime. One of the people who take part in the ceremony might have seen something—the town crier perhaps. You could talk to him."

"He knows you?"

"Not well, but we have met." He took a sip of his drink, looked around appreciatively and abruptly changed the subject. "My father loved this place," he said softly. "He would come in here and discourse on Bermuda's history. Once a history teacher, always a history teacher, I suppose."

Apart from the odd remark about his wife's eyes, it was the first time he'd said anything of a personal nature. Jamie couldn't resist following up. "Your father's retired?"

"Partly. He still does some teaching at the University in Aberystwyth."

"Aber what?"

A glimmer of a smile appeared at the corner of his mouth. "Aberystwyth's a seaport in Wales. My great-grandparents left there to come to Bermuda. My father retired there two years ago. My mother died almost four years ago, soon after my wife...well, there was no connection of course, but there were my father and I, both alone."

Remembered grief touched his eyes briefly but acutely. "I moved in with my father. It seemed a practical arrangement. It took me two years to realize that he was getting grayer and quieter by the month. Under pressure he finally admitted that the memories were painful for him, but he felt I needed him here. I convinced him I could manage perfectly well without him." He hesitated. "Which doesn't mean I don't miss him."

Jamie nodded. "I know what you mean. My folks left Boston to open a bed and breakfast on Cape Cod. My brothers are all married and living in various parts of the United States. I visit them all frequently, but it gets lonely in Boston." She hesitated. "I'm sorry about your mom," she added. "And your wife." Immediately she remembered the remark he'd made about his wife having rough nights. She looked down at the bar, fiddling with her glass.

"My wife was a drug addict," Turner said. Judging by the look in his eyes it had cost him to admit that.

What could she possibly say? Nothing.

"My wife hated my job," he volunteered after a silence. "She said it consumed me, that when I was home, my mind wasn't, and when the phone rang she ceased to exist for me. I don't think I was quite that insensitive, but that's how she perceived me. Obviously I wasn't making her happy, so she found comfort in drugs. I discovered later that she had been a user since her teens. She was clean when I met her. I had no idea." He sighed deeply. "When I found out, I got her into a program and she seemed to be doing well, but then she...slipped back. This time she got behind the wheel of a car. There was an accident. She was killed instantly."

Jamie swallowed. "I don't...I can't even imagine how terrible that must have been for you," she said.

He had banished all expression from his face. "At least the experience taught me something."

"What?" Jamie asked.

"Not to get married," he said shortly. He shook his head as though he was disgusted by his own frivolous answer, then looked at her directly, his eyes empty. "I don't make a habit of talking about my wife. Forgive me."

She put her hand on his arm. "Turner, there's nothing to apologize for. You obviously—" She had no idea what she'd intended to say. He was looking down at her hand on his arm, and she was suddenly conscious that a feeling of intimacy had sprung up between them. Because he'd revealed himself to her, of course. That's all it took, usually.

Turner was suddenly sitting upright. Following his gaze, Jamie saw a young black woman, wearing a period dress and apron like Catherine's, hurrying into a room behind the bar. The missing Linda, no doubt.

"Why don't you join the group in the banqueting hall?" Turner suggested, settling his sunglasses in place.

She took her hand off his arm and looked at him with narrowed eyes. "You want to get rid of me?"

"Yes."

He'd finally given a straight answer, but she was damned if she was going to let herself be railroaded. "I've about had enough, Turner Garrett. I don't know what you're up to, but it seems to me you're more interested in blackening Derry's good name than finding out what happened to him. Apparently you have some secret project all your own. And while all this running around may be giving you the answers *you're* looking for, it isn't doing a thing for me. You go ahead with whatever you have planned for Linda, but I'm not leaving. And tomorrow, with you or without you, I'm going aboard the *Coral Queen*."

His mouth tightened. Lifting her chin, she stared unblinkingly into the opaque dark lenses of his sunglasses. After a long moment he sighed. "All right, Jamie. I have no choice but to bow to your superior judgment."

Although his voice was clipped and sarcastic, she thought she detected a note of admiration in it. But then he added, "Try not to come up with any opinions on therapy, all right?" And she decided she had been mistaken.

"What you want with me?" the young black woman asked, keeping her voice low. She was very pretty, slim, medium height, short black hair curling around a hostile oval face. "I don't know who did that shooting. Told the police that. Tell you the same thing."

Considering he hadn't asked her who did the shooting, that was an interesting start, Turner thought. "Catherine tell you I'm a writer? From the States?" he asked.

She stared at him for a long moment, and he had to stop himself from stiffening. Her gaze flickered away to Jamie, then down to the bar. Picking up a beer glass from the counter she started tracing with one finger the ring it had left. "Don't care who you are," she murmured at last.

He tried a bullying tone. "I know you were working at the tavern that night, Linda. I understand you quit working there afterward?"

He could almost hear her mind testing the question. Finally she nodded. "Pretty scary, huh?" Turner said. "You want to tell me about it?"

"No." She darted a glance round the room, flicked a quick look at his face, then just as quickly averted her eyes again. *Had* she recognized him?

"You sure you don't have any idea who the men were who did the shooting?" He leaned forward over the bar. "How about the man who hired them? My magazine would pay you for any information at all."

She shook her head, her fingers continuing to play with the beer glass. "They had stockings over their heads," she said flatly. "Couldn't see their faces. Soon as they started I went down on the floor. Didn't come up till it was over."

Someone sitting at a table behind Turner laughed and Linda almost shot out of her skin. Her hands went to her throat, then to her mouth. "Maybe you heard something afterward," he persisted, keeping his voice harsh. "Everybody talked about the shooting. Maybe somebody guessed who ordered it."

She shook her head almost violently this time. Her slender body was trembling so uncontrollably he could hear the rustling of her starched apron. Was she afraid because she'd recognized him? Jamie was staring at him as if she had a question or two herself, but at least she wasn't interrupting.

"Did you know the men who were shot?" he asked, trying a different tack.

"Never saw them before."

He was glad he was still wearing the dark glasses. He didn't want a flicker of an eyelash to let her know he recognized that as a lie. The two drug dealers were regular customers at the Tudor Tavern.

"They just happen to be there, happen to get themselves shot," she blurted out in a harsh whisper. "Could have been anybody else, lots of people there."

That was what the citizens of Bermuda had been led to believe. But it wasn't the truth. And he suspected she knew that. "Look, Linda," he said, softening his voice in an attempt to soothe her. "My magazine isn't interested in capturing the killers. I just have to know for sure if anyone recognized them. I can't write that nobody knew who they were, if it turns out somebody did. That would make me look stupid."

Jamie was looking questioningly at him again. What was her problem? He put a cajoling note in his voice. "That's all I want to know for my money, if anyone at all recognized them or guessed who hired them. It's a lot of money, Linda. A lot. And your name would never be mentioned."

Once more she shook her head. "I don't know anything."

Turner sighed. Touching his arm, Jamie slid Derry's photo face down in front of him. He'd almost forgotten it. Picking it up, he said. "Okay, Linda, one more question and I'll leave you alone. Do you recognize this guy?"

He watched her face carefully. If anything her eyes had become more frightened than ever. But when he turned the photo over and she looked at Derry, a long sigh of relief escaped her lips. "Don't know who *he* is," she said. "Never saw *that* man."

"Are you quite sure?" Jamie asked.

Linda nodded firmly. The fact that Turner was convinced she was telling the truth this time made it all the more obvious she'd been lying earlier.

Linda's body language had given rise to another question, however. She'd been terrified right until the moment he turned the photo over. Whose photo had she expected it to be?

Chapter Six

Along with eighty or so tourists, Turner and Jamie boarded the *Coral Queen* at the ferry terminal in Hamilton, taking a seat in the back row on the upper deck. It was one o'clock on Sunday afternoon. Enough breeze was blowing to keep the temperature comfortable. Puffy white clouds floated in the shiny blue sky like patterns on Chinese porcelain.

Jamie had on another awful sweatshirt, a purple one this time. It hung to her knees, loose enough to be a pup tent. With it she wore opaque purple tights and flat black canvas shoes. Her floppy-brimmed denim hat was pulled down to her sunglasses.

It was amazing, Turner thought as the boat scudded over the turquoise water, that her sexuality beamed through such unattractive clothing. What an intriguing mixture she was: stubborn but flexible; tough yet compassionate; feminine, but apparently lacking in vanity—he had yet to see her wearing makeup. At the same time, there was something vulnerable about her that made him want to take her in his arms and ...

"I'm not sure we should sit together," he murmured. "I think the barmaid last night recognized me."

"Catherine?"

"The other one. Linda Belant."

"Oh." They were leaving Hamilton Harbour, and she turned aside to look at the Royal Yacht Club, just slipping past to starboard. Her back was ramrod straight. He could almost feel her bursting with the questions she'd wanted to ask the previous night. So far he'd managed to keep her from asking them, but any minute now...

"That shooting you keep talking about," she said, keeping her voice low. "Someone hired the men to do it?"

"So it would seem."

"Why?"

He didn't answer and after darting a glance at his face, she didn't ask again. After an all too brief silence, she said, "There was something about the way you questioned Linda I didn't like. All that emphasis on whether someone recognized the killers. You really frightened her."

"I know." He hesitated, unused to explaining himself, but for some reason wanting to. "It seemed necessary."

"Is that why you beat up Walter Seaton, because it seemed necessary?"

He stiffened. "I'd rather not talk about that, Jamie."

She lapsed into silence again, but it was not an easy silence. He could almost hear questions whirring around in her head. If he had known how intelligent she was he would never have agreed to use her. It was obvious that while she had no way of knowing exactly what he was up to, she was putting apparently unrelated events together with lightning swiftness.

"Linda has nothing to fear from me," he said to distract her. "Apparently she doesn't know anything." That wasn't strictly true. Linda had *said* she didn't know anything. But no one who was completely ignorant—or innocent—would have looked so terrified. Her fear was understandable up to a point—the shooting had been violent enough to frighten anyone—but why had she looked around so furtively when he questioned her, as if afraid that someone was listening?

Why had she trembled? *Had* she recognized the killers? Had she recognized *him*?

To be on the safe side, he'd worn a different shirt today, a tartan one that was as baggy as yesterday's choice. Both had been gifts from a woman friend who was admittedly color-blind. He'd also exchanged his billed cap for an ancient tan gabardine fishing hat that featured multiple stains of unknown origin. He'd been encouraged by Jamie's momentary lack of recognition when he knocked on her hotel door this morning.

The skipper of the boat had started his commentary over the PA system. Turner smiled at the young man's ripe cockney accent. An ex-pat, obviously. Under cover of the narrative, he said, "I think it might be a good idea for you to get friendly with the captain. Sound him out about the accident when you get the chance, without saying you knew Derry."

"What exactly do you mean by 'get friendly'?" she asked.

"Flirt a little, perhaps."

She turned her head to stare at him through her owlish sunglasses. "Looking like this?"

"You look fine, Jamie."

She grunted. "I look like a bag lady."

Bag ladies don't usually have luscious pink mouths and long elegant legs, he wanted to object, but didn't. His reaction to Jamie Maxwell worried him. He was aware of inner stirrings he hadn't experienced for a long time. He'd actually considered inviting her to stay on at the restaurant bar for dinner last night, then realized they could hardly eat in the elegant dining room wearing hats and dark glasses. He'd even thought perhaps he could take her home and *cook* dinner for her. A ridiculous idea that could easily have led to complications. He couldn't afford complications.

She smelled wonderful, he realized. Generally he didn't care for perfume—so many women poured it on indiscriminately. But hers was a light scent, barely discernible, slightly spicy, as her manner often was. A body lotion, perhaps.

That thought aroused an interesting image.

"I'm going to move round," he said, standing up abruptly.

"Doing what?"

"Just looking at the boat, getting the feel of it."

Immediately, Jamie looked suspicious. "You still don't trust me, do you?" he said.

"Why should I?" she asked, and of course he couldn't answer her.

He wandered around for a while, looking hard at every crew member on deck and below. Going topside again he stood watching the boat's wake. Derry Riley had fallen from the starboard side of the boat, near the stern. There wasn't much space between the last row of seats and the rail, considering the ladder that went down on the port side to the fantail. Some of the space that was left was used up by life preserver lockers. Odd that Derry Riley would squeeze himself into that limited space and then fall over. Today, the blue-green water was smooth, barely ruffled by the light breeze. The boat was completely stable. He was beginning to wonder just how choppy the water had been when Derry Riley fell to his death. Had it really been choppy enough to cause him to fall overboard?

"HELLO DUCKS, what can I do for you?" the skipper asked.

"I thought I might use some of the sun block you mentioned earlier," Jamie said.

He handed her a brown plastic container. "You don't need to worry, you've a good tan. I like your titfer, by the way."

"My what?"

"Tit for tat—hat. Cockney rhyming slang, ducks. Invented by Londoners who didn't like working with Irish immigrants. So they could talk without being understood. Bo Peep—sleep. Duke of York—fork. I use rhyming slang a lot over 'ere. Drives me mates barmy. Where are you from?"

"Boston." She replaced the lotion in its niche and smiled at him. "Maybe I should tell you my ancestors were Irish."

He grinned back. "Oops."

She had no idea how to go about getting information from this man. Flirt, Turner had suggested, but she'd never been much good at flirting—had never wanted to be a game player.

The skipper was not unattractive. Tanned. Thirty something. Average height. Stocky. Tow-colored, wind-tossed hair down to his shoulders. A friendly smile. More than friendly. *He* knew how to flirt, obviously.

"Pretty houses," she said, gesturing at the shoreline. Way to go, Jamie, she thought—a terrific opening line.

"The older ones were mostly built of limestone," he informed her. "Same stuff the island's made of. Nowadays, new 'ouses are built with concrete blocks."

"The roofs are interesting," she said. "Why are they terraced like that?" Game playing. She already knew that Bermudians relied on rain for their water supply, catching it on the roofs, which directed it into underground storage tanks.

"Fascinating," she said when the captain told the same story.

Now what?

"Clyde Kane," the skipper said, removing one hand from the wheel to shake hands. Yes, he was better at this than she was.

She almost gave her real name, but stopped herself in time. "Rose," she said, hoping he'd settle for that.

"Rosie Lea—tea," Clyde said promptly. The breeze was plastering her sweatshirt against her body. She wouldn't have noticed if his glance hadn't raked her up and down.

"I enjoyed your commentary," she said lamely. "You're not a Bermudian, are you?"

He grinned. "No, ducks, I'm a Londoner born and bred. Used to run a sight-seeing boat on the Thames. Came out 'ere on a work permit for a couple of years. Thought I'd get a little sun. Get away from the trouble and strife."

He'd placed a lot of emphasis on the last phrase and accompanied it with a grin. She hazarded a guess. "Wife?"

"Got it in one."

She laughed obligingly, then Clyde shook his head. "Thought I'd like being married but it was all pain and no gain as me body-building mates might say. You married, Rosie Lea?"

"No way," she said.

His smile was suddenly wily. Maybe she was succeeding at this flirting business.

"I'm going back to Blighty in October," Clyde said. "It's nice 'ere, all right, pink sand, good weather, great food, and the Bermudians are a rare treat, except for the older Brits—stuffy, some of them, think they own the whole bloody world."

They were approaching a wide band of brilliant turquoise water. "Sorry ducks, got to do me duty." He picked up his microphone. "You might 'ave noticed that we are passing coral formations on either side, close to the surface," he said into the mike, easing back on the throttle at the same time.

Coral such as that on which Derry had struck his head, Jamie thought, and immediately felt sick.

"We 'ave now reached the Sea Gardens," Kane continued. "Will everyone below in the bar please come on deck so we can open up the hatches down there. In a few minutes we'll 'ave you all go down the steps at the rear—that's the ladder at the stern in shipboard talk. Thank you."

He replaced the microphone in its holder and concentrated for a minute on steering between the fingers of coral. Then he glanced at Jamie. "You all right, ducks? You look dicky."

"I'm fine." Oh, she was doing really great. Mata Hari had nothing on Jamie Maxwell.

"ANY LUCK?" Turner asked her as the passengers streamed past them a few minutes later.

"All I got was a description of how Bermuda houses are built," she admitted despondently.

"Perhaps you can try again later," he said. What had the skipper said to make her laugh, he wondered. He hadn't heard her laugh before. Watching her leaning toward the man he'd felt a pang of jealousy. For what? Young carefree laughter? Or Jamie Maxwell herself?

Jamie herself, he admitted. "Let's go," he said abruptly, as the last group of passengers passed them.

"What's eating you now?" Jamie demanded in a low voice as she followed him down to the lower deck. "Are you mad because I didn't get any information out of the skipper? You were the one who said to be subtle."

He didn't answer.

On the viewing deck, hinged hatches had been lifted away from the windows in the bottom of the hull and folded against the rails that surrounded them. Still irritated, Jamie leaned on a rail and watched the fish swarming below—angelfish, gray snapper and sergeant majors according to the ponytailed young woman doing the commentary. The engines were ear shattering. People were pressing close, excited by the sights below, gasping when a diver wearing scuba gear swam into view and waved at them. The boat was moving very slowly now, passing directly over a wrecked ship. The *Montana,* the narrator said.

Immediately Jamie thought of the men who must have gone down with the ship, which brought Derry vividly to mind. He would have hated looking down into that deep water, hearing stories about men drowning. Tears filled her eyes. Without saying anything to Turner, she eased her way through the intent tourists and headed for the upper deck. Leaning on the port rail, she realized the breeze had come up a little. She wished she could take off her hat and let the wind blow through her hair, but supposed she'd better not.

"Are you all right?" Turner asked, coming up behind her. He had not previously seen her look so vulnerable. Head bent, hair tucked up inside her floppy denim hat, she was the picture of depression. The back of her neck looked fragile. She was biting her lower lip in the way she did when she was thinking deeply. Obviously she'd entertained high hopes of obtaining information on today's trip.

"I started thinking about Derry," she said as he leaned next to her on the rail. "Do you know where . . ."

"It was somewhere in this area," Turner said softly.

Jamie swallowed. "I've wondered all along why he would fall, Turner. Now I think maybe he felt dizzy after being down below, looking down into all that water."

Turner looked down at the water himself. It wasn't easy to see below the surface with the sun shining on it, but he could make out a wide strip of coral close to the boat.

"One thing puzzles me," Jamie went on. "You told me the doctor said he'd hit his head on the coral. At the time, I thought something seemed wrong with that suggestion. What I wonder is, could he really have hit his head on the coral hard enough to knock himself out? Given that the boat probably wasn't going very fast, you'd think if he *fell* he might graze a hip or an elbow at the most. If he dove in head first, it would be something else, but there's no way he'd do that." A frown creased her forehead. "Can we be sure the man who said he was a doctor really was a doctor?" she asked.

He shook his head. "Alexander's report stated only that the man *said* he was a doctor. And as I told you before, there was no reason for anyone else to even look at his report, never mind question it."

"Seeing the actual place where Derry drowned—" She broke off again, hands clenching the rail. "How do you manage—how *did* you manage, I guess I should say, dealing with this kind of thing all the time?"

A fair question. He rubbed his hand over his beard, which was getting to the itchy stage. "Mostly by distancing myself," he answered honestly. "It's not always easy to do, but necessary." He gazed out at the horizon. "Unfortunately," he added, almost to himself, "once you learn to close off your feelings, it's hard to turn them on again."

"Nonsense," she said briskly. "Feelings don't go away. You've just repressed some of them, that's all. Give them half a chance and they'll come floating to the top."

Would that it were so easy. "Jamie Maxwell, girl psychiatrist," he said mockingly.

She scowled at him. At least he'd banished her depression, Turner thought dryly. Just in time, too. Most of the passengers had come on deck again and Jamie needed to get back to work.

This time he suggested she sit closer to the skipper in case there was an opportunity to talk to him again. He would keep to his seat in the stern.

He watched her walk forward, her back straight, head held high in the ridiculous hat. Several male heads came up to watch her pass. Even sloppily dressed she commanded attention. Don't command too much attention Jamie, he wanted to say.

EVIDENTLY there was to be no commentary on the return journey. Just as Jamie was deciding to go speak to the skipper, a young black man in a red tank top and white shorts came forward and took over from Clyde.

Clyde started aft, then stopped as he caught sight of Jamie. "By yourself are you, Rosie Lea?" he murmured.

She nodded.

"Thought I saw you with a chap earlier."

"He just happened to sit next to me."

He smiled widely. "'ow about a drink, then?"

She followed him to the stern, not letting her eyes meet Turner's, though she was very aware of him watching her.

On the lower deck, the hatches had been bolted down over the viewing windows and several tables and chairs set up. A few people were already imbibing.

Jamie asked for a tonic water, Clyde the same. "Not my tipple of choice, but I am supposed to be working," he said.

He grinned at her over the rim of his glass. "You feeling better? What was it, a touch of the old *mal de mer?*"

Jamie shook her head, seeing an opening. "I'm nervous around boats," she said. Then she added, "Someone told me about the young man you lost from this one a while back. He drowned, I understand." She assumed what she hoped was a worried look. "Do you lose many tourists?"

"Cor blimey no," he said, setting his glass down on the table. "Never 'ad anyone go overboard on this boat long as she's been in commission. Never would 'ave 'appened if I'd been on board. Always warn the passengers to be careful moving around if there's the least little bit of chop, I do."

Jamie tried not to let her disappointment show. "You weren't working when it happened?"

"No." He swallowed some tonic water, grimaced then looked thoughtful. "Bermudian named Jordan Lathrop was on that day," he said. "Surprised me, the accident I mean. Jordan's a good skipper. Owns 'is own boat. Takes parties out fishing. Every once in a while he fills in for one of us when we're sick."

"You were ill that day?"

"Blotto the night before, ducks. Whopper of a 'angover in the morning." He frowned. "One of me problems with the missus—no patience with drinking. Churchy, you know?"

Jamie felt a distinct sympathy for Mrs. Kane and wondered if she'd welcome her errant husband home in October.

"How did the man fall overboard?" she asked, hoping she sounded far more casual than she felt.

Clyde shrugged. "Dunno, love, that's a fact. Didn't ask Jordan much about it—'e can be touchy sometimes. The crew didn't want to talk, neither. Felt responsible, didn't they?"

Evidently deciding it was time to change the subject, he leaned back and looked at her. "Where you staying?" he asked, eyes bright with interest.

"With friends," she said hastily.

He looked disappointed. Then the wily look reappeared. "Lucky, 'aving friends to stay with. I first came 'ere and I 'ad this one room in 'amilton. I've a better flat now, above a restaurant, up the apples and pears—" He paused expectantly.

"Stairs?"

He beamed approval. "Bit of all right, you are, Rosie Lea. Catch on quick, you do." He hesitated, looking her up and down again in a way that made her want to slap him. "Gets flippin' lonely sometimes," he added, raising his eyebrows. "Going up those apples and pears to Fakey Ned, I mean."

"Fakey what?"

"Ned, love." He leaned forward, bright eyes fixed on her face. "Rhymes with bed."

"So it does," she said coldly. Standing up, she excused herself, leaving Kane with a 'what did I do to upset *her*' look on his face. Without even glancing at Turner she marched to the stern.

"What's the matter?" Turner demanded, joining her at the rail. "You look extremely pink around the gills."

"The skipper propositioned me," she said shortly.

His mouth tightened. But he spoke lightly. "Want me to challenge him to a duel?"

She glared at him.

"I believe I warned you detective work can have its rougher moments," he said evenly. "Are you saying you wish to give up?"

"You'd like that wouldn't you?" she snapped. "No, I do not want to give up."

"Then perhaps you can give me a report."

"Kane didn't say much that was useful," Jamie retorted, still angry. "He wasn't on duty the day of the accident. He said a Bermudian named Jordan Lathrop was in charge and *he* didn't want to talk about it."

"Jordan Lathrop," he echoed flatly. "Well, well. You did make some progress."

"You know him?"

He nodded, his face impassive. "My father and I went fishing with him a few times."

He was silent for a few moments, then he straightened up and looked at her. "Jordy used to keep his boat in Hamilton, but he moved a while back. I'm not sure where he is now. When we get in to Hamilton we'll find a telephone. It'll be a bit late for a meeting with him today, but you might be able to set something up for tomorrow."

She looked at him, narrow eyed again. "You're telling me I'm going to be on my own for this one?"

"I'm afraid so. But I'll be close by, I promise."

"Is that supposed to make me feel safer?" she asked.

Chapter Seven

"Dammit!" Jamie muttered under her breath. She couldn't go more than an hour without being made sexually aware of Turner Garrett. It sure didn't help to have him listening in on this phone call, which meant he had to stand right next to her with his head crammed up against the telephone receiver, his face no more than a couple of inches from hers. To balance himself, he'd put an arm around her shoulders. She could feel the heat that arm was generating throughout her entire body.

"Don't you think I'm capable of making the arrangements myself?" she said hotly as she dialed.

Turner raised expressive eyebrows, but didn't comment or move.

"Yeah?" a gruff voice said loudly in Jamie's ear.

"Jordan Lathrop? My name's Jamie Maxwell." Turner gripped her shoulder convulsively. Her stomach cramped as she realized she'd forgotten to use her alias. It was too late now. Hastily she plunged into her usual explanation. "I'm a meeting planner for an American company," she said. "I'm looking into entertainment possibilities for a group of executives. Somebody told me you might be able to help."

"Okay."

"May I meet with you somewhere tomorrow?" she asked.

There was a silence at the other end. Just as Jamie wondered if he'd put the receiver down and gone away, he said, "I'm working on my boat. You'll have to come to the marina."

"Where is it?" she asked, when it seemed Lathrop wasn't going to offer anything more.

"Coulston Marina. Sandys Parish." After another pause, he gave her more specific directions.

"Would tomorrow morning be okay?" she asked.

"Don't usually show up before midday. Or later."

"I'll come at noon, then," she said. He hung up without another word.

"Not your typically friendly Bermudian," she said as she replaced the receiver.

"Jordy's an old salt," Turner said. "He's all right once you know him."

Jordy. Just how well *did* Turner Garrett know Jordan Lathrop? Jamie wondered.

MOPED ENGINE WHINING, they rode down a hill into a village that could have been taken right off a picture postcard. On the left a large bay embraced sparkling aquamarine water. A strip of pink sand was edged with coconut palms, purple morning glory and hibiscus bushes. Small pleasure boats bobbed at their buoys, serene under the midday sun.

Jamie found Lathrop's boat easily enough, but no one was in sight. Going into the wheelhouse she listened to indistinguishable sounds coming from below. "Ahoy?" she called uncertainly. She never was sure about nautical matters.

A muffled voice answered, giving what she took to be an invitation to come down. Stepping out of the wheelhouse, she glanced at the shore to make sure Turner was where he was supposed to be. They'd arranged that he would keep watch from the deck of a nearby waterfront restaurant.

She couldn't miss the tartan shirt. He was sitting at an umbrella-shaded table, fishing hat and sunglasses in place, sipping something cool by the look of it.

She settled her denim hat firmly on her head, removed her sunglasses and descended to the lower deck, her heart pounding against her rib cage like a paddleball. She had never felt so alone in her life. Her steps slowing as the silence grew around her, she walked past a small cabin, an even smaller galley and what she took to be the head, and into the aft compartment.

Lathrop was below the deck, crouched on a platform beside a large engine. For one heart-stopping moment, she thought he was naked, but then she saw he was wearing brief shorts. He was a big man, black, with cropped hair and a bushy moustache shot through with gray. He didn't have the ready smile of most Bermudians; his dark eyes assessed her suspiciously.

Squatting down by the open hatch, she held out her hand. "Jamie Maxwell," she said.

He waved his hand to indicate it was grimy, picked up a socket wrench and fitted it over a spark plug. "When you going to want to charter the boat?" he asked over the ratcheting sound of the wrench, getting down to business right away.

Jamie decided to throw caution overboard. She was tired of the oblique approach. "The charter request was a ruse," she admitted. "I wanted to see you about something else."

He grunted and went on working. Not a man to waste words, obviously.

"A friend of mine, Derry Riley, drowned last month when he fell overboard from a glass-bottomed boat named the *Coral Queen*. I understand you were the skipper that day."

The big hand holding the socket wrench stayed steady. Perspiration glinted on his forehead, but it was hot down here. Also smelly. There was a strong fish smell overlaid with a tarry odor and something very like creosote. Jamie concentrated on breathing shallowly.

"I thought perhaps you could tell me exactly what happened," she said. "Derry's mother was so shocked when she got the news she didn't ask many questions. She's a widow," she added, hoping sympathy might make him open up.

"I was below when it happened," he said. "Had to give the undersea commentary. Girl who usually does it didn't show. She'd been at the same party as the guy I filled in for."

Two people had missed that day's work? Coincidence? "Who gave the party," she asked.

"Fellow named Kyle Hammond. Works for Rex Putney."

Rex Putney. The philanthropist she'd read about in the newspaper. She shook her head. They were getting off the track. "Let me get this straight," she said. "Somebody else was at the wheel, the helm, whatever, and Derry drowned while everyone was below looking at the Sea Gardens?"

He nodded.

The police report had said several people saw Derry fall. But if everyone was below... "Do you know how he came to fall?" she asked.

"You ever been out on a glass-bottomed boat?" he asked.

"Yesterday. I went on the *Coral Queen* and talked to Clyde Kane. He told me about you."

He nodded, then took a Feeler gauge from his tool box, shook out the blades and checked the gap on a new spark plug. "Biggest shock of my life," he said as he installed the plug. "Not long after I started the commentary. Everybody leaning over the rails, looking at the fish, oohing and ah-ing, same as always. All of a sudden this here redheaded fellow shows up, in the water, going down, looking dead. People start screaming. Next thing I know the diver's following him down, bringing him back up. I had to fight my way through hysterical passengers to get to the fantail. One of the crew was there, helping the diver get the guy on board. Looked like he'd bashed his head on the coral going in. Some old guy yells he's a doctor, so I let him take over. He and Bobby Kenyon tried to revive him on the way back to Hamilton, but they didn't have any luck.''

Pretend he's talking about some stranger, Jamie told herself as nausea clutched at her throat. Pretend this is just some story he read in the newspaper, a story that has nothing to do with Derry. She swallowed hard.

Lathrop glanced at her. "Get yourself a glass of water in the galley if you need it," he said gruffly, but not unkindly.

She shook her head. "I'm fine." She thought for a moment, going back over everything he'd told her. "Do you know the doctor's name?" she asked.

He paused in his labors. After his spurt of talkativeness, he was back to pondering before he spoke. Finally he shook his head. "Police took over when we got to Hamilton. They might know."

"This Bobby somebody. He's on the *Coral Queen*'s crew?"

He dropped a used spark plug in the lid of his toolbox. "Was that day."

"He's the one who took over when you went below?"

"That's him."

"Is he still on the crew?"

"I don't think so." There was distaste in his voice. Why? Jamie wondered.

"Please, Mr. Lathrop, I'd appreciate anything you can tell me about this man. Where I can find him, what he looks like. It's very important to me."

His dark eyes regarded her steadily for a full minute. Then he nodded. "He's a white Bermudian. Average height, stocky, dark eyes, straight black hair, receding on the forehead. The kind of five o'clock shadow that's so dark it looks tattooed on, know what I mean? Bobby's not bad-looking except he's cross-eyed. Can't help that, I suppose."

"I didn't see anyone like that yesterday," Jamie said.

"Your lucky day."

Jamie waited.

"Not one of my favorite people, Bobby. He's a sneery sort. Unreliable, too. Turned up stoned a couple of times when I was helping out on the *Coral Queen*." He snorted. "Anything I hate it's a druggie."

"And this man was at the helm when Derry went overboard?" Jamie said unbelievingly. "Was he stoned then?"

"Wouldn't have let him take over if he had been." He dropped another used spark plug and picked up a new one.

"What about the diver?" she asked. "Do you know his name?"

"Joe Hokins," he said. "Also white. Tall. English ex-pat. Dark curly hair, blue eyes. Lifts weights and shows it. Women think he's handsome."

She hadn't seen anyone answering that description on board the *Coral Queen* either.

"Something off about Hokins, my opinion," Lathrop said. "Has a hair-trigger temper for one thing. Some people act first, think later. Hokins acts first, doesn't ever think. Goes looking for trouble. *Likes* trouble." He paused again. "I heard Bobby had done a bunk."

"Done a bunk?"

"You know—taken off, disappeared."

Jamie's stomach turned over. "After the accident?"

"A few days, maybe." He looked up at her in a startled way. "You saying it might be connected?"

The officer who investigated the "accident" had taken off, now it seemed one of the crew members had done the same. How could it not be connected? "What do you think?" she asked.

Looking perturbed, he began removing the ignition wire from another spark plug. Realizing her tights were cutting off her circulation, Jamie stood up, then remembered she was supposed to show herself to Turner every few minutes. Excusing herself, she went up on deck, breathing deeply when she reached fresh air. What Lathrop had said about the two men on the Coral Queen had disturbed her.

Turner was still sitting on the restaurant's deck, his face turned toward her. His whiskers were fast turning into a beard—she could see it even from here. She felt comforted by his presence, which was pretty stupid considering that newspaper story. Not to mention his often suspicious behavior.

Face it, Jamie, she told herself, because you're physically attracted to the man, you're too ready to overlook the reason he's in disgrace.

"Damn!" Lathrop exclaimed as she rejoined him. He held up the spark plug he'd just removed. It was brand new. "I already changed this one," he muttered.

"Why don't you tell me what's bothering you," she suggested quietly. "It's obvious something is, or you wouldn't have told me so much about those two men."

"You're a sharp one you are," he muttered as he replaced the offending plug. For a minute she thought he was through talking, but then he suddenly said, "I never was satisfied about that accident."

Jamie's stomach jerked. Squatting again, she gave him her complete attention. "Why not?" she asked.

He returned his attention to the engine. "Nobody but Joe Hokins saw the guy fall," he said slowly. "Oh, people told the police officer they saw him fall, but what they saw was him going past the viewing window. Bobby said *he* didn't see the guy fall. So that makes Hokins the only witness. And I wouldn't trust Hokins far as I could throw him."

"I didn't see anyone of Hokins's description on the *Coral Queen*, either," Jamie said.

He shrugged. "Doesn't always work there." His eyes narrowed. "Maybe he did a bunk, too."

Jamie's breath caught in her throat. "Did Hokins tell the police how Derry fell?" she asked.

Wiping his hands on an old bandana, Lathrop went into one of his brown studies. "Said he came up on deck, staggered hard against the rail, lost his balance and fell over."

"The water was rough that day?"

"Breeze was brisk. Little chop, that's all." He frowned. "Your friend might have been seasick, I suppose. Doesn't take much for some people. Horizon jerks up and down a bit and off they go. Hokins said *he* was at the bow, getting into his scuba gear. Took him a minute to finish, then he jumped over the side and went after him."

"Did you tell the police officer you weren't convinced it was an accident?" Jamie asked.

"Never said I wasn't convinced," he protested. "Said I wasn't satisfied."

"Did you tell the police officer *that?*"

He shook his head. "Learned long ago not to volunteer things, especially when you've no proof." He shrugged. "Besides, once I said I hadn't seen anything, the officer didn't ask me any more questions."

"Was that Sergeant Cornell Alexander, a West Indian?"

"Sounds familiar."

What now, she wondered. "So you never even saw Derry?" she murmured, more to herself than to Lathrop.

"Didn't say that. Said I didn't see him fall. Saw him earlier when he came aboard and again when he came forward to take pictures. Talked to him a little bit then."

Jamie had frozen in place. It was a full minute before she could speak. "He took pictures?"

He nodded. "Took quite a few along the shore—houses, trees. Watford Bridge when we went under it."

Derry's Minolta had been empty. There had been no rolls of film in his equipment bag or his suitcase. Jamie hadn't even attached any significance to that, until now...

Quite suddenly she couldn't wait to tell all she had learned to Turner and find out what he made of it. "Thank you for your help, Mr. Lathrop," she said, holding out her hand.

This time he shook it.

She had stepped onto the dock and started for shore when she heard him call her name. She came back. He was standing next to the wheelhouse, looking at her, frowning, wiping his forehead with the rag he'd used earlier. He was even bigger than she'd thought. "I just thought of something," he said. "Did you talk to the girl?"

Chapter Eight

"What girl?" Jamie asked.

"The girl who came on the *Coral Queen* with your friend."

Jamie stared at Lathrop blankly while his statement rattled through her brain. "I didn't know he had a girl with him," she said faintly. She stepped back onto the boat. "This could be important, Mr. Lathrop. What did she look like?"

Tugging at his bushy mustache, he screwed up his face. "Messy blond hair, skinny, small, pretty, I suppose."

"Did you tell Sergeant Alexander about her?"

He shook his head. "I didn't even remember her."

"Blond hair, skinny, small," Jamie muttered. "It's not much to go on."

"You want to know where she works?" Lathrop asked.

Jamie tried not to let her exasperation show. "Where?"

"Beauty parlor. The New Woman. Name's Anna. Don't remember her surname. I drove my wife there one time. They have some fancy kind of facial they do and she wanted to try it."

"Can you tell me where the beauty parlor is?"

He considered again, while Jamie dug her nails into her palms. She was very conscious of Turner watching her. Probably he was wondering why she'd come aboard again.

"Near the causeway that goes to St. George's," Lathrop said at last.

"I'M FINALLY getting somewhere," Jamie said excitedly as she joined Turner on the restaurant's deck.

He raised a cautionary hand and she realized for the first time that a waiter had followed her to the table with a menu.

"I'm not sure I'm hungry," she began.

"Maybe we *should* have lunch, Rosie?" Turner said with enough emphasis to remind her to be careful.

Right—they could hardly sit here without ordering something. She glanced at the menu without making sense of the words. "A cheese sandwich," she said finally.

"Same here," Turner said.

As soon as the waiter left, she leaned forward. "Jordan Lathrop was down below giving the commentary when Derry drowned. Somebody else was at the helm."

"Who?" Turner asked.

To her horror, she realized her mind was blank. "I can't remember the guy's name." She started to stand up, meaning to run back to the boat, but Turner put his hand on her arm.

"Wait a bit," he suggested. "It will come back to you."

She subsided, racking her brain. "He mentioned another man—the diver—Joe Hokins."

He repeated the name under his breath.

She gave him a few seconds to think, then told him what Lathrop had said about Hokins. "He said the other guy— why can't I remember his name?—he said he was sort of sneery. And here's another thing—Clyde Kane told me he wasn't on board because he had a hangover. Lathrop says the girl who was supposed to do the underwater narration was at the same party the night before and get this—neither of them were well enough to come to work the next day. The party was given by a guy called Kyle somebody. Hammond. He works for Rex Putney—he's a philanthropist—Putney, I mean. I read about him in a newspaper when I first got here.''

She was suddenly conscious that Turner's interest had intensified. About to question him, she realized she hadn't told him the most important thing yet. ''Listen,'' she began, then stopped as the waiter approached. The sandwiches were arranged on flowered china plates, cut diagonally into four pieces, accompanied by a pot of tea and two delicate cups. Jamie realized she was hungry after all. Picking up a triangle she took a bite, then looked at the sandwich accusingly. ''It's stuffed with onions.''

''Certainly,'' Turner said, as though that was to be expected.

Oh well, it tasted great anyway. ''There was a woman...'' she began, but Turner stopped her with a hand on her arm.

''Perhaps this isn't the time or place,'' he said, gesturing to indicate the tables that had filled up around them.

Willing herself to be patient, she concentrated on her lunch, poking into her brain every once in a while to persuade it to come up with the missing name.

They were back in her hotel room when her brain finally obliged. After ducking into the bathroom to wash up and change into cuffed white shorts, Reebok running shoes and a khaki shirt she'd sent to be ironed the previous day, she ran a pick through her hair, which evidently stirred up some brain cells. ''Bobby Kenyon,'' she blurted out as she sat down in the chair opposite Turner.

Recognition flared in Turner's eyes. He'd taken off his hat and glasses and she could see what he was thinking much more easily. He was practically simmering with shock. She stared at him. ''You know who he is,'' she said, making it a flat statement rather than a question.

For one millisecond, he lowered his gaze. Then he looked at her directly. ''I'm afraid not,'' he said smoothly.

She stared at him.

"Perhaps you'd better tell me all of it before we get into a discussion," he said before she could demand an explanation.

That seemed reasonable enough. Excitedly she recounted everything Lathrop had said, including his dissatisfaction with the circumstances of the "accident." "He didn't tell any of this to the investigating officer," she told Turner. "Said he didn't ask him."

Turner muttered under his breath.

"He said he'd heard Kenyon had 'done a bunk,'" Jamie added. "Don't you think that's significant, considering Cornell Alexander did the same thing?"

"Alexander did *not* do a bunk," Turner objected. "His resignation was properly submitted and accepted."

"The beauty parlor is near the causeway that goes to St. George's," Jamie went on, ignoring his objection.

He didn't comment. "Let me think for a minute, Jamie," he said.

She sat back in her chair, but couldn't help fidgeting. Patience was not among her virtues. A stray sunbeam glinted on an object that was lying on the carpet next to Turner's chair. Investigating, Jamie came up with Derry's enameled four-leafed clover. Returning to her seat, she studied the charm, casting her mind back. She couldn't remember opening the side pocket of her duffel since she'd hunted for Derry's letter. In any case, why hadn't the charm been picked up by the maid's vacuum cleaner? Maybe the maid hadn't vacuumed for a few days. Getting up, she replaced the charm in the duffel.

"I almost forgot," she exclaimed. "Mr. Lathrop told me Derry came forward during the trip out to the Sea Gardens to take photographs of the scenery. But Derry's camera was empty and there were no containers of film in his luggage."

Turner's dark eyes glinted again. "You're sure?"

"I unpacked his suitcase. His mother couldn't bear to look in it." She paused. "Now there's a thought." Jumping up she picked up the telephone and asked for the manager.

"What are you doing?" Turner asked, looking alarmed.

"It's okay," she said, then heard Charles Hollingsworth's public school accent. "This is Jamie Maxwell," she said.

"Hello, Jamie." His voice had warmed considerably.

She made her own voice brisk. "I spoke to you about my friend Derry—the man who drowned. Can you tell me who was responsible for sending his suitcase back to the States?"

There was a pause. "I'm afraid I have no idea," he said.

"Could you look into it and get back to me?"

"Of course," Charles said promptly.

"He's going to check up on it," Jamie said as she hung up.

To her surprise, Turner was on his feet, looking extremely stern. "What did I do?" she asked.

"You don't think the manager will wonder why you are so curious about your friend's suitcase? I warned you to be discreet, Jamie."

"I've already talked to him about Derry," she pointed out. "He knows I'm trying to find out what happened to him. If I can trace whoever sent the suitcase maybe I can find out what happened to the film."

"He might have turned the film in but didn't have a chance to collect it." He put his hands on her shoulders. "Slow down, Jamie, think before you act. Please."

Lifting her chin, she gave him an unrepentant smile. "You might as well accept that I have a bull-in-a-china-shop approach to life. I'd have thought you would have noticed by now." She was very aware of the strength of his hands through the cotton of her shirt. A quiver of reaction, impossible to ignore, vibrated down her spine.

"Where to next?" she asked, hoping he wouldn't notice the tremor in her voice.

"To the New Woman. I'll go there tomorrow. Alone."

She stared at him, exasperated. "That doesn't make sense. I'm the obvious one to see Anna. Nobody's going to believe you in a beauty parlor, especially in your Digby persona."

"I could ask for a shave," he pointed out, letting go of her shoulders to rub a hand over his beard.

She ignored both his statement and the bereft feeling she'd experienced when his hands left her shoulders. "It would be much easier for me to bring up the subject of the *Coral Queen* casually," she insisted. "I can lead the conversation around to Derry and see what Anna comes up with."

He was shaking his head again, with finality this time. "Your stint as a detective is over, Jamie."

She was so stunned she couldn't seem to locate her voice. Once again, the image of Turner Garrett bending over the prone body of the old man, Walter Seaton, nightstick in hand, flashed in her mind, sickening her. What was she getting close to? Why had he decided it was time to stop cooperating?

"You've got to be kidding," she said hotly. "There's no way you're going to shut me out of the action now. Derry was *my* friend. I'm the one who instigated this investigation. Wild horses can't stop me from going ahead with—"

His fingers touched her mouth to silence and started a whole slew of sensations in other parts of her body. "If you stop right now, I promise you..."

"No way." His hands were gripping her shoulders again, harder this time, perhaps because she had tensed with anger. His jaw had lifted perceptibly to match the angle of hers.

"Why do you want me off the case?" she demanded. "Is it something Lathrop said? As soon as I mentioned Kenyon's name, you got excited. Until your Mount Rushmore look took over."

"My what?"

She winced. God, she had a big mouth. "Sometimes you look like one of the presidents on Mount Rushmore," she said lamely. "Sort of granite faced."

"That's hardly flattering." She thought she'd insulted him beyond forgiveness, but then he smiled and his grip on her shoulders loosened. "I want you off the case, as you put it, because I'm concerned for your safety." He paused as if considering what to say next. "I don't recognize Kyle Hammond's name," he said, "but I do know who Bobby Kenyon is, and Hokins by reputation. What I know of them isn't good."

So. He *had* lied to her. How many times?

"But Hokins and Kenyon don't have anything to do with Anna, surely," she protested. "Anna was obviously somebody Derry picked up, the way he almost picked up Catherine. Let me at least go to see her, Turner. I can be tactful if I put my mind to it." She tried her best to look innocent. "Let me do this and I'll do whatever you tell me to after that."

Wry laughter entered his dark eyes. He studied her face, his hands rubbing her shoulders now in an absent-minded way that felt like a caress. Her nervous system was going into overdrive. "How can I refuse such an offer?" he murmured, then added, "If I do, you'll probably go, anyway." He sighed. "All right. Anna's yours."

"Great! I will be careful, honestly."

His face was so close. The planes and angles of it were becoming familiar to her, she realized. Quite suddenly the air seemed to sing between them, and an expression she hadn't seen before came over his face. He looked . . . fond.

More than fond. How wonderful it would be if for once she could dispense with suspicion, distrust, fear. Was it possible? Could they come together simply as man and woman? For a little while.

Drawing in a breath, she laughed nervously. "We both smell of onions."

He sniffed and smiled. "That's not onion, Jamie, that's ambrosia, the food of the gods and immortals."

His gaze had found her lips, his eyes midnight dark. She was conscious of warmth and a storm of sweetness invading her body. At the same time she felt as if she were riding upward on a current of air. Inside her bemused mind a thought stirred to life, an admission that she didn't want him to let go of her, wanted instead that he should draw her closer, hold her, make love to her. Slowly.

"Jamie." There was such tenderness in his voice.

Without consciously meaning to, she put up her hand and touched his face, shivering with sensual delight when she felt the rasp of his beard against her fingers.

Taking hold of her hand he held it against his cheek for a long moment. His free hand moved slowly down her back, easing her close to him, while his face came down to hers and his mouth touched gently against her own. There was an aching in her throat that made her tremble.

"I've wanted to do this from the beginning," he said against her lips, and then his gentleness gave way to something much more insistent, and she parted her lips to him and let her body lean into his. A wonderful lassitude seemed to have taken control of her body. Her eyes drifted closed, all of her feelings concentrated on the sensations he was bringing to life as his mouth moved hungrily on hers and his hands slid urgently down her back and over her bottom and lingered there.

Her knees were definitely going to give way, she decided as she returned his kiss with a passion she hadn't known she possessed. This man had a debilitating effect on her knees.

As if she'd spoken aloud, he drew her to the bed and sat on its edge with her, all without moving his mouth from hers. There was no doubt about it, she thought, a beard definitely added interest to a kiss.

His hands moved to her breasts, his thumbs teasing her nipples erect. Giving in to her own impulses, she unbuttoned his shirt and ran her hands over the soft mat of dark hair. His skin was smooth and browned by the sun, hard with muscle. She slipped her arms around his back, under his shirt, then touched her lips and tongue to the hollow above his collarbone. He tasted warm and clean and slightly salty. She could feel his breath stirring her hair, feel the beat of his heart, as erratic as her own.

He was easing her shirt from her shoulders now, gazing at her with obvious pleasure, a smile curving the corners of his mouth. How had she failed to notice what a seductive mouth he had? Hadn't she thought it was stern?

Her gaze fixed itself on his face as she wriggled out of her shorts and panties. His fingers were fumbling with the fastening to her bra. She let him fumble, enjoying the suspense and the frustration showing in his eyes. Finally the hooks came free.

He folded her bra. She hadn't even know a bra *could* be folded, but he did it very neatly, then folded the rest of her garments, too, and placed them on the bedside table.

She laughed and his eyebrows questioned her, but she shook her head, smiling. This was no time for even friendly criticism. Besides, his neatness was sort of endearing.

Returning to her, he ran his hands over her wild hair, dividing it between his hands, pulling it in front of her shoulders, attempting to smooth it, then letting his hands slide down to cover her breasts. He laughed when her hair sprang free. She had never seen him look so carefree.

Disposing of his own clothing, tidily of course, he didn't take his gaze from her for a moment. "You are so breathtakingly lovely, Jamie," he murmured.

"You, too," she said with a smile. Her heart was pounding as if she'd run several miles. Which was hardly surprising. She and Turner had suddenly come a long, long way.

As he took her in his arms and pulled her down beside him on the bed, there was one moment when she understood with great clarity that she was playing with fire. According to the old maxim, people who played with fire were pretty sure to get burned. For one more moment she lay taut, staring up at the bars of light cast by the sunshine that was streaming in through the window. Then Turner's lips closed over her nipple and she felt a tug of need and desire slice through her like a silver sword. His hands caressed her, lifted her. Her own hands lifted to his face, her fingers sliding over his beard, then going behind his head to bury themselves in his crisp hair and pull his head close so that she could once again savor his wonderful, exciting, skillful mouth.

He wanted to touch every part of her, it seemed. While Jamie was soon ready for a deeper intimacy, he continued to touch and kiss and admire. When she tried to pull his body closer to her, he resisted and went blithely on with what he was doing. After a while, she stopped pressuring him, beginning instead her own journey of discovery. He was a sensual man, she learned, a man who liked to be touched.

For a long time they moved together and apart and touched and kissed and murmured to each other. Until finally he kneeled over her, looking down at her, and gently, carefully, eased himself into her.

Again there was a moment, just as he entered her, when his face became stern and she felt a flicker of fear, but then his body covered hers and pressure started to build inside her and there was no more thought, no more suspicion. There was only movement and heat and mouths exchanging breath and soft words that had no meaning. Their kisses quickened then slowed as their bodies grew still and the sweet pressure built. A moment later the bars of light on the ceiling shattered into small particles that might never again come together.

SOMEONE SHOUTED in the street outside. A car door slammed. A breeze strayed in through the open window and sent a shiver across Jamie's fevered skin. Turner's left arm was under her neck, his long legs wrapped around her. Her right arm was caught under his body and had lost its feeling. But she had no desire to move. She sighed, feeling like a cat that had lain overlong in the sun.

Turner smiled at her. Then he leaned over her and she thought he was going to kiss her, but he checked his wristwatch instead. And groaned slightly.

"What?" she asked.

"I have to meet someone. Much as I'd rather stay here." He kissed her lightly, absentmindedly, as though his mind had already moved on.

"Someone? Who?"

"Someone who might have information to add to what Jordan Lathrop told you."

He was back to giving evasive answers. And Jamie's contentment was beginning to fray around the edges. "Does this someone have a name?" she asked, making no attempt to disguise the caustic note that had crept into her voice.

He smiled at her. "Everybody has a name." If that wasn't a fatuous answer she didn't know what was.

With one lithe movement, Turner unwound himself and stood by the side of the bed, looking down at her. God, he was a gorgeous man—lean and hard-muscled. Gently he touched a finger to her breast. "Please believe that I don't want to go," he said.

She wanted to believe him. But a feeling of disappointment was gnawing inside her. What had she expected then, that he'd stay with her through the evening and the night? It wasn't going to happen, obviously.

They showered together and soaped each other and almost recaptured the passion that had engulfed them earlier. But Turner was holding back, deliberately, Jamie felt sure. And afterward they dressed in silence, Jamie putting her shorts and shirt and Reeboks back on, Turner getting back into the awful baggy slacks and tartan shirt.

Letting down her hair, which she had pinned out of the way for her shower, she dragged her pick through it, wondering how to break the silence that had come between them. Silences grow from a lack of trust, she thought. All the lovemaking in the world couldn't erase a lack of trust.

"Turner," she said, not sure what she was going to say but feeling she needed some reassurance.

He had just finished tying his sneaker laces. "Jamie," he said, with another of his brilliant smiles.

Then someone knocked on the door.

Chapter Nine

Turner and Jamie both started, guilty as a pair of randy teenagers caught by their parents. Jamie's heart ricocheted against her rib cage. "Ignore it," Turner murmured.

Jamie glanced at the door—she hadn't set the safety latch. "It might be the maid with my laundry," she whispered. "If I don't answer, she'll let herself in." God, what if the maid had walked in while they were still on the bed!

"Go on into the bathroom," she urged. "I'll get rid of whoever it is."

He sighed, giving in. As soon as he was in the bathroom, Jamie opened the outer door, and there was the golden boy himself—Charles Hollingsworth, slim and elegant in tailored jacket and Bermuda shorts. She was so disoriented he had moved past her before she could stop him. He headed straight into the sitting area and settled himself for a visit. "Have you had dinner?" he asked.

"I had a late lunch. I'll probably skip dinner altogether." Not bad for a spur-of-the-moment invention.

"How disappointing. I was hoping you'd join me." His mouth had gone charmingly wry and that flirtatious note was back in his voice. Conscious that Turner could hear him, Jamie felt increasingly flustered. Yet she could hardly go on hovering in the doorway. Closing the door, she went to sit on the edge of the chair facing Charles. This situation was straight out of an old-fashioned farce.

"I have the information you requested," he said.

Information? *Derry's suitcase.* she gazed expectantly at him. "Actually," he added, "I also have something else in mind. I'd hoped we could discuss it over dinner."

"Something about Derry?"

"Something personal."

Oh, God! What should she do now? "My time here is pretty well scheduled." *Don't give excuses,* she scolded herself.

He looked hurt. "How can I have dinner with you?" she said lightly, making a joke of it. "I'm allergic to your smoke, remember?"

He raised a hand, Boy Scout fashion. "I vow never to smoke in your presence, so help me, God."

It was certainly flattering to be pursued so strenuously. "I'm sorry," she said.

"Another time? Tomorrow?"

"Maybe. What did you find out?" Damn, she'd sounded too anxious. She was supposed to be subtle. Trouble was, subtlety came no more naturally to her than patience did.

He was obviously startled by her sudden intensity.

"You said you had information for me," she prompted.

"Oh, yes. It seems my assistant, Loretta Dean, packed your friend's clothing. A police officer picked up the suitcase, she says."

"Did she get his name?"

His smile was regretful. "I didn't ask. Is it important?"

"Yes. No. I mean . . . I want to cover all bases before I report back to Derry's mother. She's so anxious..." Her voice trailed away as she realized Charles was gazing fixedly at Turner's fishing hat and sunglasses, which Turner had left on the coffee table. Before she could think of a way to distract his attention, his gaze roamed around the room and settled on the closed bathroom door.

"Maybe I could talk to Miss Dean myself," she said hurriedly, standing up and picking up her purse.

"Now?" he asked, rising with obvious reluctance.

"Perhaps you would take me to her? She might be more inclined to answer my questions if she feels I have your approval."

He smiled. "You certainly have that, Jamie."

Jamie winced, almost convinced she could see the gleam in Turner's eyes as he eavesdropped on this conversation.

"Shall we?" she asked, gesturing at the door.

To her relief, he accompanied her without question, though it seemed to her he cast one last glance at the bathroom door. Was she imagining suspicion where none existed?

"What was it you wanted to discuss with me?" she asked as they entered the elevator.

"I wanted to invite you to a party," he said with another of his engaging smiles. "But if your schedule's full..."

She certainly didn't have anything against parties, but it didn't seem wise to encourage Charles Hollingsworth's obvious interest; she didn't need any more complications right now.

"The host is one of Bermuda's leading lights, Rex Putney. Delightful man. British. I think you might enjoy meeting him."

Rex Putney. The man she'd read about in the newspaper. The charity guru for whom someone named Kyle Hammond worked.

"Putney's a very influential man in these parts," Charles continued as they exited the elevator. "He was president of a chain of department stores until his retirement."

"Oh, he *is* that Putney," Jamie said, surprised. "He has a store in Boston."

Charles nodded. "He is also a noted philanthropist. He has established countless scholarship funds. He also founded a museum and a hospital, sits on several charity and arts boards and helps to raise funds for all of them. Contributes a great deal himself, actually. He's a multimillionaire."

"He sounds too good to be true," Jamie said, amused by the almost holy light that appeared on Charles's face whenever he talked about wealthy people.

He looked shocked. "Oh, no, Rex Putney's the genuine article," he said loyally. "He's even involved in trying to prevent criminals from constantly returning to prison. He's instituted a program that tries to catch convicts as soon as they are released, provides them with clothes, money and jobs. I'm told the project has been quite successful."

Jamie had known the minute Putney's name was mentioned that she would accept Charles's invitation, but before she could do so, she realized they had reached Loretta's office.

Loretta was plotting a line chart on her computer, wearing another equally attractive silk suit, an ivory one this time. She kept her gaze fixed on the screen as they entered.

"Miss Maxwell is still concerned about her friend's effects," Charles said.

"Effects?" Loretta queried without turning around. Her voice was quite harsh.

"The suitcase you packed and gave to the police." There was an apologetic note in Charles's voice. He really was a little too timid. Any other boss would be annoyed rather than apologetic when his assistant was being rude.

Loretta shot him a murderous glance. "What about it?"

"Do you know the officer's name?" Jamie asked.

The young woman swung around in her swivel chair, giving Charles another hostile glance on the way. She shook her head.

Could she go to the police station and ask about Derry's suitcase? No, Turner had warned her to be discreet. "What did the officer look like?" she asked.

Loretta's mouth turned down at the corners. "Looked like a policeman. Blue uniform, hat. Like that."

"Loretta," Charles said in a chiding but even-tempered way. "Didn't you tell me he was a tall, good-looking man?"

She made a slight snorting sound. "Aren't they all?"

"Was he..." Jamie tried to think of a tactful way to put the question, then decided it wasn't necessary to be tactful in the face of the woman's rudeness. "Was he a white man?"

Loretta glanced again at Charles, as though impatient with Jamie's questioning. Charles smiled affably at her and she swung back to her computer and exited the program with a couple of brisk keystrokes before swinging back. "He was a white man," she said with exaggerated patience.

"Young, old? Thin, fat?" Jamie asked.

"How many times do you see a fat police officer?" Her forehead wrinkled. "He had a pretty good build, I suppose. I don't remember much about him. It didn't seem important."

"I'm sorry to disturb your work," Jamie said, hoping to disarm her. "Derry Riley was my best friend, you see."

Sympathy gleamed in Loretta's dark eyes, which was at least an improvement over hostility.

"Was the police officer fair or dark?" Jamie asked.

Loretta rubbed her nose. "I think he kept his hat on."

Abruptly Jamie decided to cast all caution aside. "Do you remember seeing any thirty-five-millimeter film in Derry's room?"

Loretta shook her head. "Not my place to go through the man's stuff. All I did was dump it in the suitcase."

It hadn't looked as if it had been dumped. It had been a far neater job of packing than Jamie had ever managed.

"So there might have been film in there for all you knew?" Jamie asked. "I *know* Derry took pictures while he was here, but there wasn't any film in his camera or his suitcase when it arrived in the U.S., which seems sort of..."

Loretta narrowed her eyes. "You implying I stole—?"

"Good grief, no."

"Your friend might have dropped the film off for developing," Charles suggested, just as Turner had.

Would there be any point in checking places Derry might have left the film, Jamie wondered. How many places would there be? Dozens? She sighed.

"If you do remember the police officer's name, could you let me know?" she asked Loretta.

Loretta nodded, but her expression was so negative Jamie was quite sure she wouldn't hear from her.

Why on earth was the woman so hostile, she wondered as she walked with Charles toward the lobby. Was it possible *she'd* been involved in Derry's death, or the subsequent cover-up—if there had been a cover-up.

The thought brought Jamie to such an abrupt halt that Charles, walking slightly behind her, bumped into her. Apologizing, he looked at her curiously. "Sorry," she said. "I was just...thinking."

"Thinking about that party?" he asked with a smile.

She'd almost forgotten about his invitation. Rex Putney. "When is the party?" she asked, making her voice casual, aware that the young women at the registration desk were watching.

"Day after tomorrow," Charles said. "Two o'clock in the afternoon. It's a garden party. The gardens at Stonecrest are remarkably lovely."

"Stonecrest?"

"Putney's home. I'm taking several guests in the boat. I'd be delighted if you could come."

A group excursion. That ought to be okay then. But on Wednesday she and Turner were supposed to go to the ducking ceremony in St. George's. "What's your connection to Mr. Putney?" she asked. It was none of her business of course, but she couldn't help being curious.

"Heavens, I'm not important enough to have a connection. I've merely contributed to some of his causes and served for a time on one of the arts boards. That's all."

The corners of the blue eyes twinkled, his mouth curving in the genial smile that was one of his most attractive features. "Actually, if your question is why on earth I've been invited, I should tell you I'm a rarity in Bermuda, Jamie— an eligible man who isn't just passing through. I'm invited to any number of parties for that reason." He laughed so infectiously Jamie couldn't help laughing with him. "I really do need you, you see," he continued. "You can protect me from the ladies."

Kyle Hammond had worked for Rex Putney, and Kyle Hammond had given a party the night before Derry drowned. After the party Clyde Kane and a young woman had been unable to report for work. Having met Kane she was prepared to believe that happened to him fairly often. Which probably meant Kyle Hammond had nothing to do with anything. All the same, it was worth taking a look at Rex Putney and maybe finding out whatever she could about Hammond. She might even meet someone who knew Kenyon or Hokins, or even someone who'd met Derry. A long shot but surely worth exploring.

"Okay," she said, then realized how ungracious she sounded. "I may have a conflicting appointment, but if that doesn't work out I'd love to go to a party." She glanced down at her shirt and shorts. "I'll even wear a dress."

"Good show," Charles said, sounding delighted. At the prospect of her accompanying him, or the thought of her wearing a dress, Jamie wondered.

TURNER HAD LEFT her room, though she really hadn't been gone all that long. Of course, he hadn't known when she'd be back. And he'd said he had to meet someone. There was no reason to feel so...deserted. It was probably as well to have some time to think very seriously about Turner Garrett.

He'd left her a note, propped up against her overflowing duffel, written on Victoria Hotel stationery. "It seemed politic to withdraw. I'll give you a ring later."

The last sentence startled her until she realized he meant he'd telephone. Someone had once said the United States and the United Kingdom were two countries separated by a common language, she remembered, smiling.

He'd added a postscript. "I'm not sure the creases will fall out of that dress, Jamie, it looks like a lost cause."

She'd forgotten about the dress she'd left hanging on the bathroom door. She laughed, then frowned at the loving note that had crept into her laughter. Abruptly she remembered Loretta's description of the police officer who had picked up Derry's suitcase: a tall white man, good-looking, with a good build.

Turner was well built. Yes indeed. He wasn't aggressively muscular, but everything he had was in terrific condition.

On the heels of that memory, she was visited by another—Derry Riley's suitcase, so neatly packed. Turner, she had noticed, was a man to whom neatness counted.

Though Jamie hadn't turned on the air-conditioning in her room all day, it suddenly felt very cold in there.

Chapter Ten

If Turner felt any lingering sexual desire when he called, he disguised it well. "I won't be able to come back tonight," he said briskly.

"Are you at home?" she asked, realizing she didn't yet know where he lived.

"No."

Was someone with him? Was his taciturnity due to caution, or was he one of those men who started beating a retreat as soon as he'd been intimate with a woman? She'd run into a man like that once. What woman hadn't?

"I've made an appointment with Anna," she said into the silence. "Ten tomorrow morning. Her last name is Campbell. Does that mean anything to you?"

"Not that I recall." He was silent again for a moment, then said, "I had intended accompanying you to the New Woman, at least as far as the door, but I've changed my mind."

So. She wasn't going to see him tomorrow, either. *Did* he regret making love to her? Don't be so insecure, Jamie, she scolded herself. "Okay," she said briskly.

"I think my time might be better spent trying to get a lead on the current whereabouts of Kenyon and Hokins." It wasn't caution that was making him distant if he felt free to mention those two names.

"I'm quite capable of taking a cab," she said evenly.

"Good. We can meet afterward to exchange results."

He wasn't trying to avoid her altogether then. She felt a lift of spirits that dismayed her, because it meant she cared too much, and she didn't want to get in over her head here. Caring about a man made a woman vulnerable—and gullible.

"At one o'clock?" Turner continued. "The White Horse Tavern in King's Square?"

"Fine." Another awkward pause. "I talked to Loretta Dean," she told him.

"Ah, yes." He sounded relieved to have something to talk about. "Did you get any new information?"

"She confirmed that she packed Derry's suitcase. You probably heard Charles say so."

"Charles," he echoed. "Yes, I did hear him."

There was a note of distaste in his voice. She decided abruptly that she wouldn't mention the party. "She gave it to a police officer whose name she couldn't remember. Someone tall, not fat, white, well built."

"Not too specific a description."

"It could be a description of you."

"Or John Doe," he said after a short pause. Another evasive answer. "As it happens," he continued, "I heard Hollingsworth tell you Loretta had given the suitcase to a police officer. I checked on it straight away, but no one knows anything about it."

"You went to the police station?"

"I telephoned. I do still have some contacts. I had thought the officer in question might be Cornell Alexander, but if Loretta said he was white, I'll have to look further."

"Loretta didn't remember any film in Derry's room," Jamie said when he didn't go on. "Charles made the same suggestion you did—that Derry might have dropped it off to be developed. Can that be checked on, or would it be too big a job?"

"Possibly," he said. Which question was he answering?

"Loretta seemed hostile," Jamie offered.

"Did she indeed?"

"I think she was mad at Charles for telling me she'd packed the suitcase. Do you know her? Could she have had anything to do with covering up whatever happened to Derry?"

"I can't say I know her well," he said.

Did that answer seem slightly ambiguous?

"I'll see what I can find out about Loretta," he added, then hesitated. "Look, Jamie, I don't want to upset you, but..." Another pause. What the hell was he going to say? "I do want to remind you to be discreet. You have a way of being very straightforward and direct."

"Damn the torpedoes, full speed ahead," she commented.

For the first time a note of amusement entered his voice. "Directness is a laudable trait, but in the circumstances, you need to be devious." She heard him take in a breath, let it out. "I don't want you to take any risks, Jamie."

He was concerned for her. Her heart sang. "I'll walk on eggs," she promised.

"Until tomorrow, then."

She had no business feeling disappointed because he wasn't able to return, she told herself after hanging up. But somewhere in the back of her mind she'd held out the hope that they'd spend the night together, talking over the results of their investigation, planning the next move. Making love.

AFTER HE'D RUNG OFF and pushed the telephone back into place on his companion's desk, Turner sat staring at it for several minutes. His friend Tom, who was on his usual window seat perch, finally stirred, brushing a hand through his hair. "Problems?" he asked.

Turner laughed shortly. "You might say that, I had this foolish idea I could *use* Jamie Maxwell for a while, then drop her when it suited me. It's not working out that way. She's a very headstrong young woman."

"And from what you tell me, too smart for her own good."

"Much too smart."

"Which could be hazardous to our health."

Turner nodded, scowling. "And to Jamie's."

To ADD TO her general irritation, Jamie was hungry. And as she'd declined Charles's invitation to dinner she could hardly eat in the hotel or call room service. She would just have to go out. Maybe, she thought, with a sudden quiver of excitement, she'd eat at one of the Hamilton restaurants Derry had gone to. Sorting through the coasters and matchbooks Derry had sent her, she selected one, picked up her purse and headed for the door, then hesitated before opening it. Turner was right, her damn purse *was* heavy. Pulling a small fanny pack out of her duffel, she strapped it on over her shorts and put her billfold, hotel key and Derry's photograph in it.

The Hog Penny was within walking distance of the hotel. Jamie was encouraged to discover it was a tavern, thus a place Derry had probably spent some time in. Standing up as a waitress approached, she retrieved Derry's photograph from her fanny pack and put it on the table. The waitress, a middle-aged black Bermudian, was cheerful and helpful about describing the specialties of the house. Just as cheerfully, she agreed to show Derry's picture to her fellow workers. "He has red hair and blue eyes," Jamie called after her as she walked away.

She turned and smiled and nodded, but when she returned with Jamie's curry, she had a doleful look on her round face. "Nobody's seen this man that they remember," she said. "The cook, he remembers a red-haired man coming in several days ago, but we get a lot of British tourists—quite a few redheads."

Handing the photograph back to Jamie, she asked, "Is he your ace boy?"

"Ace boy?" Jamie queried.

The woman smiled. "Close friend. *You* know."

"A friend, yes. I was hoping to meet up with him."

"Sorry," the woman apologized.

Rather than stand up again, Jamie stuck the photo in her shirt pocket and attacked her curry, pausing to order a tall glass of water as soon as she discovered how spicy it was. The Hog Penny was obviously a popular meeting place for young people. While she ate, Jamie watched several conversations start up in the bar area. Occasionally they led to subtle pairings. Two brightly dressed young black women standing at the bar had turned around to look encouragingly at an attractive black man who had followed Jamie in and now sat at a nearby table reading a paperback book. Evidently he wasn't interested, though he was obviously aware. When he caught Jamie watching, he winked at her, then continued reading.

Jamie grinned. It was always fun to watch people and it was a relief to be just an ordinary tourist. She wasn't going to allow herself to speculate on her coming meeting with Anna Campbell or to dwell on the change in her relationship with Turner Garrett, she decided. She was going to let tomorrow take care of itself.

"It's pouring out there," the waitress said when she brought Jamie's bill. "You want me to ring up a taxi for you?"

Jamie shook her head. "I don't have far to go."

She might have changed her mind if she'd realized it was now full dark and the rain was a cloudburst. But the minute she moved out from under the restaurant's canopy, she was drenched, so it hardly seemed worthwhile going back.

Jogging in place, she waited impatiently for the signal to change at the pedestrian crossing at the corner, then jogged rapidly along Front Street. The whole area was deserted. Head down, she ran steadily, swerving as she approached the hotel to head for the side door and stairs rather than drip all over the lobby. Just as she stepped on the dimly lit pathway, she heard footsteps pounding behind her and pulled to one side to get out of the way.

But instead of going past her, the other person, a man, collided with her. He must have been blinded by the rain, she thought, as she fought for balance. The man grabbed her from behind and she really believed he was keeping her from falling, until a strong arm crushed her breasts and a voice whispered harshly in her ear. "Hold still, stupid."

Her heart jerked. Adrenaline shot through her body, driving out every thought but the urge to fight. Bringing her right elbow back sharply, she felt it jar against the man's body. Her satisfaction was short-lived. His hand immediately went to her throat and tightened so that she couldn't scream if she tried. Nor could she turn her head to look at him.

He was wearing gloves. Somehow that made the whole thing more frightening. Her own fingers went to her throat, trying to bend his little finger back so he'd have to loosen his hold. His free hand grabbed her hair, pulling it back so sharply she thought it would come loose. Lifting her from behind with his knee, he pushed her around a bush and up against the wall of the hotel. "Hold still or I'll squeeze the life out of you," he muttered, and there was something in his voice that made her believe he meant it.

She let herself go limp, hoping to put him off guard, then realized he was trying to open the zipper on her fanny pack. Her fury, as she realized he meant to rob her, overcame her fear. She renewed her struggle, but the man was strong, and try as she might she couldn't loosen the stranglehold he had on her throat.

With a muttered curse he threw her billfold down, then swung her to one side and put his knee to her back again. "Get the hell out of Bermuda," he said harshly. And pushed.

She fell to the ground, sprawling on the soft, wet grass, her breath wheezing through her throat. The second she landed, she pushed herself to her feet, stumbled blindly around the bush and squinted through the densely falling rain. Visibility was nil. She couldn't see anyone at all.

Scrabbling around, she found her billfold and stuffed it in her pack, checked that her hotel key was still there, then stumbled around the corner and in through the hotel door. Staggering up the stairs, her breath still whistling in her chest, she didn't stop to rest for a second until she reached the safety of her room.

All the money that had been in her billfold was intact. She stared at it unbelievingly. Then she panicked for a moment, thinking Derry's photograph had dropped out of the pack, until she remembered putting it into her shirt pocket. It was okay, though slightly creased.

Quite suddenly she began shaking uncontrollably. Her throat hurt. Water was dripping steadily from her hair. She was soaked to the skin. She recognized that she was not only cold, but in shock. She had to get warm or she was going to be sick. Pulling off her clothes, she kept her mind fixed on the wonderful image of a hot shower. Once she was warm, she could figure out what to do about the mugger—who to call....

By the time she emerged from the bathroom, feeling much calmer and certainly a whole lot warmer, her fear had abated, though it certainly hadn't gone away. Rummaging through her purse, she finally came up with the card Turner had written his home number on. The phone rang on unanswered.

What now, she wondered, propping her elbow on the desk and leaning her head on her hand. She couldn't see calling Charles. Getting involved with the police might be a mistake. Probably it would be better to wait until she could talk to Turner.

Maybe she shouldn't even tell Turner, she thought as she sank wearily into bed. He might use it as an excuse to stop her investigating Derry's death, even though it was obviously not connected. She had been mugged, yes, but the mugger hadn't got away with anything. Apart from some slight bruising on her throat, there was no real harm done, except to her nerves.

ANNA CAMPBELL was exactly as Jordan Lathrop had described her—pretty and small, with a mane of frizzed blond hair that made her head look too large for her anorexic body. She wore a creamy silk shirt tucked into jeans that couldn't have been over a size two, and red shoes with four-inch heels.

She had beautiful skin, fine pored, pink and white, smooth as porcelain. There might be extra benefits to be gained from this visit, Jamie decided, as she signed the client register. Hoping Anna wasn't familiar with rhyming slang, she signed in as Rose Lea, the name she'd given when making the appointment.

The salon featured a lot of glass and chrome. There were three operators, each with their own suite of rooms. On the walls of Anna's section, 1920s murals depicted long-legged flappers in cloches, fur collars and daringly short skirts, accompanied by escorts in top hats.

"This is terrific," Jamie said. Her voice was still a little husky, her throat slightly sore.

Anna agreed. "I'm verra fortunate." Lathrop hadn't mentioned that she was a Scot. "If it hadna been for Mr. Putney," she went on, "I'd never have managed to buy the place. He's a wonderful man is Mr. Putney, forever helping people."

It was curious how Rex Putney's name kept coming up. As Charles had suggested, he seemed to have his fingers in several pies. All the same, she didn't want to question Anna about him and get distracted from her true purpose in coming here.

Within minutes she was lying on a white chaise, her hair tied up in a blue scarf, a matching drape covering her jeans and the aqua cotton turtleneck she'd worn to cover the bruise on her throat. The piped-in music was soothing, and she could feel residual tension draining from her as Anna cleansed her skin with a fragrant lotion. She'd better get down to business before she got too relaxed. Be subtle, she reminded herself.

"My skin dried out this weekend," Jamie said tentatively. "I went out on a glass-bottom boat and the sun was pretty fierce. I guess I should have used some moisturizer."

If she hadn't been watching, she might have missed the slight jerk of Anna's head at the mention of the glass-bottomed boat. Likewise the tightening of her fingers on the cotton ball she was using on Jamie's face.

She recovered fairly quickly. "We've a verra good moisturizer," she said. "It's made from cucumbers and includes a sun block. I'll give you a sample to try."

"The boat was the *Coral Queen*," Jamie mused aloud. "A very flirtatious skipper—Clyde Kane. Do you know him?"

Anna shook her head.

"It was lovely. All those fish and anemones and things. The water's such a beautiful color here, isn't it?"

Anna's cheeks were suddenly pinker than before. "I'm going to put an organic cereal on your face now," she said. A husky note had appeared in her voice.

"Cereal?" Jamie queried.

"A mixture of grains that will draw out the impurities."

"I'll take your word for it," Jamie muttered. She needed a different approach, obviously.

"How's the male situation in Bermuda?" she asked brightly. "I had curry at the Hog Penny in Hamilton last night and saw several pickups." She laughed. "A couple of young women weren't having much luck though."

Anna made a snorting sound. "Och, the male situation's all right if you just want a good time. You want something permanent, forget it. You can't get serious, it's all parties. You here on holiday?"

Jamie nodded as best she could. Her face was beginning to tighten up.

"Then it's probably all right for you. Me, I thought I would come to glamorous Bermuda and find a husband. I've been here several years. The Bermudians are lovely people, but they have their own cliques. So then there's the ex-pats. They love it here. Women coming in on holiday, just what men like, isn't it? No strings, natural time limits, wham bam and put them back on the cruise ship or the aeroplane."

"You ever date tourists?"

She paused. "Sometimes." So okay, Jamie thought, how do I lead the conversation around to Derry in a subtle way?

"You're what's called an ex-pat yourself? Did you have to get a work permit? Is it difficult? Could I get one?"

"Depends on what you do," Anna said, sounding much more comfortable now. "I'm an aesthetician. I teach as well as practice. So I have a skill that's helpful for training the local people. I'll apply for status after a while.'' She chuckled. ''Then I'll be known as a paper Bermudian.''

''I'm a meeting planner for a software company,'' Jamie said. ''Clerico Corporation.''

No reaction. So Derry hadn't talked about his job.

''I live in Boston,'' Jamie added.

Anna's fingers stilled, then trembled. ''Have you met anyone from Boston before?'' Jamie asked.

Anna shook her head, then excused herself to wash her hands. ''We'll just wait awhile for the face pack to set,'' she said from the doorway without turning around.

When she returned she was calm again. She began carefully removing the face pack. Jamie's face felt wonderfully fresh. But Anna wasn't through with her yet. Next she put on a jellylike substance that smelled distinctly off, which she said was made from putrefied plant materials.

''Like compost, you mean?'' Jamie asked with some alarm.

Anna laughed. ''I suppose you could say that, but it's prepared under sterile laboratory conditions. It's good for you, really it is. Don't talk now, I need you to relax.''

After a few minutes she began cleaning the gel off with brisk movements of her slender fingers. Obviously she was just about finished and Jamie was no further forward. She sent a mental apology winging Turner's way. She would just have to do this in her own blunt way.

''I haven't been quite honest with you, Anna,'' she said as soon as Anna eased the chaise back to a sitting position.

Anna looked questioningly at her reflection in the mirror, removed the scarf from her head and began untangling her hair with a plastic pick.

''I wasn't asking idle questions about you dating tourists,'' Jamie said. ''I came to Bermuda to look into a so-called accident. I'm a friend of Derry Riley's.''

Anna's hands shook convulsively so that she almost dropped the pick. "What's that to do with me?" she asked, her voice sounding strangled.

Drawing on memories of "Murder She Wrote" episodes on TV, Jamie said firmly, "Would you rather speak to me, or to the police? I know you went on board the *Coral Queen* with Derry—somebody saw you."

A look of terror appeared in Anna's eyes. Dropping the pick, she sank down onto a stool as if her legs had given out. All color had left her face. "I didn't, it wasn't..." She buried her face in her hands and started sobbing so hard her bony shoulders shuddered under the creamy silk.

"Damn," Jamie muttered. She hadn't meant to bring on this strong a reaction. Fighting her way out from under the blue drape, she swung her legs over the side of the chaise and patted Anna's shoulder awkwardly.

Eyes streaming, Anna looked up at her. "He was a nice laddie, Derry," she said brokenly. "I liked him a lot. I was that upset by the accident."

At least she'd admitted knowing Derry. Handing her a box of tissues, Jamie sat back down, watching sympathetically as Anna wiped her eyes and regained her composure.

"Where did you meet him?" Jamie asked.

Anna hesitated a fraction of a second. But when she answered, she sounded candid enough. "I was on my lunch break," she said. "I met him at the ducking ceremony in King's Square."

Which explained why Derry hadn't returned to see Catherine.

"He was taking pictures, and I got between his camera and the action," Anna continued. "He asked me to move in the politest way. Lovely manners, he had."

More pictures unaccounted for. "There were no pictures in Derry's luggage when it was returned to the States,"

Jamie said. "No pictures, no film, not even in his camera. Do you know if he left it somewhere to be developed?"

Anna picked up the scarf that had been wound around Jamie's head and twisted it between her hands. Was she trying to remember or avoiding the question? After a moment she shook her head. "I don't know anything," she muttered.

Jamie was sure Anna wasn't telling the truth. But accusing her wouldn't help. She'd probably just shut up altogether. "You were talking about the ducking ceremony," she prompted.

Anna lifted her head. "I dinna approve of it, myself. It's funny enough, those lassies being dunked in the water on that stool, but think of the origin of it—just for scolding a man or gossiping. Everyone watching, jeering, it must have been horrid for the poor women who were sentenced to it."

Why had she gone to it if she disliked it so? Jamie wondered. "So then you got talking to Derry," she prompted.

"Aye. He told me he really liked St. George's—because of its history. He said he had come back that day to catch a glass-bottomed boat at the wharf, but it had left early."

One mystery cleared up.

"That's Bermuda for you, I told him," Anna went on. Her voice was stronger now and she'd stopped knotting the scarf. Which probably meant she was telling the truth now. *Had* she lied earlier? Why would she?

"I explained the ceremony to him," Anna continued. "After we'd talked awhile, he invited me to dinner. He took me to the Carriage House. Lovely salad bar they have there."

She seemed to be lost in thought for a moment, then she shook herself a little. "He was disappointed not to see the sea gardens, he said, so I told him there were glass-bottomed boats leaving from Hamilton every day." She paused, her eyes filling again. "He asked me to go with him the next day. Said he needed a hand to hold because he was frightened of the water."

"So you agreed to go with him," Jamie said hastily before she could break down again.

"Aye, I did that," Anna agreed. Under the stress of her emotion, her Scots accent was getting even stronger. "The next day was a Thursday, my day off. He came for me here. He'd rented a cycle—a moped."

"Where were you when the...accident happened?" Jamie asked when it seemed Anna had nothing more to say.

"Down below, watching the fish," Anna said promptly. "Derry was there for a wee while, but he didn't like all that water, and he went back on deck." She took a shaky breath. "The next I knew he was in the water and everyone was screaming. I knew right away it was Derry. The red hair..." She broke off, covering her face with her hands. "I've seen him in my dreams every night since," she moaned. "I can't sleep for seeing him as soon as I close my eyes. I'll never forget it, never."

Whether she was telling the whole truth or not, there was no doubting her distress. "What happened then?" Jamie asked, her voice stern.

"Why then—" She reached for a tissue and blew her nose. "The diver brought him up on the back end of the boat and some man said he was a doctor and he and—" She hesitated again. "He and one of the crew tried to bring him round, but then the doctor said he was dead. He'd hit his head." She made a gulping sound, then went on in a rush. "When the boat got into Hamilton, a police officer came aboard. People were rushing round, getting in each other's way, everybody trying to tell him what had happened, so I just left."

Jamie stared at her. "You left?"

She looked stricken. "I know I shouldn't have, but I was that upset, and I didn't see how I could help Derry. And it worried me, talking to the police—I was afraid it would affect my status. I just wanted to go away and try to forget what had happened. But I canna do it. I canna forget it.''

Her distress was once again so obvious that Jamie reached for her hand and squeezed it lightly.

"You're no going to tell the police I was there with him, are you?" Anna asked.

Jamie shook her head. It wasn't really a lie. She *was* going to tell Turner, but he didn't qualify as "the police," right now. "Did anyone else talk to Derry?" she asked.

"No," Anna's expression was suddenly alert. "Why do you want to know that?"

If she gave a reason, she'd be telling Anna she suspected Derry's accident was not an accident. Did she want to do that? What did she have to lose?

"I'm trying to make sure it was an accident," she said.

Anna's face turned as white as the wall behind her. "Of course it was an accident. What else would it be? He stumbled against the rail and fell over. He banged his head on the coral. I heard the doctor say so."

"I guess I'm just trying to get it clear in my mind," Jamie said soothingly. "His mother wanted to know more about it. That's why I came to Bermuda."

"She must be verra upset. His mother."

"Yes." Jamie swallowed. One last try. "Did you know any of the crew who were on duty that day?" she asked. "Bobby Kenyon or Joe Hokins? Jordan Lathrop was the skipper."

Anna shook her head, but she avoided making eye contact. Her mouth was set in a tight line. Jamie stood up. "I'd better go. Thanks for talking to me, Anna. I know it wasn't easy."

"That's all right." Her voice was unsteady, her face creased with worry lines.

"If you think of anything else, would you get in touch with me?" Jamie reached into her purse for her card case, then realized she'd be giving herself away. Which didn't seem to matter now. "My name's really Jamie Maxwell," she said, writing the Victoria Hotel's name on her business card.

Anna's eyes widened as she took the card. "Derry talked about you. He said you were his best friend in all the world."

Jamie swallowed again. "He was mine, too."

Anna studied the card. "Why would you give me a false name?"

Jamie couldn't think of an answer. Luckily Anna didn't press for one. "I'm sorry about Derry," she said, her hazel eyes bright. There was no mistaking her sincerity.

All the same, she did seem relieved Jamie wasn't asking any more questions. Why was that?

Chapter Eleven

Jamie entered the White Horse Tavern right on one o'clock, then realized she had forgotten to disguise herself after leaving the New Woman. Some detective she was. Ducking into the rest room, she put on her floppy hat and dark glasses, noting in the mirror that her skin looked great—she would have to find out more about Anna's products before she left Bermuda.

Turner had procured a table on the deck next to the water and was serving himself from a pot of tea. He'd gone back to his braid-decorated cap and his Hawaiian shirt. Jamie was glad she'd put on her sunglasses. In bright sunshine, that shirt was a fearsome thing. Turner sniffed the air as she sat down opposite him. "You smell like a fruit salad," he commented.

"Fruit compost," she corrected, then laughed at his horrified expression.

His answering smile seemed strained. There was a sudden emptiness in Jamie's stomach that wasn't due to lack of food.

"How did you do?" he asked.

"Anna Campbell *was* on the *Coral Queen* with Derry," she told him.

Abruptly he leaned forward to look at her closely. "Is that a bruise on your throat?"

She'd forgotten to check if the turtleneck was still covering the spot after Anna got through with her. Did she want to tell him the truth or not? "I was mugged last night," she said finally.

He looked stunned. "You were what?"

"Mugged. It means assaulted in a public place."

"I know what it means, Jamie. Talk."

"Okay," she said with another sigh. "Here's what happened. I decided to go to the Hog Penny for dinner last night. As long as I was there, I thought I'd show Derry's picture to the waitresses. Nobody recognized him. When I left, it was raining hard. I ran for the hotel and this guy came up behind me and tried to throttle me so he could get into my fanny pack."

Turner blinked.

"It's a small bag you tie around your waist and—" she broke off as Turner's face tightened. Hastily she filled him in on the rest.

"Did you call the police?" he asked when she was through.

She shook her head.

"Hollingsworth?"

"I didn't call anybody."

"Why not?"

"Visibility was poor, and the guy didn't give me a chance to get a look at him. I couldn't even tell if he was black or white. And he didn't take anything. What was the point of calling anyone?"

"You were hurt, dammit!"

She touched her throat. "I was raised with four brothers, remember. We were all pretty wild. If no bones were broken and blood wasn't flowing, nobody worried much." She thought for a minute. "The mugger was American," she exclaimed. "That's funny, I hadn't realized that until now." She suddenly remembered that Turner could turn on an American accent at will. She shook her head. "He said, 'Hold still, stupid,' and 'Get the hell out of Bermuda.'" Another thought struck her. "Somebody mentioned an American recently. Who was—" She broke off, feeling a chill spread down her spine. "The bartender at the Tudor Tavern. He said one of your killers might be an American." Her voice rose. "Turner?"

Turner's eyes had narrowed to dark slits. "Why would a mugger tell you to get out of Bermuda?" he murmured almost to himself.

"Maybe he hates tourists."

He looked at her narrow-eyed.

"You think the incident's connected to your investigation?" she asked.

His face closed. "I don't know, Jamie. You say he didn't take anything. Yet he seemed to be looking for something."

Jamie shivered. "I don't think I want to talk about it anymore."

"You could have rung me," he said accusingly.

She gave him a narrow-eyed look of her own. "I did. There was no answer. I remembered you'd said you were meeting someone, so I didn't try again. I was bushed, anyway, I just wanted to sleep."

He took in a breath, let it out. "Jamie..."

"About Anna..." she said, before he could start in again. She went on to tell him everything the young woman had said, stopping when a waitress brought the fish chowder they'd asked for. "I'm convinced Anna Campbell was not telling the whole truth and nothing but," she added after the waitress left.

He raised an eyebrow. "You don't believe too many people, do you?"

"I have a built-in lie detector," she said, looking him as directly in the eye as she could, considering he was wearing his opaque sunglasses.

Apparently Turner didn't recognize that as an innuendo. He placidly stirred sugar into his tea. His beard was getting to the scruffy stage, she noticed.

"We haven't accounted for much of Derry's time," he said after a short silence. "Judging from what Anna told you, he must have met her a short time after he met Catherine. And that was evidently on April seventeenth, the day before—" He broke off.

The day before he died, Jamie filled in.

Turner was frowning. "Does Derry's letter offer any more clues to his activities?"

Jamie pulled the letter from her purse and scanned it. "He watched the cruise ships come in. And there's a mention of a bobby directing traffic. All of which take place in Hamilton. We haven't really done much in Hamilton. Derry did send me a few matchbooks and coasters from there. There was one from the Hog Penny, that's why I went there."

"You had no business going there alone for that purpose," Turner said grimly.

"I had to eat somewhere," she pointed out. "I'd turned Charles down, so I could hardly call room service."

He sighed but didn't chastise her as she'd half expected him to. "Charles appears to fancy you," he remarked.

"I've noticed." She went on before he could comment further. "Maybe we could bum around Hamilton tomorrow morning. There's not much point in checking out the ducking ceremony now that we know from Anna what Derry was doing there."

He set his cup carefully in its saucer. "You're forgetting that your detecting days are at an end."

"I never said I agreed with you."

"You said if I let you interview Anna you'd do whatever I told you after that."

"I lied."

He sighed and reached for her right hand, holding it between both of his own, effectively defusing her anger. "Jamie, please. Leave the rest of this investigation to me."

"What have you found out?" she demanded. "What's come up that makes you want me out of the way? You haven't even told me what you did this morning *or* last night."

"Too much knowledge can be dangerous, Jamie." His voice had acquired an edge again.

"To who? Whom. You or me?"

"My concern is for you."

"Then let me worry about it." She wished he would take off his sunglasses so she could see his eyes.

He leaned forward. "If I tell you what I've found out, if I promise to keep you informed, will you agree to take a back seat in this investigation?"

"Let's hear what you have to say, then I'll decide," she said flatly.

She was the most exasperating woman he'd ever met. "You're a tough lady, Jamie Maxwell," he said, not without admiration.

"Right."

He wanted to cup that belligerent chin in his hand and kiss that luscious pink mouth, trace those fine bones with his fingertips. But he'd realized, in the cool of the previous evening, and had his suspicion confirmed the minute she told him about the mugger, that there was a real danger of Jamie Maxwell getting in the way of his current project. He couldn't allow that to happen. It had been a mistake to let his hormones run away with him, and it seemed wiser to back off a little, let things cool down between them. A difficult decision out of her presence, an almost impossible vow to keep when she was here in the flesh. Such superb flesh.

"First of all, then," he said, letting go of her hand, "there doesn't seem to be any film waiting anywhere for Derry Riley to collect."

Her eyes widened. "How did you find that out so fast?"

He'd underestimated her intelligence again. He had to stop doing that. "I've already told you I still have a few contacts," he said, hoping she'd let it pass.

Her eyes narrowed and he went on rapidly. "I also checked on Bobby Kenyon and Joe Hokins. The general consensus is that they haven't been around for at least three weeks, maybe more."

"Maybe not since Derry's accident?"

"Possibly. However, there's no record of them leaving the island, so I should be able to trace them eventually."

"No record where?" she asked. "Who formed the consensus?"

It was impossible to bamboozle this woman. "Just people in general," he hedged. He turned to look out toward the harbor, pretending to admire the view of the bridge to Ordnance Island, the tall masts of the *Deliverance II*. Even when both of them were wearing sunglasses, it was difficult to meet her gaze when he was dissembling. She was so direct herself, she seemed able to pull the truth out of him at the oddest moments, something he was learning to guard against. He certainly wasn't able to answer questions about his sources.

"Are we going to check out Hamilton tomorrow?" she asked.

He shook his head.

Just as she'd expected. "Why not?"

"I have something else to do."

"More people to meet?"

"Possibly."

Possibly. What kind of answer was that? "Are you going to check on this American—the mugger?"

"I'll see what I can find out. Unfortunately there are a lot of Americans in Bermuda."

"You think my mugger is the American the bartender talked about?"

"I sincerely hope not. But just in case there is a connection, I want you to spend the rest of today and all of tomorrow being a simple tourist. I want you to frequent only public places. And I want you in the hotel before dark." He leaned forward to give weight to his request.

"Okay," she said. Turner looked surprised that she'd agreed. Evidently it hadn't occurred to him that a simple tourist could check out the restaurants and pubs in Hamilton. And in the afternoon a simple tourist could go to Putney's party with Charles.

He smiled at her. "I promise you, Jamie, I'm not neglecting our investigation of Derry's death." He glanced at his watch. "In fact, I have a meeting with someone in Hamilton in less than an hour, so I'd best get you back to the hotel."

"I'm not some kind of parcel you can just drop off," Jamie said stiffly. "I can find my own way back."

She was offended. Understandably so. But it was far better for her to be angry with him than for her to weasel the truth out of him. "I'll give you a ring tomorrow," he promised. "It may be late afternoon, but I will be in touch."

"I may not be in," Jamie said. "I'm meeting someone myself tomorrow afternoon."

"Who?" he asked.

She raised her eyebrows. He realized she wasn't going to tell him. Was she making it up to pay him back? No, he didn't think she was capable of that kind of small-mindedness. Which made his own deceitfulness seem worse. It was necessary, he reminded himself.

REX PUTNEY'S HOUSE was a huge, two-storied, contemporary structure painted blue and white. Surrounded on three sides by oleander hedges backed by woods, the grounds were private, the setting spectacular, with sweeping views of the Great Sound and its myriad small islands. The terraced lawns looked as though each blade of grass had been trimmed with manicure scissors. Flowers bloomed riotously in several beds.

Two canopied bars had been set up, along with several buffet tables overflowing with food. Waiters passed among the well-dressed guests, dispensing cocktails and wine.

"People really do live like this," Jamie murmured.

"Rex can certainly afford to," Charles said, helping himself to a glass of wine from a waiter's tray.

He raised an eyebrow at Jamie, but she shook her head. "I'll nurse my mineral water for a while." Once in a while she liked a glass of wine, but right now she was having enough difficulty balancing herself on her high heels, which kept sinking into the velvety lawn. "Where's our host?" she asked.

Charles nodded at several people spread out in a semicircle as if posing for a group portrait. Opposite them a stocky man with a thatch of white hair was holding forth. From here he looked like a cross between Donahue and Onassis.

Charles went on to point out an "important" representative of the Department of Tourism, two "powerful" government officials, an "honorable" or two, and several members of Bermuda's "oldest" families. Wasn't everybody's family old, Jamie wanted to ask. Didn't everybody date back to Adam?

Tailored Bermuda shorts and blazers were apparently de rigueur for men. Jamie was glad to see that her dress, a silk, scoop-necked designer number in varying shades of green, rescued from the bathroom door and ironed by one of the hotel's obliging maids, compared well with those worn by the rest of the female guests.

Nearby, a group of guests broke apart, laughing. To her dismay she caught sight of a familiar face beyond them. Ducking behind Charles, she peered around his left shoulder.

Turner Garrett. Looking as he had the first time she'd seen him—well groomed, clean shaven, dark hair brushed within an inch of its life. He was dressed impeccably in the Bermuda gentleman's fashion—dark blazer, white shirt, dark tie, Bermuda shorts, kneesocks and polished shoes. She'd almost forgotten how gorgeous he was when he wasn't pretending to be Digby. Glancing around a little wildly for a place to hide, she stopped herself abruptly. She had a right to be here; she was an invited guest. Besides which, what was *he* doing here? All that mystery about what he was going to do today, and he was attending a *party!*

Charles was still cataloging the distinguished guests. This seemed to be one of his favorite occupations.

Turner was leaning against one of the bars, holding a tall glass whose contents looked suspiciously dark. There was an empty area around him that seemed to have been left there deliberately. As she watched, Turner took a deep swallow of his drink, then straightened and looked around. A moment later his gaze met Jamie's and sharpened. The horror that spread over his lean face would have been funny if it hadn't been so infuriating.

He turned away almost immediately. Obviously Turner Digby Garrett was not pleased to see her here and intended to ignore her. Which she wasn't about to let him do.

The crowd eddied and blocked her line of sight. Dislodging her right shoe, which had sunk again, she craned her neck as discreetly as she could. Rex Putney had joined Turner and was talking to him.

"Could I meet our host?" Jamie blurted out, interrupting Charles in mid-flow.

"Certainly," Charles said, without any sign of being offended.

Several female guests turned their heads to follow their progress. As their glances discovered Jamie, their expressions changed from approval to curiosity tinged with envy. Charles hadn't exaggerated his eligible status.

He presented Jamie to Rex Putney as if she were a debutante meeting royalty. She was half inclined to curtsey. That was a beautifully cut jacket Mr. Putney was wearing, she thought, and she was willing to bet his tie was Parisian silk. He *looked* like a multimillionaire, well dressed, confident, solid, his legs spread slightly in a "king of the hill" stance.

"I've done a lot of shopping in your basement," she informed him as he shook her hand. When nervous, she had a habit of blurting out entirely the wrong thing.

A familiar glint appeared in Turner's eyes, but to her relief he didn't laugh. Rex Putney's warm brown eyes beamed at her through his tortoiseshell-rimmed spectacles. "Are you enjoying your holiday?" he asked, ignoring her faux pas.

About to tell him she wasn't a tourist, Jamie was stopped by a warning twitch of Turner's black eyebrows. "Bermuda is wonderful," she said lamely.

"I heard about the terrific thing you did for the Barrett family," Charles said to Mr. Putney.

The older man waved a hand dismissively. "Always happy to help," he said.

"But to resettle a large family like that, after they were burned out, that was truly kind."

Jamie winced at the sycophantic note in Charles's voice. Mr. Putney caught her eye and winked. "No sense waiting until you're dead to give your money away," he said. "Much more fun to do it while you're alive and can see the results."

"I like your philosophy," Jamie said.

He grinned, dipping his head.

"Aren't you going to introduce me to your young lady, Hollingsworth?" Turner asked. His voice sounded slurred. Obviously he'd had more than one of his dark cocktails. Jamie was shocked and disappointed. She would never have pegged him as a drinker.

"Forgive me," Charles said at once. Evidently he'd been concentrating so hard on Mr. Putney he hadn't noticed Turner's presence. "Inspector Garrett, Jamie Maxwell," he said hastily.

"You can call me Turner," Turner said, smiling rather sloppily. "I'm not too inspectorial at present."

Switching his drink to his left hand he held out his right. She could hardly refuse to shake, she supposed. His hand gripped hers almost painfully. Was he trying to convey some kind of message? "Charming, charming," he murmured. "I must say you have excellent taste, Hollingsworth."

The air around him smelled heavily of rum. Disgusted, Jamie tugged at her hand. He let it go, bowing gallantly, if unsteadily.

Jamie felt sick.

"Inspector Garrett and I were discussing his recent problems," Mr. Putney said.

"You've certainly been shabbily treated by the press, old boy," Charles said to Turner.

"Rubbish," a new voice said. The tall man standing next to Putney at the bar had turned sharply. He was seventy-five or so, with a military bearing, a ruddy complexion and a toothbrush mustache. He was unsuitably dressed, considering the weather, in a tweed jacket and cords. He had rather small brown eyes. He looked like a retired English army officer, Jamie decided—the kind who had served in India in the days of the Raj. "You're *defending* Garrett?"

he asked Charles, the words coming out like individual explosions.

Charles's gaze slipped sideways. "I don't know that I was defending him exactly, Gordon, old boy," he protested. "It just seemed unsporting of the media to turn on him without waiting for the results of the hearing. One would think..." His voice trailed off apologetically, as if he'd realized the man had stopped listening to him.

"Don't suppose Walter Seaton would think you were badly treated by the press," the man said to Turner in what was apparently his characteristically explosive manner. "If he were capable of thinking, that is."

Turner raised an eyebrow. "That's clever, old chap," he said admiringly. "I do believe you made a medical joke."

The man pressed his lips together. "Not meant as a joke."

Turner laughed, then took another swig of his drink.

The man glared at him.

"A fine turnout," Charles said, spreading his own slightly obsequious brand of oil on the troubled waters. "Might I introduce Miss Jamie Maxwell, Gordon?" he asked the man. "This is Gordon Stacey," he continued smoothly to Jamie. "One of Bermuda's leading attorneys."

The leading attorney gave Jamie a cold glance, said "Harrumph" and glared at Turner again.

Mr. Putney diplomatically asked Charles how things were going at the Victoria, and Charles replied enthusiastically. Including Stacey in the conversation, he managed to ease his attention away from Turner. At the same time, a foursome moved up to the bar and Jamie and Turner stepped aside. For the moment they were unobserved.

"What are you doing here?" Turner muttered from behind his glass.

"Charles invited me," she said stiffly.

"You said he was an idiot."

"I did not. I said he was a bit of an airhead."

"So that's why you came? To spend time with an air-head?"

She felt her cheeks flame. "I don't think I told you that Lathrop said Kyle Hammond worked for Rex Putney," she said.

Turner didn't look surprised.

"You knew that?" she asked.

"I discovered it." His mouth had its stern look.

"I thought Hammond might be here and I could ask him if he knew Kenyon or Hokins," Jamie explained.

"You haven't talked to anyone about them, have you?" he asked, looking alarmed.

"Not yet."

"Don't," he said. "And that's an order."

Annoyed, Jamie looked pointedly at his glass. "What the hell are you drinking?" she asked.

He hugged the glass close to his chest as if afraid she was going to snatch it away. "I told you about our dark-and-stormies." He chuckled. "This is a dark-and-turbulent."

She scowled at him. "Don't you think you've had enough?"

He looked at the glass, then at her. "No." To prove his point, he drained the glass and set it on the bar.

"I hope you're not going to ride your moped in this condition," Jamie said.

"Don't you fret," he said, wagging a finger at her. "I've got my car. You're forgetting I'm my real self today."

"This is your real self?"

His eyes glinted with something that might have been amusement—or irritation. Then he peered at her owlishly, breathing rum all over her. "I do believe you're wearing makeup, Jamie Maxwell," he said. "Eyeliner, mascara, lip gloss, the works. *Very* nice. Our man Charles must rate high on the 'must make an impression' scale. Pretty dress, too. I'm glad to see the wrinkles did drop out after all."

He shook his head. "Go home, Jamie," he said thickly, then turned on his heel, almost bumping into a young woman in a clinging pink dress that exposed a lot of tanned bosom. She smiled in response to Turner's muttered apology. Then she either recognized him, or smelled the rum he reeked of. Whatever the cause, her immediate recoil was very apparent and brought a bitter smile to Turner's mouth. Jamie ached for him, even though she was disgusted by him at the moment.

"I'm surprised to see Garrett here," Charles said to Rex as the bar area cleared again. "I'd heard he was lying low."

Putney raised his bushy white brows. "You agree with Gordon then? You believe he's guilty?"

Jamie forced herself to forget her own distress and concentrate on the conversation. But whatever it was that Charles muttered, it was unintelligible to her.

"What did the inspector do?" Jamie asked, widening her eyes in an attempt to look ingenuous.

"He's being investigated for police brutality," Gordon Stacey said. Then he snorted, looking at Rex Putney. "Can't understand why you keep insisting he's innocent. The newspaper ran a vivid description of the way he beat that poor old man. So far I haven't seen any retraction. Far as I'm concerned, Garrett's a disgrace to the force."

"Now, now, Gordon," Mr. Putney put in mildly.

The attorney shrugged impatiently. "Makes me hot under the collar," he said unnecessarily. "Got to keep our police officers under control. Can't have them taking the law into their own hands."

How safe was the law in *his* hands, Jamie wondered. This was not a man she would trust with administering her estate, supposing she had one. Nor was he the kind of person she could imagine caring about someone like Walter Seaton.

"I've already told the commissioner he should make an example of Garrett," he said.

"You want him to boil me in oil?" Turner asked, suddenly towering over them again. He had a fresh drink, Jamie noted.

Stacey didn't look at all embarrassed. "It would seem a fitting punishment."

"Got me convicted already, have you?"

"If you mean do I think you're guilty, the answer is yes."

Mr. Putney intervened again. Putting a hand on Turner's arm, he looked at Stacey and said quietly, "I think we'd better wait for the results of the investigation, don't you?"

Stacey curled his lip. "Man's not guilty, let's hear him say so. Been waiting to see a statement from him in the newspapers. Not a thing so far."

Tension stretched almost visibly between him and Turner. Nobody was talking in the immediate area. Jamie sensed ears straining to hear what Turner would say. To her dismay Turner looked down at his drink in a way that made him look...furtive. No, not furtive. Guilty.

"I don't have to prove my innocence," he muttered. "Law says somebody has to prove me guilty." After glaring at Stacey one more time, he turned sharply and strode off in what might have been an impressive manner if he hadn't swayed slightly as he walked.

Jamie felt sicker than ever. "Mr. Putney," she said as Gordon Stacey snorted and walked off in the opposite direction. "What makes *you* so sure the inspector is innocent?"

He grinned cheerfully at her. "Can't expect him to go pussyfooting around when someone's resisting arrest."

"You're saying it's okay for an officer to use excessive force when it's called for?"

"A police officer risks his life every day. He has a right to protect himself."

It wasn't exactly the reassurance Jamie had hoped for. The recurring image of Turner looming like Goliath over that poor man flashed through her mind again. "The inspector seems to have had a little too much to drink," she said.

Putney nodded agreement but his expression was sympathetic. "Can't really blame the guy. It's certainly natural that he'd be bitter. His occupation's in jeopardy. His reputation's in shreds. As Charles here said—the media have given him a rotten time. All because he did his job." Behind his spectacles, his eyes gleamed suddenly. "I'm hoping he'll decide to—" He broke off, then smiled charmingly. "I'd love to stay and chat with you, Miss Maxwell, but I'd best circulate. Can't have my guests feeling neglected. Come and see me again, won't you?"

"Phew," Charles said as they watched Putney walk away. "That got a bit sticky, didn't it?"

Jamie decided it was time he gave a proper answer instead of agreeing with whoever happened to be speaking. "You never did say if you thought the inspector was guilty or innocent."

"Don't have an opinion," he said with a charming shrug. "Don't believe in getting involved in discussions like that. Diplomacy's my game. Be nice to everybody, everybody will be nice to you. Makes life much pleasanter all round."

"Is that why you were nice to that boorish Gordon Stacey?" Jamie asked. "I thought maybe he was a friend of yours."

"Good Lord, no," he said with so much feeling that she laughed. "Don't quote me," he added hastily.

"I won't." She looked at him curiously. "As you obviously don't like him, why do you bother being nice to him?"

"Have to, my dear. Man's one of the owners of the Victoria. Has a winter place in Florida along with the rest of the owners of the group. They don't only own the Victoria, of course. These are major investors, Jamie."

This information struck Jamie as important, but she didn't know why.

Charles smiled approvingly at her. "Rex liked you," he said with satisfaction. "I knew he would." He paused as if for emphasis. "Just as I do."

Taking hold of her arm in a rather intimate fashion, he led her over to one of the buffet tables and handed her a plate. Jamie felt embarrassed as she moved along the line. She didn't think Charles was really talking about "liking" her. Judging by the gleam in those blue eyes, he had something else in mind, but she felt nothing for him. He was nice enough, she supposed. *Innocuous* was the word she would choose to describe him. She found herself looking around for Turner.

"Mr. Putney's charming," she said after she and Charles made their way to some bistro chairs overlooking the Great Sound and settled themselves with their plates on their laps.

"Charismatic," Charles said.

Jamie nodded absently. She had just caught sight of Turner at the far side of the grounds. He was standing under a stone archway, one of Bermuda's traditional moon gates, looking down a long flight of wooden steps that led to the water. There was a yacht tied up at the dock. As Jamie watched, Turner started down the steps, appearing definitely unsteady. Half-afraid he would fall and make an ass of himself, she kept an eye on him until he reached the dock safely and sat on a wrought-iron bench. He had a fresh drink in his hand, which looked as dark as the last one.

She was furious with him. How could he possibly think drinking would help anything? She had thought him to be intelligent. But intelligent people did not look for solutions to their problems in the bottom of a bottle, especially when they were already under a cloud.

Would anyone notice if she was to go down there? Jamie wondered, then dismissed the idea at once. By pretending he didn't know her, Turner had made it clear he didn't want anyone realizing there was a connection between them.

She was feeling more confused than ever about Turner Garrett. Gordon Stacey was convinced he had beaten Walter Seaton without cause. Rex Putney had said he was only doing his job. Turner had told her the man was resisting arrest. Who was right? And did the motivation really matter? How could she possibly be in love with someone who could hit an old homeless man hard enough to put him in a coma?

In love?

Despair washed over her.

Chapter Twelve

"Heavens!" Charles exclaimed. Jamie glanced at him. His face was undergoing a swift change of expression. He was looking beyond her, frowning. Was he watching Turner, too?

"What are you doing here?" he asked, sounding almost as surprised as Turner had done when he'd greeted Jamie earlier.

The object of his surprise turned out to be Loretta Dean, looking beautiful in an icy pink dress that showed off her formidable bosom and lovely skin to perfection. Maybe she patronized Anna's salon, too, Jamie thought.

"I belong here as much as you do," Loretta said, glaring down at Charles.

Once again Charles folded, as he seemed to do every time anyone answered him back. He had rather a weak chin, Jamie noticed. It went with his weak nature. "Well, of course you do," he said, looking flustered. "I didn't mean to imply..."

"You certainly did," Loretta said. Apparently Turner wasn't the only one who had been imbibing. Her words weren't slurred, but her voice had the careful sound that meant she was watching the way she spoke.

"For your information, Mr. Hollingsworth," she said. "I was invited by Mr. Putney himself. I do believe he considers himself my friend."

"Loretta," Charles protested. "I didn't mean..."

Loretta overrode him. Waving her drink for emphasis, she leaned toward Jamie, making her worry about the danger to her dress. "Our Mr. Hollingsworth doesn't approve of common people like me being invited to socially correct parties."

"I say, Loretta," Charles chimed in.

She ignored him. "His family owns chunks of British real estate. Lives in Beaumont Hall, Wiltshire. Upper crust. Brits love their bloody useless upper crust."

"I am not useless," Charles protested.

"Listen, Loretta," Jamie said, feeling desperately embarrassed. "I don't think—"

"Go 'long," Loretta said, looking daggers at Charles. "You manage the Victoria, that what you're saying? But who does all the work, Mr. Hollingsworth? Who takes over when you go off visiting your family? Who's in charge when you attend all those business meetings in Florida?"

Unfolding himself from his chair, Charles gave Jamie an apologetic glance. "If you'll excuse me, Jamie, I think I'll remove myself from this situation until Miss Dean calms down." Gathering his dignity, he strode off toward the buffet tables, carrying his empty plate like a shield before him.

There was a short, awkward silence. Jamie chewed on a piece of French bread and looked down at the dock below. Turner was apparently watching the crew members moving around on Mr. Putney's yacht. His glass, she noted, was empty.

"The British," Loretta declaimed, collapsing into the seat Charles had vacated, "still think they own the bloody world."

Clyde Kane had said the same thing, Jamie remembered. "Aren't you afraid of losing your job, talking to Charles like that?" she asked.

Loretta laughed. "He'd never give me the sack. He knows who runs that hotel, frees him to go off and do whatever comes into his head. Besides all that he owes me."

Leaning back in her chair, she looked up at the sky and sighed. "This is what we call a Bermudaful day," she said plaintively. "Bright, sunny, warm, cloudless sky." She glanced at Jamie. "Looks like I just ruined it for you. You don't think a woman should speak her mind?"

Jamie wasn't sure what to say to this seemingly habitually hostile woman, so said nothing, concentrating instead on eating some of the food on her plate, which was delicious but had lost its appeal. "I agree that women still don't get proper acknowledgement for the jobs they do," she commented finally.

"You too?" Loretta looked at Jamie with great interest. "You never did come back to discuss your conference."

"I've been busy," Jamie said lamely.

"Maybe we can talk it out now," Loretta said. "Take my mind off my troubles."

About to protest that this was hardly the place, Jamie mulled over Loretta's last statement and decided she could hardly refuse. For the next fifteen minutes, she outlined the details of her semimythical executive conference, while keeping an eye on Turner Garrett, who was sitting so still it seemed possible he might have dozed off down there. But at least he'd run out of anything to drink.

Loretta asked a few succinct questions, then gave Jamie an approving smile. "You know what you're about. Look good, too, get you dressed up. If I was in charge of the world, I'd offer you a job at the Victoria. We get several conferences a year—small, usually, but high-powered. We need someone to handle them properly. Hard to find someone who's detail oriented. Wouldn't be much different for you working the opposite side of the counter.''

Jamie wasn't sure whether she meant to be taken seriously. ''Thanks,'' she muttered. At least Loretta seemed less hostile now.

Just as she was wondering whether she should raise the subject of Derry's suitcase again Loretta leaned forward, shading her eyes with her hand. ''Is that Turner Garrett down there?'' she asked.

Jamie leaned, too. Rex Putney had joined Turner and was talking to him, gesticulating from time to time. ''I guess so,'' she said carefully. ''I don't really know him. I just met him today.'' Might as well get some information on him while she could, she decided. ''I understand he's in disgrace.''

Loretta made a snorting sound. ''If you ask me, that Walter Seaton got what he had coming. Seems like someone might be making too much of it, trying to get to the inspector.''

''To get rid of him, you mean?''

She shrugged gracefully. ''Who knows?''

''Was he the police officer who picked up Derry Riley's suitcase?'' Jamie asked, hoping she sounded casual.

''Turner Garrett?''

''Yes. You said a police officer . . .''

''So I did.'' She was silent for a minute, then she said, ''He helped one of my brothers out once. And I've met him socially. He's always been nice to me. Not good-natured all the time though, like our Charles.'' She made an exasperated sound. ''Gets on my last little wick, that man. I always want to make him mad, to see where his spine is.'' She shook her head. ''At least you know where you are with Garrett. He's tough, but he's fair.'' She thought for a minute. ''Never did like his wife, though.''

Frustrated as she was by Loretta's avoidance of her question, Jamie couldn't help questioning that statement. She *was* human after all. "Why not?" she asked.

Loretta shrugged. "Cold woman. One of those long British noses meant to be looked down. Good-looking woman, all the same. Blonde, blue eyes, WASP type. I only met her a couple of times. Gatherings like this. But she always put me in mind of the old story about the Snow Queen, you know? She was a coke head. Got herself on a high, she turned into a nympho, too. Talk of the island." She shook her head. "Always wondered how Turner Garrett put up with her. He strikes me as a proud man. He must have been shamed, the way Pamela rubbed herself upside the men, especially Rex Putney."

"Mr. Putney!" Jamie exclaimed. "He must be at least sixty."

"Every bit of that," Loretta said cheerfully. "Money's a powerful aphrodisiac." She grinned sideways at Jamie. "Not to me, though. Me, I like 'em young and built. How about you?"

Jamie murmured something that was unintelligible even to herself. "Loretta," she began, intending to get back to Derry's suitcase, but then she saw Charles returning.

Loretta caught sight of him at the same moment. Standing abruptly, she took off, making a wide arc to avoid running into Charles.

Charles gave Jamie a rueful grin. He looked somewhat crushed, she thought, as he sat himself down alongside her. As well as being frustrated, she felt a little awkward, unsure of what to say. "This food is wonderful," she said finally.

"Rex always puts on a good feed." He slanted a glance at her. "I'm not at all useless," he said, sounding aggrieved.

"Of course you aren't," Jamie said mildly.

"My family's not all that well off, actually," he added. "There used to be a considerable fortune, one of England's oldest and finest..." His voice trailed away. "Taxation, death duties... Women like Loretta don't realize..." He broke off again. "As for the business meetings," he went on, "as I told you, the Victoria's owners have their headquarters in Florida. If I'm summoned, I can't refuse to go, can I?"

"Of course not," Jamie said again.

Charles sighed, patted his jacket pockets, then gave her an apologetic smile. "I need a pipe," he announced. "Do you mind if I leave you again for a few minutes?"

"It's not necessary," Jamie said, standing up. "I could use a little exercise. I'll look for you back here."

"Thank you, Jamie," he said, accompanying the simple statement with a sexy glance that worried her all over again.

Setting her plate on the buffet table, she headed directly toward the moon gate at the side of the grounds. Looking down the wooden steps, she saw Mr. Putney going on board his yacht and hesitated, wondering if Turner was going to follow him.

Turner started up the steps. She waited for him. "Drink evaporated," he said, waving his glass at her. "Have to get a refill."

"I can't believe you're drinking like this," she said hotly. "An intelligent man like you. Especially considering the lousy position you're in right now. Why do it to yourself?"

He made a face at her.

"Why don't I drive you home?" she suggested, trying to hang on to her temper. "You don't seem too welcome here."

"You've noticed that have you? Makes you see why I have to go about in my Digby disguise, doesn't it?" He inclined his head to one side. "Not a bad idea of yours, actually. Going home. I've accomplished everything I wanted to."

Quite suddenly he didn't sound so drunk. "What will you do with your escort?" he asked before she could comment.

"I'll think of something," she said. "Wait for me in the parking lot. And don't try to drive."

"Yes ma'am." He sketched a mocking salute that made him stagger against the stair rail. He was still drunk, after all.

Disgusted all over again, Jamie hurried across the grass toward Charles, who was having a tête-à-tête with a loud-voiced woman who was bonily elegant in flowered silk and pearls. Apparently she was suggesting he take part in some charity dog show she was hosting the following month. She didn't seem to mind the cloud of smoke that wreathed both their heads.

"I'm sorry, Charles," Jamie said, coming to a halt a few feet away from the smoke. "I'm afraid I'm not feeling well."

"I'll take you back to the hotel," he said promptly, but not without a disappointed glance at his companion.

"That's not necessary," she said hastily. "You'd have to run the boat back to pick up the other people you brought. Stay and enjoy yourself. I'll call a cab."

"You're sure?" He was already halfway to sitting down again. She could hardly blame him for letting her go so easily. He hadn't exactly had a great time so far.

Turner saw her coming across the car park and tapped the horn lightly a couple of times. She came up to the passenger window and leaned down to stare in at him through her sunglasses. "I understood I was going to drive," she said.

"I'm actually perfectly capable of driving," Turner said. "I must confess also that I'm very proprietary about my car. I've promised her I'll never let anyone else drive her—in return, she never lets me down."

He rather enjoyed the look of shock on her face. "You're not drunk," she said accusingly.

"Only extremely awash with tea," he said. "Admittedly strong tea, made specially for me by one of the waiters. Swore him to silence with a twenty-dollar bill."

"But you stank of rum," Jamie protested. She sniffed. "You still do."

"Gargled with it every once in a while, spat it out when no one was looking." Reaching into the car's side pocket, he came up with half a roll of breath mints and popped a couple into his mouth. "Come along, Jamie, get in, do," he said. "We don't want to be seen together, remember."

Still looking stunned, she got in and sat down. "You were playacting? Why on earth would you *pretend* to be drunk?"

Without answering, he started the car and drove out of the parking lot. Pausing at the end of Putney's driveway, he leaned over and kissed her lightly on the cheek. "Close your mouth, Jamie," he suggested as he pulled out onto the road.

Surprise had apparently robbed her of her voice. It was a while before she recovered it. "Who was all the drama intended to fool? Rex Putney?"

He nodded. How smart she was. "I wanted to convince him that I'm bitter about my suspension."

"Aren't you?"

He glanced at her with admiration. He did so enjoy intelligent women. All the same, he had to be careful here. "Of course I'm bitter. I just wanted the fact to be obvious."

"Why?"

"I was trying to nudge Rex into offering me a job. He's known for helping down-and-outers. Actually he approached me as soon as the story of my suspension was published. At the time I wasn't sure how useful working for Rex would be. Now that I've decided it would be useful, I wanted to give him another chance to make an offer. It worked, too. He wants me to take over security arrangements for his various enterprises. I accepted at once, but he insisted I sober up before giving him a final answer.''

She was frowning, absorbing.

''I do apologize, Jamie,'' he added. ''I had no idea you would be turning up. Big shock, that was. I certainly didn't want you to see me behaving so badly, but once begun I had to keep up the pretense.'' He produced a smile that he hoped was disarming. ''I appreciate the lecture you gave me, however. I'll bear it in mind if I'm ever tempted to drink.''

''I must have sounded pretty pompous,'' she said flatly.

He smiled at her fondly. ''You were trying to save me from myself.''

''You could have told me,'' she said.

He glanced sideways at her. ''I wasn't sure how convincing an actress you could be. You have this thing about honesty.''

''I do, indeed,'' she snapped. ''You might try it yourself.''

Sitting back, she looked straight ahead. He could almost hear the wheels spinning in her brain. He was willing to bet she was replaying everything he'd said and done at the party. As traffic permitted, he glanced at her, gauging the play of expressions across her face. About the time her expression cleared and sharpened and he could sense her gearing up to ask questions, they arrived at their destination.

She looked startled as he drove into the car park. ''What is this?''

''It's a lighthouse,'' he answered, taking off his jacket and tie. ''Gibbs Hill Lighthouse. More than a hundred and forty years old. One of the few lighthouses in the world made of cast iron. Brought over in bits by ship from England.''

She dismissed these fascinating observations with a shake of her head. ''I meant, what are we doing here?''

''You'll see.''

''What if someone sees us together?''

He opened his shirt collar, rolled up his sleeves and adjusted his sunglasses. "I think we can chance it. It's near closing time and lighthouse visitors are usually tourists."

She followed him obediently enough as he bought tickets and led the way inside, but she glanced nervously back at him as he indicated the circular staircase. Did she think he was going to push her off the top?

They passed two other people who were coming down. American tourists by the look of them. Overweight. "One hundred and eighty-five steps—they ought to put an elevator in here," the woman said seriously. "In the Bahamas, they put an elevator in everything."

Jamie laughed. Good, Turner thought, perhaps the incident would put her in a more receptive mood.

But when they emerged on the observation walkway, she was no longer laughing. She barely spared a glance for the breathtaking view of the South Shore. "I take it this expedition is meant to give us privacy?" she said. "You're going to tell me everything you should have told me from the beginning?"

He certainly wasn't going that far, but after a quick look at that belligerent chin, Turner decided it might be wise not to say so.

Taking hold of the rail with both hands, her bright mass of hair and the full skirt of her dress blowing out behind her, Jamie stood looking straight ahead, her face solemn. She was obviously waiting for his explanation. For a moment, lost in contemplation of her, he couldn't remember what it might be.

She glanced at him questioningly, suspiciously.

"Right," he said. "I'm going to trust you with some information. In order to do so, I have to go back to April fifteenth and the shooting at the Tudor Tavern."

She looked startled.

Even with the sunlight shining directly on her, her skin was flawless, he noticed. He wanted to touch her. How had he ever thought her not beautiful?

"It was about eight o'clock in the evening," he began. "Two men wearing Burberries—trench coats—and stocking masks entered the lounge of the Tudor Tavern carrying handguns. The place was crowded. Quite calmly the two proceeded to shoot up the place, apparently at random. When they were done, several people were injured, mostly from flying glass, or from banging themselves on the furniture as they dove for cover. Two men, one white, one black, lay dead on the floor. Just as calmly as they had entered, the two gunmen walked out and drove away. As you can probably imagine, there was considerable chaos. Nobody managed to get a license number."

"You said—*apparently* at random. What did you mean?"

Once more she had proved how intelligent she was. She'd picked out the most significant aspect of the entire incident.

"That's a part of this story that's not generally realized," he told her. "If the gunmen had really shot at random, more people would have been hurt or killed. Four guns hold a lot of bullets. But only two men were hit."

"Which means they were the intended victims?"

"That's how it looked to the investigating officers."

"You were involved in the investigation?"

"I was. I wasn't first on the scene, or the detective in charge, but I was in the neighborhood and I arrived soon after it happened." He paused, reacreating the scene in his mind. "Officers were questioning witnesses, medical personnel were dispensing first aid, there were photographers, people examining the bodies, ambulance people. After an event like this, it's important to gather physical evidence and start diagramming, so that's what I elected to do. I diagrammed the place, marking the locations of the bodies and the bullets and so on. I found lots of spent cartridges on the floor. But no bullets. All the bullets, except for those in the dead men, were in the walls and the ceiling.''

''So the hit men were definitely after those two men and no others.''

''Precisely. There are very few murders in Bermuda, Jamie, so this was an unusual case. Handguns are strictly prohibited. Even the police are unarmed. Bermuda's a fairly peaceable place. Some of the bad guys do have guns, obviously, and usually they just shoot at each other, as they did in this case.''

''What was the motive?''

''The two victims were known drug dealers. It seems pretty obvious the shooting was connected with that fact.''

Drug dealers. The words made a connection in Jamie's mind. Turner's wife had been a drug addict. Drugs had *killed* her.

He was watching her face. She needed to say something before he wondered what she was thinking. ''One of the two killers was an American, the bartender said.''

''He said that was the story. It has yet to be confirmed.'' He sighed. ''Some sort of internecine warfare seems the most likely explanation for the shooting. However, nobody on the scene would admit to recognizing the killers.''

He paused to gather his thoughts. ''There has been a tremendous increase in drug activity in recent years, here as well as everywhere else in the world. There is evidently a sizable organization importing cocaine into Bermuda. We know some of the people involved, but only the small-fry, like the two who were killed. The people we normally depend on for information seemed to be running scared. Probably because of the shooting. If we can find out who was responsible for the shooting, we'll be a lot closer to finding out who's importing the drugs.''

He frowned. "It's possible nobody in the lower echelon knows who the top man is, of course. Rumor has it he's known only as the chief. Such secrecy is not unusual...those at the very top in the drug business usually keep their distance from those who work beneath them on the various levels of sales and distribution—the growers and producers and wholesalers, the pushers and peddlers."

"You sound as if you're still very much involved in the case," she said.

He froze for a second, then shook his head. "Not officially." He was silent for a while, trying to decide how best to ease her away from the areas of this story that he didn't want her snooping into. "As I told you before, if I can crack a case or two, it will look good on my record as far as the internal investigation is concerned."

A troubled expression appeared on her face. It appeared whenever the subject of Walter Seaton came up, even by implication. The question of his culpability bothered her a great deal, obviously. But there was nothing he could do about that. He kept hoping she would just accept what had happened and let it go, but she didn't seem inclined to.

"As you know, I have a personal reason for wanting to solve this case," he said, hoping to forestall the questions she was obviously assembling. "But even before my wife's...involvement, it was my ambition to see drugs cleaned out of Bermuda altogether. This is some of the fairest land anyone could hope to see, a paradise on earth. We've been blessed by nature with a wonderful climate, trees, flowers beyond compare, birds, whistling frogs, waters teeming with fish. And all of it measures only twenty square miles, approximately. If we can't get rid of the drug scourge here, where can it be wiped out?

"The drug trade is a sore that festers and suppurates and poisons everything and everyone with whom it comes in contact. Politicians pump money into antidrug programs, law enforcement agencies keep fighting the cartels and knocking them down and they keep getting up and carrying on, business as usual. I can't do much about the rest of the world, but I want drugs out of Bermuda. Now. I especially want this man they call the chief. And I intend to get him.''

He broke off abruptly, aware that his voice had risen. Jamie was staring at his face, frowning, her eyes troubled. ''Sorry,'' he muttered. ''I didn't mean to get on a soapbox.''

She continued to stare at him for several seconds, then she shook her head a little, looked away, glanced back. ''Didn't you say, when you showed me that newspaper article about Walter Seaton, that he was a person of interest in a murder investigation?''

Damn.

''Was he a person of interest in the Tudor Tavern murders?''

''He often takes up residence in the car park at the Tudor Tavern. It was thought he might have seen something.''

''Had he?''

''He said not.''

''Is that why you beat him?''

Double damn.

''It's obvious you feel very strongly about this whole business,'' she said flatly. ''I must admit I agree with what you said about drugs, and I admire your...passion, but judging by the speech you just gave, it seems to me your feelings are quite violent.''

She wasn't going to leave it alone. And he couldn't give her an answer that would satisfy her. He certainly couldn't tell her the truth. ''My problem with Walter Seaton is not connected to the shooting at the Tudor Tavern,'' he said, hedging.

She gave him the kind of disgusted look an answer like that deserved. Then she began moving around the walkway. He followed her. When she reached the north side of the lighthouse, she stopped, apparently noticing the scenery for the first time. "That's the Great Sound there, isn't it?" She pointed toward the Belmont Hotel. "Stonecrest must be on this side of that building? I hadn't realized it was so close."

There was a vagueness to her voice that told him she wasn't really thinking about what she was saying. She was using small talk as a cover while her agile brain ticked over. Recognizing this, he wasn't astounded when she looked at him directly again and said, "Is Rex Putney the chief?"

"What makes you think that?" he asked, truly interested in how she'd managed to come up with that name without him having to tell her.

Holding up her left hand, she started ticking off fingers with her right. "One— I read in the newspaper, a couple of days after I got here, that Rex Putney had recently returned from delivering some kind of charitable supplies, medicine and stuff, to the West Indies. Which means he gets around on that yacht of his. Two— Charles Hollingsworth told me all about Putney's philanthropy when he invited me to his party, including the bit about him being connected with criminals. Three— Catherine said she'd heard one of the killers was an ex-con."

She frowned. "Anna Campbell told me he helped her to get *her* business started."

He hadn't known that. He tried not to show the burst of interest that flowered in response to that statement. She noticed it, anyway, and looked at him narrowly before going on. "Four— Rex offered you a job, which you accepted. And I asked myself, why would you want to work for Rex Putney, philanthropist? And I remembered saying to Charles that Rex sounded too good to be true." She raised her eyebrows. "He is too good to be true, isn't he?"

"I'd no idea you knew so much about Rex," he said rue-fully. "If I had..."

"You were down there on his dock, looking at his boat, giving the crew the once-over," she interrupted. "Are the drugs coming in by boat?"

Lord, she was quick. "We've beefed up security at the airport in recent years," he said. "But the stuff's still com-ing in. It seems logical to assume it's coming in by boat."

"And I'm right about Rex Putney?" She frowned fero-ciously at him. "You're getting your carved-in-stone look again. Don't try to put me off, Turner. I know I'm right."

He sighed. "Rex Putney is a person of interest. That's all I'm prepared to say."

"You think he might have had a hand in the Tudor Tav-ern shoot-out?"

He winced at her continued use of movie-style language. "Not personally, perhaps, but possibly indirectly."

Jamie's brow was furrowed with obviously strenuous thought. "So if you go to work for Rex you'll be able to snoop around and see what he's up to."

And that's not all, she thought but didn't say. According to Loretta Dean, Turner's drug-addicted wife had made a play for Rex Putney. Did Turner carry a personal grudge against Rex? Was he engaged in some kind of personal vendetta? Was that the reason for his occasional secretive-ness? He had sounded most violent when he spoke of "get-ting" the chief. Had he beaten Walter Seaton into a coma because he got in the way of his investigation into the Tu-dor Tavern shoot-out? A shoot-out that might involve Rex Putney. If Rex did turn out to be the chief, what might Turner do to *him?*

Turner studied Jamie's face carefully. She was chewing on her lower lip and obviously indulging in some high-level thinking. If he wasn't very careful here she would soon have it all. "Look, Jamie," he said hastily before she could get carried away. "I want you to understand that I have no proof Rex is involved in drug smuggling. He's a suspect only because he has means and opportunity.

"As you pointed out, he does have a yacht, and he frequently takes it down to the Bahamas, Haiti and Jamaica, as well as to the U.S. The fact that he assists ex-convicts is another reason for suspicion. Several of the people he employs are *known* to have been involved in drugs."

He broke off and continued more slowly. "It's entirely possible, however, that his motives are as philanthropical as they appear. Those medical, food and building supplies do get delivered. And he's always been quite open about employing ex-convicts. It is his stated belief that once a man has paid his debt to society he deserves a new beginning. Which is absolutely true."

She took off her sunglasses and studied his face. She was adding two and two and making at least half a dozen, her eyes narrowing with suspicion as she stared at him. Suspicion of him? Possibly. "There's more," she said accusingly.

He nodded. "One of the men who was killed in the Tudor Tavern worked for Rex. The other had gone through Rex's rehabilitation program. It seems . . ."

"What about Bobby Kenyon?" she blurted out, her voice tight. "Jordan Lathrop told me Bobby Kenyon often came to work stoned." All at once her eyes were as cold as the green light that often appeared at the tops of cresting waves. "You got very interested when I mentioned Kenyon in connection with Derry's so-called accident. You said you knew something about him. And Joe Hokins." Her eyes narrowed again. "You told the bartender at the Tudor Tavern that the gunmen had disappeared into thin air. You said yesterday that Kenyon and Hokins can't be found. They're involved in all this, aren't they?"

His scheme to give her part of the story without revealing all had backfired on him. There was no way she would let this matter drop now. Mortified that once again he'd underestimated her intelligence, he was impressed by her at the same time.

Fortunately for him she hadn't figured out all of it yet. What he had to do now was to keep her mind so occupied that her fertile imagination wouldn't have a chance to make any more lightning leaps—which could be at the least, uncomfortable and at the most, dangerous.

"Bobby Kenyon and Joe Hokins were in Casemates together last year," he told her. "When they were released they both went through Rex's rehabilitation program. At various times they've crewed for him."

"When did you find all that out?"

"I knew it all along."

For a moment she gazed at him blankly, then she started speaking very quickly. "Kyle Hammond worked for Rex Putney too. Hammond, Kenyon, Hokins, they've all worked for Putney. Kenyon and Hokins were on the *Coral Queen* when Derry died. Clyde Kane wasn't, because he got drunk at a party the previous night—a party hosted by Kyle Hammond."

She stared at him, her glorious green eyes as cold and hard as jade. "Derry's death is connected with the drug trafficking and the Tudor Tavern shooting in some way," she said accusingly. "You knew *that* all along, too, didn't you? You *used* me."

Before he could quite grasp what she was saying, she had turned abruptly and hurried away from him. It was a minute before he had the sense to go after her. By then she had reentered the lighthouse and was running down the spiral staircase at top speed. Good Lord, he thought, she was wearing heels—she'd break her neck at the rate she was going.

"Jamie," he yelled after her. "It's not like that at all. Wait, Jamie, wait."

All he could hear was the sound of her leather-soled shoes clattering on the steps.

Chapter Thirteen

She was standing by his car, leaning both arms on it, her head down, her face flushed with exertion.

"That was a bloody foolish thing to do," he shouted.

She bit her lower lip, then glanced at a nearby bench where a young couple were sipping soft drinks and watching them with interest. "Get in the car," he said, lowering his voice.

He expected her to argue, but instead she moved around to the passenger side of the vehicle. To his dismay, he saw that she was limping. "You've hurt yourself," he exclaimed, following after her and taking hold of her arm.

She shook his hand away. "Did you twist your ankle?" he asked. "We'd best get it X-rayed. Is it swollen?"

"I broke the damn heel off my shoe," she snapped.

Relief showed in his eyes. He really had been worried about her. Which made it difficult to hang on to her fury.

Getting into the car, she kicked off her ruined shoe and its mate and leaned back, trying to catch her breath. Hurtling down that steep winding staircase hadn't been the most intelligent thing to do.

Turner was breathing heavily, too, as he slid in beside her. His dark eyes glowed with anger. "Would you please inform me why you found it necessary to do such a stupid thing?"

"I was mad at you. I *am* mad at you. You knew right from the beginning Derry's death was tied in with your own investigation, didn't you? That's why you agreed to help me."

Guilt showed clearly in his eyes. But he shook his head. "I didn't know straight away. I was interested when you mentioned Cornell Alexander, because his name had come up previously in connection with a couple of incidents that weren't as fully investigated as they might have been. I was intrigued by the similar lack of information in Derry's file. I became even more interested when we found out Derry had visited the Tudor Tavern. But I didn't suspect any real connection until Lathrop brought up Bobby Kenyons's name."

He pushed an impatient hand through his hair. "Bobby Kenyon has been in trouble with the law for years. He's served several short sentences in prison for breaking and entering. He has a history of stealing the type of goods that can be sold easily to support a drug habit. As I told you, last time Bobby was released, Rex enrolled him in a drug rehabilitation program—along with Joe Hokins." He glanced at her. "That's why I didn't want you mentioning your job to Rex. Because of the connection to Derry. *If* Kenyon or Hokins had anything at all to do with Derry's death, and if Rex *is* the man I'm—the police are looking for—you could have been exposing yourself to risk."

He touched her face. "I did use you as cover for my own enquiries on the first day of our investigation, Jamie. At that time I was still fairly convinced Derry's death was an accident. By the time the day was over, I was committed to helping you for your own sake, and that was *before* I suspected a connection."

"You think he was there, don't you? At the Tudor Tavern?"

"I think it's possible. But I think Linda was telling the truth when she said she didn't recognize him. It's also possible she might not have noticed him. But there are too many coincidences for me to discard the theory.'' He hesitated, then went on. ''You have to trust me, Jamie. I'm one of the good guys.''

Everything that was honest and direct showed in his dark eyes. But how could she believe him? He'd admitted—and shown—that he was a very good actor. Confused, Jamie let her cheek rest against his hand. She wanted desperately to believe he really was one of the good guys, but the image of poor Walter Seaton lying unconscious on the ground was as vivid as ever in her mind. ''I'm sorry I acted so childishly,'' she said without committing herself.

''And I'm sorry I ever thought of using you for my own purposes, even for a brief period.''

The car seemed suddenly smaller, and lacking in oxygen. Turner's hand was warm on her face, his eyes had darkened. As she gazed at him, his thumb grazed her lips, tracing the outline of her mouth.

All at once her reasons for distrusting him seemed insubstantial—maybe she had an overactive imagination, maybe Walter Seaton could be explained, maybe Turner wanted only to bring ''the chief'' to proper and legal justice.

''Jamie,'' Turner murmured, his face inches from hers.

Her body felt lethargic. She couldn't even remember why she'd felt so angry. Yes, Turner had used her, but did that really matter? Surely the important thing was that Turner was as committed as she was to finding out what had happened to Derry. ''What do we do now?'' she asked.

He smiled, his dark eyes filling with light in the way that always enchanted her. ''I think I'm overdosed on investigation for today,'' he said. ''At this moment I have something else on my mind.''

When she looked at him questioningly, his thumb worked its way across her lips again, this time pressing gently until they parted. With his gaze on her mouth, he said, ''You insisted a while ago that everyone has feelings. If I stopped trying to suppress mine, you said, they'd come floating up to the top." He cocked an eyebrow. "Am I quoting you correctly?"

"I think so." Her voice sounded hoarse. Which was hardly surprising, considering that her throat was so tight.

"You were wrong," he said. "They didn't float, they exploded."

She nodded agreement, unable to speak. She was noticing again how seductive his mouth was. Somewhere in the dim recesses of her mind a warning sounded. The man was tough. The man was stubborn. If, as she now suspected, he was planning some personal vendetta against Rex Putney, he would be quite likely to pursue his goal to whatever end he deemed necessary, no matter who was in the way. She must not forget he was also an accomplished actor. Was he capable of wooing her, seducing her to lull her suspicions?

"What I'm trying to decide is this," Turner continued slowly, his strong fingers tangling in her hair. "Why is it that a man can know very well that it's wisest not to get emotionally involved with a woman, he can assemble all the reasons very logically in his mind—she's here temporarily, he's working on something that consumes him, and he can't handle anything extraneous, he's made it a practice to stay uninvolved ever since his marriage...ended. And then in spite of all his good resolutions, he finds that he's involved right up to his eyebrows, anyway?" He brushed her lips with his own, then laid his face against hers. His smoothly shaven skin felt just as sensual as his beard had. "Can you explain this phenomenon, Jamie Maxwell?" he asked.

"Hormones?" she whispered in a last-ditch attempt to break the spell he was weaving around her.

He laughed, his breath brushing against her skin; that slight, small friction setting off a spark that seemed ready to burst into flames that would soon engulf her entire body.

"You are so romantic," he murmured. With one finger he traced the scooped neckline of her dress, setting her nervous system vibrating. "I'm remembering something, Jamie Maxwell. When I made love to you, you didn't say 'Come off it.'"

She was puzzled for a moment, then recalled telling him that growing up with four brothers had left her unable to take men seriously when they got romantic.

"You don't remind me in any way of my brothers," she said. "You seem to be a different species altogether."

"The lover species, perhaps?" he asked.

As she stared at him, his hand moved slowly to her shoulder, her upper arm, her left breast.

She groaned as her body yearned toward him, shuddering slightly. "I want to make love to you again, Jamie," he said softly. "I must confess I didn't intend to. I was afraid of getting too...involved. I'd made up my mind to be this strong dedicated person who couldn't possibly take time out to indulge his emotions. But I can't resist you, Jamie. I truly can't. Please let me make love to you again."

She could feel her body loosening, leaning into his. Surely, just for tonight, she could pretend to herself that she had no reason to fear his motives, no reason to disbelieve him?

He must have read her weakening in her face. His mouth came down urgently on hers and took all of her breath out of it. Then he set her away from him. "The hotel?" he asked.

She hesitated once more, wondering why he didn't suggest taking her to his home. Then he kissed her again and location didn't matter. Deliberately she shut off that part of her mind that wanted to advise caution. "The hotel," she agreed.

Surprisingly, considering the heat that was generated between them on the drive, they had enough sense to remember not to enter the hotel together. Jamie went first, walking from the parking lot around to the front door and in through the lobby, carrying her ruined shoes, relieved when no one noticed her and she didn't run into Charles or Loretta. They were probably still at Rex Putney's party, she realized.

Turner came up the back stairs, arriving right after she did, as out of breath as if he'd run up all three flights.

She locked the door carefully, adjusted the safety catch, fastened the chain, then turned and walked directly, blindly, into his arms. On the drive there, she hadn't allowed herself to think, concentrating instead on the sensations coursing through her body, sensations too strong to deny. She was driven by a need so strong that she had forgotten all the questions her mind had formerly produced. She wanted Turner Garrett, and she wanted him now.

His kiss ignited a thousand tiny explosions along her nerve ends, as though they were fireflies, bursting with light inside her body. Every instinct she possessed was telling her to move impatiently against him. Turner's own impatience showed in the clumsy way he helped her take off her clothing, the haste with which he removed his own. Smiling at the thought, she wondered if he was impatient enough to leave their clothing on the floor.

He wasn't. Turning away, he picked everything up and draped it neatly over a chair. She laughed shakily. "You are the tidiest person I've ever met," she informed him.

He was puzzled for a moment, then he glanced at the clothing and felt sheepish. "My mother trained me too well, I'm afraid. Does it bother you?"

She grinned. "It certainly does. You make me look even messier by contrast."

Her smile faded as he took her in his arms and looked into her splendid green eyes. There was no mistaking the message that blazed in them—a message of hunger, of passion banked but ready to explode. Cupping her face in his hands, he kissed her gently, then traced her mouth with the tip of his tongue. Her lips parted to give him access to the sweetness that was more delicious each time he tasted it. His hands moved downward to pull her against his aroused body.

Holding her with one arm, he reached out and yanked the covers down on her bed, then rolled with her onto it, his mouth clinging to hers in a kiss that swamped him with passion.

Her mouth felt wonderful on his, hot and demanding now, answering and provoking his own intensity. Ever since that first time, he had dreamed of running his hands again over her surprisingly strong body. Her skin felt wonderful against his own, warm and smooth. He eased her gently on top of him, and she came willingly, kneeling over him, her amazing hair glinting with light around her flushed face and smooth shoulders. He stroked the satin skin of her back, applying just enough pressure to bring her closer. But she shook her head and began trailing soft kisses down his throat and onto his chest. She had her own plans for this scenario, it seemed, and he was more than willing to let her set the pace.

There was plenty of time. He could think of nothing that was more urgent than his need to make love to this beautiful, endearingly zany woman. It was what the Americans called *time out,* he thought. Time out to look wonderingly at each other's body, time out to rediscover one another's intimate places, to follow exploring hands with lips and tongue. He felt the swell of her breasts against his palms and saw the pupils of her eyes dilate until there was the merest rim of green around them. He touched his lips lightly to the bruise on her throat, feeling anger knife through him as he considered the savage hand that had marked her.

Aware of his sudden tension, she stroked his back gently, lovingly, and moved against him in a teasing way. Then she knelt over him again and allowed him access to her warmth. By then his blood was singing through his veins and he was afraid he would climax long before he was ready to.

"Slowly," he muttered as he entered her. "I want to do this slowly. I want it to last forever."

Forever, her mind echoed. Forever.

There were no more words between them. There was only the astonishing experience of two bodies moving as one in perfect harmony, as though they had spent hours in rehearsal. Timing his movements to coincide with her own rocking motion, Turner thought that no woman had ever excited him like this. He couldn't seem to get enough of her mouth, her warm, willing mouth. Nobody existed in the universe except himself and the radiant, passionate woman in his arms.

"Jamie," he groaned, as raw heat raced to where they were joined together.

"Wait," she urged him and he felt her sudden stillness and interpreted it and rolled over so that she was under him and he could move more freely. And then Jamie said, "Now," and a wave surged out of nowhere and picked him up and carried him away.

"THAT WAS some kind of lovemaking," Jamie murmured when her breath finally came back to her.

"It could be used in seminars," Turner agreed sleepily.

She could feel the languor stealing over her body. Probably she should get up and shower. But that much effort seemed beyond her, especially when Turner was holding her, his warm breath feathering against her face. Maybe she could just rest for a little while....

They woke at nine o'clock. The sun had set half an hour ago. They were both hungry. Gathering up his clothes,

Turner camped out in the bathroom again while Jamie, her robe wrapped around her, accepted the gargantuan meal she'd ordered from room service, tipping the bellman lavishly so he wouldn't wonder about the number of dishes.

They ate every crust of bread, every leaf of lettuce and chunk of tender chicken, then drank coffee, smiling at each other and talking in desultory fashion about nothing they would ever remember, until at last the tray was safely outside the room and they were back in each other's arms.

HOURS LATER, when the telephone rang, Jamie assumed it was her wake-up call. In what seemed an even denser form of her usual morning daze, she reached for the receiver and grunted into it.

"Jamie?" a female voice queried, which seemed somewhat familiar for a desk clerk.

She acknowledged with another grunt, at the same time allowing several pieces of information to penetrate her fuzzy brain. One—the bedside clock's hands pointed to 8:30 and she'd left a standing order for a 9:00 a.m. call unless otherwise notified. Two—at some time in the night, Turner Garrett had hung up her dress and his jacket, pants and shirt and had folded the rest of their clothing neatly on the bedside chair. Anyone else picking up after her would have irritated her, she felt sure, but Turner's compulsive neatness seemed as lovable as his occasional bouts of stuffiness. The third bit of information to come her way was that Turner's hand was moving gently over her bare abdomen, indicating he was either awake or was dreaming he was still making love to her.

Whoever was on the other end of the line was breathing but not speaking. "Who is this?" she asked, pushing herself to a sitting position, widening her eyes to force sleep out of them.

"Anna. Anna Campbell."

Jamie was awake now. Flattening a hand over Turner's wandering fingers, she flashed him a warning and saw his eyes light with interest. "What can I do for you, Anna?" she asked.

Turner raised himself on one elbow, gazing at her face.

"I wondered could I see you today," Anna said. She was speaking so softly Jamie could barely make out the words.

"I can be out of here in fifteen minutes," she said.

"No, that's too soon. I have appointments all morning and most of the after—" She broke off and Jamie heard her speak to someone else, then she heard a door close. "Could you meet me at four o'clock?" Anna asked.

"Sure. At the salon?"

"I'm not certain that would be a good idea." There was a silence. "Next door at Treasure Cave, perhaps. In the lobby. I often go there to chat. Nobody will think anything of it."

"Is anything wrong?" Jamie asked.

"It's, well, I didn't tell you everything. I was that afraid, you see, and I wasn't certain I was right."

Jamie felt a sudden chill. "Can't you tell me now, Anna?"

"Och no. The telephone—I'd rather see you, try to explain. It's important to me that you understand...." She was beginning to sound agitated.

"Okay," Jamie said hastily. "I'll meet you at four."

The phone clicked almost immediately.

"Anna Campbell?" Turner queried as she hung up.

She nodded, still regarding the telephone thoughtfully. "She wants me to meet her at Treasure Cave at four o'clock. Says she didn't tell me everything."

He plumped a pillow behind himself and leaned back against it, obviously turning this new information over in his mind. After a while, he nodded. "We need to be careful. If

I show up with you, Anna's liable to take fright even though she doesn't know me.''

"I'll take a cab.''

"A bus would be better. I can follow on the bike more inconspicuously.'' He put an arm around her in an absent-minded way. Already his embrace felt familiar to her. She wasn't going to worry right now about how she would feel if her suspicions about him turned out to be well-founded, she decided. She was going to live only for the moment.

"I'll try to get to the cave ahead of you,'' he said. "I can stand about in the lobby and keep an eye on you when you meet Anna.''

"Okay,'' she agreed.

The phone rang again. Could it be Anna calling to say she'd changed her mind? Jamie picked up the receiver.

"Good morning, Jamie,'' Charles Hollingsworth said.

Lying naked against Turner's arm she felt herself blush. "I wanted to make sure you've recovered,'' Charles said.

"Recovered?'' Even as she echoed the word, memory returned. Yesterday. At the party. She'd excused herself because of illness. "Completely recovered,'' she said heartily, then added quickly, "Sorry if I seem dense, Charles. I was in the shower. I'm dripping.''

He let her go like the gentleman he was. Hanging up, she glared at Turner, daring him to comment, then forgot Charles as her worry about Anna returned. "What can she want to tell me?'' she asked. "It has to be about Derry, don't you think?''

He kissed her lightly on the forehead. "We've no way of knowing *what* she wants with you, Jamie. And there's no use worrying about it all day.''

"What shall we do, then?''

"We could check some more of the restaurants and taverns in Hamilton. Though most of them won't be open until noon. We can have lunch while we're working. Then I'll go home and change clothes and meet you in time to follow your bus.''

His arm tightened around her shoulders, pulling her over against him. His smile had a mischievous slant to it this time. Quite suddenly the air was crackling merrily away between them. ''Perhaps if we put our heads together we'll think of a way to fill in the time until then,'' he suggested as his mouth met hers.

Chapter Fourteen

On the bus, Jamie tried to watch out for Turner's moped, but eventually lost sight of it. There was a lot of traffic, and apart from one other white woman and a young black man who was slumped down in his seat with a cap over his eyes, the rest of the passengers were high-spirited schoolchildren, who spent the journey hopping up and down and changing places so often they completely obscured her view. She wondered where they found the energy on such a hot day.

When the bus stopped at the cave, Turner was still nowhere to be seen. Considering the number of times the bus had stopped, he'd probably arrived ahead of her. Jamie walked up the pathway marked Entrance and entered the building. There were a couple of dozen people milling around in the lobby, but no Anna. No Turner, either.

Jamie glanced at her watch. She was eight minutes late. Surely Anna would have waited that long? Maybe one of her appointments had taken longer than she'd expected. But why wasn't Turner here? She took up a post near the door. After ten minutes or so, a slender young black man came to gather everyone together for the next tour. "Have you got your ticket?" he asked Jamie.

Jamie shook her head. "I'm waiting for a friend."

He looked concerned. "We're starting now and this is the last tour of the day."

"Oh." She'd have to take a chance, she decided. Anna had said the people here knew her. "I was supposed to meet Anna, from the New Woman," she told the young man.

The guide smiled. "Anna's already in there, miss," he said. "She went in with the last lot. You go in with us, we'll overlap with them along the way."

Why the hell had Anna gone inside? And where was Turner? Should she *wait* for Anna? What if the tour came out in a different area? Hurriedly Jamie bought a ticket, and the young man escorted her to the cave entrance, gathering up the rest of his group on the way. He and Jamie were in the lead as they trooped down the wet sloping walkway. "Watch your step," the guide shouted over his shoulder. "It's slippery underfoot."

The vast cavern was brightly lit. The colored lights seemed to dance eerily on the gnarled amber surfaces. The stalactites were reflected in an enormous subterranean lake along with the lights, so that it was difficult to tell which were real and which were images. The planked pontoon walkway that bridged the lake was equipped with a stout wooden handrail but gave a little with each step and was slimy enough underfoot to make Jamie feel very insecure.

Fantastically shaped stalagmites thrust upward through the water and from shelflike formations in the limestone walls. It was an awe-inspiring display, mysterious and slightly scary. The air smelled overused as though it had been inhaled and exhaled by too many people. Water dripped constantly. Jamie shivered in her shorts and cotton shirt as she looked up at the limestone "daggers" aimed straight at her head.

In the distance the walkway branched in two directions. One section disappeared behind a particularly large outcropping. The tour must wind around and come back in this direction, Jamie decided, which meant Anna should show up there eventually. She would wait just beyond the intersection.

A few minutes later the guide led his group into a small grotto. "This whole cavern was found accidentally," he said, his voice echoing. "As it was discovered fairly recently it escaped damage from the pre-electric-age practice of burning palmetto leaves for illumination, which marred the beauty of many of Bermuda's other caves."

Early-style pollution, Jamie thought.

Worrying about Anna, she looked beyond the guide to see if the other group was in sight yet. It wasn't, but as her gaze returned to the grotto, she saw something in the water a little way beyond the guide—something that didn't seem to belong. The reflections of the stalactites distorted the surface, so she couldn't be sure what it was, but the colors were definitely different. Hanging on to the handrail, she leaned out as far as she could in order to change her angle of vision.

It wasn't some*thing,* it was some*one.* A woman in blue jeans and a white blouse was lying facedown in the shallow pool that covered the floor of the grotto. A skinny woman with a mane of long frizzy blond hair. A woman wearing red shoes.

Anna Campbell.

Jamie's heart seemed to explode. For a split second she was frozen in place, unable to move. Then she gripped the guide's arm and pulled him to the spot. A scream rang out as the woman standing next to him caught sight of the body. The sound bounced off the limestone walls, echoing throughout the cavern. The scream was joined by others as the rest of the group crowded around and people at the rear began calling out to ask what had happened.

Jamie dropped to her knees at the edge of the walkway and reached out to take hold of Anna's shoulder. "We have to turn her over," she yelled at the guide.

The young man squatted down beside her but didn't seem to know what to do. "Women," he moaned. "Look at those high heels. This walkway's slippery. We try to warn them."

"I'll support her neck. You'll have to help me roll her," Jamie ordered. He took a deep breath and stretched an obviously reluctant hand toward Anna, but then was unceremoniously yanked aside by another man who knelt beside Jamie. The newcomer was wearing a garish Hawaiian shirt, baggy pants and a tan fishing hat. Jamie had never been so relieved to see anyone in her life.

Together she and Turner lifted Anna's limp body out of the water and laid her gently down on the walkway. Water streamed from her. Her eyes were open, sightless, her mouth flaccid. Turner rolled her onto her side. "Call for an ambulance," he said sharply to the guide.

"I've had CPR training," Jamie said, and Turner gave her an approving nod. As he opened Anna's shirt collar, she used both hands to tilt Anna's head back and clear her airway. Then she pinched the woman's nose closed, covered her mouth with her own and gave her four forceful breaths of air. She tried to close her mind to the fact that it wasn't at all like practicing on the Red Cross dummy—this was human flesh; though bordering on cold it was still pliant. Pausing to listen for return breathing, though she was quite sure there wouldn't be any, she watched Turner check Anna's carotid pulse.

"Nothing," he said and started compressing the young woman's chest, counting out loud. Jamie came in on cue to deliver two more breaths. The crowd had gone silent now, except for a sort of muffled sobbing that was coming from someone in the group.

Though Jamie was concentrating hard on the rhythm of compression and breathing and turning Anna on to her side to drain water from her, she became aware that the tourists in the earlier group had finished the circuit and were crowding in behind the people she'd come in with. Their guide, a stocky black man, pushed through and took charge. "Clear the area," he shouted. "Go back to the lobby and wait. Do not leave the building."

Jamie's group immediately began retreating, mingling with the newcomers, excitedly answering their questions. It was probably not a couple of minutes more before the walkway trembled as a pair of paramedics raced in, but it seemed like an hour. Within seconds, the paramedics had taken over. Jamie stood up, her legs trembling so hard she had to grip the handrail for support. Reaction was setting in.

Turner stood up next to her. They were both fairly wet. "We have to get you out of here," he muttered.

She hung stubbornly onto the handrail. "I have to wait and see if Anna's all right," she protested.

"There's an exit this side of the door to an alley. We'll go out that way."

"Turner..."

"Move," he said forcefully.

She moved. As she and Turner emerged through the side door into a shadowed alleyway, a police car drove up in front of the building—a white car with a neon-bright orange slash bisecting it. Turner grabbed her arm and propelled her toward the rear of the building. The moped was parked there. Surely he didn't intend that they should just get on it and take off?

That *was* what he intended. Ramming a safety helmet onto her head, he pushed her onto the bike's pillion, grabbed his own helmet, climbed on and started the engine.

She had no choice but to hang on to him. "We can't just leave," she yelled after the moped swerved around a corner.

Turner didn't answer. A mile up the road he stopped the bike, got off and ran over to a phone booth, leaving Jamie to balance the moped as best she could. A minute later he was back, shaking his head at her before she could even frame a question. This time he didn't stop until they reached the Victoria Hotel. Parking behind the building, he dumped both helmets in the basket, then took her hand and hauled her through the rear entry and up the stairs to her floor. Not until they were in her room did he pause to even take a breath.

"Anna's dead," he said curtly. "I would guess she'd been dead several minutes before we got her out. We had to try, but there wasn't anything we could do for her." His mouth was grim, his eyes hard.

She forced breath through her clenched teeth. Now that the crisis was over, she couldn't seem to stop shivering, even though her clothing had dried on the way over. "She was murdered?" she asked, though she already knew the answer.

His mouth tightened. "I don't accept the guide's interpretation for a minute."

He seemed to realize all at once that she was trembling. His expression softened. Finding her terry cloth robe behind the bathroom door, he put it on her and began to rub her back briskly. "We were quite a team, you and I," he said. "Where did you learn CPR?"

"My company has the Red Cross come in every so often." She swallowed, visualizing Anna's poor bedraggled body. "It's not the same when it's real."

He held her closer for a minute, then set her away with obvious reluctance. "I want you to stay here," he said. "Don't open your door to anyone. Keep the safety latch and the chain on. Don't answer the telephone. Make yourself some hot tea on the machine. Put lots of sugar in it."

He turned as if to go. "Turner," she wailed. "You can't just dump me in here and take off."

"I must see what I can find out."

"Then I'll put on my hat and glasses and come with you. No one will—"

"No, Jamie."

"But it's my fault she's dead. If I hadn't questioned her, she'd still be alive."

He took hold of her shoulders and looked directly into her eyes. "No, Jamie. I'll grant you it's obvious that Anna *knew* something. *That's* why she was killed, not because she was going to tell you what she knew, but because she knew it in the first place."

She let out a shaky breath, feeling slightly better. "Who did you call?" she asked.

He seemed to consider not answering her, but thought better of it. "A friend of mine—Tom Reynolds—a reporter."

She was shocked. "You gave the story to the newspapers?"

He shook his head, hesitated, then raised his hands in a gesture of surrender. "Tom and I have an agreement. He helps me with certain parts of this investigation, I give him the whole story when it's over."

"Did he know I was going to meet Anna?"

Again he hesitated, then nodded. "I rang him up earlier while I was home changing into these clothes."

"What could a reporter do in this situation?"

"You aren't going to leave it alone, are you?"

"No way."

"Then I suppose I'll have to tell you that I first tried to reach Superintendent Baldwin. He wasn't in his office, so I rang Tom, told him what had happened and asked him to track Baldwin down and repeat the information to him."

She felt alarmed. "Won't we get in trouble for leaving the caves before the police arrived?"

"One hopes not."

"Superintendent Baldwin won't care?"

He sighed. Because of her persistence, probably. Tough.

"Dunch Baldwin's my friend, Jamie. That's why I asked Tom to ring him. I knew he'd protect my rear."

"If you knew that, why did you rush us out of there?"

His face had become expressionless. "Think, Jamie. If Anna was killed minutes before she was supposed to meet you, to tell you something she'd omitted telling you previously, then you might also be in danger. Having determined that nothing could be done to help Anna, my first priority was your safety."

That sounded reasonable. "What happens now?" she asked.

"You wait. Here. Just as I said. No phone calls, no answering doors. Don't talk to anyone. Don't trust anyone."

"You're going back to the caves?"

"Just to take a look round."

"But the police may still be there."

"I'll wait until they leave." He touched her cheek. "I'll be back as soon as I can. All right?"

His dark gaze was intense, forbidding refusal or discussion. "Okay," she said reluctantly.

As soon as the door closed behind him, she regretted not insisting on going with him. And as the hours passed, doubts began fretting at the edges of her mind like mice nibbling on a board. Turner had sounded fairly convincing when he explained why he'd rushed her away from the caves. But what if he'd had another reason for leaving the scene in such a hurry? What if he'd been anxious to get *himself* out? Why had it taken him so long to get to the caves in the first place? Somewhere in the back of her mind a cold voice questioned further. Was it possible that Turner had arrived ahead of Jamie, met Anna himself, lured her into the cavern and pushed her down into the water, held her down until she was dead?

Why would he do that?

Because he had been present on the *Coral Queen* when Derry drowned, and Anna had been about to tell her that?

The abyss that yawned at Jamie's feet with this thought was so unbearable a sight that her mind shut down for several minutes.

When she let it crack open again, she thought of how Loretta hadn't actually answered when Jamie had asked if Turner was the officer who'd picked up Derry's suitcase—Derry's neatly packed suitcase.

And then she thought once again of Walter Seaton lying unconscious on the ground with Turner Garrett looming over him.

Why had Turner agreed to help her investigate Derry's death, anyway? So he could unofficially investigate the Tudor Tavern shooting, he'd said. But what if he hadn't wanted anyone else investigating Derry's death because he was involved in it!

Turner had gone fishing with his father and Jordan Lathrop, which might mean Lathrop was a family friend, which might have inclined Lathrop to "forget" Turner Garrett's presence on Derry's trip on the *Coral Queen*.

She was being ridiculous, she scolded herself. Simply because Turner wasn't available, some irrational part of her mind was inventing suspicions. There wasn't any reason to believe that Turner had been on that boat when Derry had drowned.

Was there any reason to believe he hadn't?

He had made love to her. Tenderly. Wonderfully. *Men had deceived women before.* But she had wanted his lovemaking, wanted him. If he'd been involved in Derry's death, she'd have known, or at least sensed something. *There's an immutable law of nature,* her mother had warned her when she began dating. *When the body gets turned on, the brain gets turned off.*

AT ABOUT SIX-THIRTY in the evening she went out on her balcony, needing to at least *watch* some activity. It was still hot. Muggy. The sun shone. Boats scudded all over the harbor. People's voices echoed happily from the swimming pool. Birds chirped. Cooking smells drifted around, but she had no appetite. Just before she went back into her room, she noticed ominous, dark clouds piling up on the horizon.

By seven the black clouds hovered directly overhead. A few minutes later they opened up and released a deluge. Inside her room Jamie watched sheets of rain flowing down the windows, then suddenly thought to switch on her television set. Anna's death was reported on the news as a regrettable accident. For some reason she had lingered behind the tour group, had slipped under the guard rail, fallen into the water and drowned. She had been wearing very high-heeled shoes.

A police officer was interviewed, but had little to say except that it was all most unfortunate. There was a shot of an ambulance leaving the cave, people milling around outside. Turner was nowhere in sight. Not as himself. Nor as Digby.

At eight she hunted out the card Turner had given her with his home number on it. There was no answer.

She called an hour later. Still no answer.

Where was he?

At nine-thirty she gave up expecting him to call and went to bed, sure she would lie awake worrying for most of the night. Instead she fell into a deep sleep almost at once, wakened some time later, after a confused dream in which Anna Campbell was telling her she was going to take the high road and Jamie could take the low road. It took Jamie a minute or two to realize the words had come from an old Scottish song about Loch Lomond. She felt a twist of anguish deep inside for the young woman who had died so horribly.

She was lying on her left side. The rain had apparently stopped. It was very dark. She remembered pulling the heavy drapes closed before going to bed. A glance at her bedside clock showed her it was only 11:00 p.m. She needed to go to the bathroom. That was probably why she had woken up.

About to sit up and swing her feet over the side of the bed, she hesitated. Then froze.

What was that sound? It wasn't one she recognized. A small sound. Somewhere between a click and a jangle. Like someone carefully setting keys down on a counter top.

Straining her ears in the darkness, she became aware that her heart was pounding erratically against her rib cage. Which made it difficult to hear anything else, though it did seem she could make out the sound of the whistling frogs outside in the grounds. She hadn't yet determined why the local people called them *whistling* frogs. The sound they made was much more like the chiming of little silver bells.

But she had closed and locked the double-paned sliding glass doors when she came in out of the rain. *She should not be able to hear any exterior sounds at all.*

The air in the room felt heavy, different, chilled. And the blackness was not as impenetrable as she'd first thought. There, between the bed and the window, was a denser patch of blackness than the rest.

Someone was in her room.

Chapter Fifteen

A sturdy figure, dressed in dark clothing, stood next to the dresser. A pinpoint of light confirmed that he was going through Jamie's purse. The contents of her duffel bag were strewn on the dresser. The intruder wasn't responsible for that—Jamie had left them that way when she'd gone to meet Anna.

The intruder was wearing gloves. There was some kind of covering on his head—a ski cap, the kind that masked the face, with holes for eyes, nostrils and mouth.

Was this the man who had mugged her? How the hell could she tell? What was he looking for?

She must have made some slight sound. The flashlight beam swung toward her so quickly she barely had time to close her eyes. She kept them closed after the light moved away, concentrating on breathing easily, her ears alert, ready to record any movement toward her bed. Part of her mind scrabbled hysterically, another part calmly weighed options.

Her impulses were telling her to jump up and race for the door. But it seemed stupid to make a run for it, considering she'd set all the locks. The burglar must have come from the balcony through the sliding glass door. Which meant he'd climbed up three stories, going from balcony to balcony. Unless she was prepared to take a nosedive from her own balcony, there wasn't much sense in trying to escape that way.

The frantic part of her brain produced a memory of a friend's husband who had awakened to find two burglars in his bedroom. He'd jumped out of bed yelling, "I'm going to shoot you guys," even though he didn't own a gun. One of the burglars had shot *him,* though not fatally. The victim had said he had no idea why he'd yelled such a thing. "Your gut takes over from your brain," he'd complained.

She had to use her brain.

If he moved toward her, she'd wait until he was right next to the bed, then fling the blankets over his head and make for the door, screaming at the top of her lungs. Interior hotel walls were never all that thick. You could hear the plumbing through them and television, why not screams?

What if he had a gun?

Then he'd shoot her. Or not.

She was naked. She always slept naked.

If necessary she'd run down the hall naked.

The flashlight beam disappeared. Cracking her eyes open a millimeter, Jamie saw that the man had replaced her things in her purse and was moving carefully toward the glass doors. She let her breath out slowly and silently. He was trying hard not to be caught. Great, she would be happy to oblige.

After he let himself out, she made herself count to one hundred, then tumbled out of bed and shot over to the doors. Feeling through the drapes, she examined the latch, which was in the open position but appeared to be intact. Maybe she hadn't closed it earlier, after all. No. She distinctly remembered locking it. She pulled the latch down again, then shot back across the room to the bathroom.

As she emerged, she started shaking uncontrollably. Stumbling over to the desk, she switched on the light and dialed Turner's number again.

Still no answer.

Should she call hotel security? The city police?

This was no ordinary burglary. An ordinary burglary would be too much of a coincidence, coming right on top of Anna's death. This burglary was *connected* with Anna's death.

She'd asked for Turner's help because of his expertise. "Stay," he'd told her. "No phone calls, no answering doors." She would have to wait for him. She might have doubts about him, but he was all she had.

She put on her robe, then pulled a blanket off her bed and wrapped it around herself. Dumping out her purse she went through everything in it. At first she thought nothing was missing. Then she remembered Derry's letter, which should have been there. It wasn't.

Unable to decide what that signified, she couldn't think of anything to do but to sit by the phone, calling Turner every ten minutes. She was still shaking so much her fingers frequently found the wrong numbers, forcing her to start over.

Turner showed up at her door shortly after midnight, his dark glasses stuck in the pocket of his Hawaiian shirt. He looked tired, she thought, when she eyed him through the spy hole.

As soon as she opened the door, she fell apart completely, shaking and sobbing and apologizing for being so weak all at the same time. "I've always thought I was so tough," she complained. "Look at me, I can't even stop shaking."

Pulling off his hat and throwing it onto the dresser, Turner folded her into his arms, blanket and all, then reached around her to lock the door. After a moment he moved with her to the bed and sat there with her in his arms. "You've a right to be scared," he said briskly, without sounding at all condescending. "It's probably the first time you saw a dead body. That's a traumatic event for anyone. First time I saw a dead body I threw up all over my shoes."

"It's more than that," she wailed. "Someone broke into my room." Taking several deep breaths, she forced herself to stop shaking. After a minute or so she managed to tell him about the burglar.

As she talked, he held her more and more tightly, as though he could protect her in retrospect. "You did the right thing—pretending you were asleep," he said, when she'd finished her story.

"I didn't know what else to do. I was *petrified*, Turner."

Turner was still holding her tightly, concern creasing his face. If his fear for her was an act, if his anxiety was an act, he had to be the best actor in the world.

Maybe he was.

"Why on earth would anyone rob a hotel room when the occupant's in it?" she asked. "He could surely have broken in while I was off somewhere." Suddenly remembering something that had completely left her mind, she pulled herself free and stared at Turner. "Derry's four-leafed clover," she said.

He looked puzzled.

"The first time you came into my room, I got Derry's letter out for you," she reminded him. "While you were reading it, I saw the clover leaf on the floor next to your chair. I couldn't imagine how it got there because I remembered closing it into the zippered compartment of my duffel."

Getting up, she went to the dresser and opened up the side pocket of her duffel bag. The clover leaf was still there and she held it up to show it to Turner. "I gave it to Derry on his sixteenth birthday," she explained. "His mother let me have it back as a memento of our friendship. It could hardly jump out of my bag, could it? But if someone had gone through my stuff, they might easily have dropped it without noticing."

"Was anything missing at that time?" he asked.

"Not that I noticed."

He seemed about to comment on that, but didn't. After a moment, he asked, "Is anything missing now?"

She nodded. Still standing by the dresser, she studied his face, that awful cold voice in her mind reminding her that she hadn't been able to reach him all evening, before or after the burglary. She didn't think the intruder had been as big as Turner, but lying down in bed it might be difficult to judge the height of a standing man. But why would Turner steal Derry's letter when he'd already read it?

What if somebody else wanted to see it?

"Derry's letter is gone," she said, inclining her head toward her purse, but keeping her gaze fixed on his face.

He showed no particular reaction. "And you usually have the handbag with you," he murmured. "The letter was there all along? You took it from your handbag to give to me."

She nodded. "I'd had it in the duffel, but I took it out, intending to follow up on the places Derry had visited. It's been in my purse ever since."

"So if the letter was our burglar's objective, and he'd checked your stuff once before when you were out, he'd have to wait until you were in, so he could look in your handbag." He frowned. "We need to determine who knew you had that letter."

His mouth twisted, bordering on a wry smile. "You are sure the letter's missing, Jamie? I don't mean to be rude, but something could hide out in that bag of yours for months."

"The letter's gone," she said firmly.

"Anything else?"

"Not a thing." Abruptly she went into mild shock. "My God," she exclaimed. "That must have been what the mugger was after. He pulled my wallet out of my fanny pack and then threw it on the ground without taking anything out. He must have been looking for the letter, too. I took the fanny pack instead of my purse, you understand, that's why I didn't have Derry's letter. I wonder..."

Shaking his head, he went over to the glass doors. Opening the drapes, he looked at the latch, lifted it with the tips of his fingers, pushed the slider to one side and stepped outside onto the balcony. Bending down, he examined the latch mechanism closely without touching it.

"He was wearing gloves," Jamie said when he stepped back into the room.

He muttered something that sounded unprintable, then frowned. "There are a couple of chipping marks. Apparently he forced the latch with a blade of some kind. The hotel should be warned to provide sturdier locks, or bars—" He broke off and looked bemused as though he'd realized he no longer had the authority to warn anyone about anything.

"You'll have to leave," he said, coming to put his hands on her shoulders. "We'll find you new quarters in the morning."

That was certainly okay with her, she didn't relish spending any more time than she had to in this already violated room. "I'd just as soon change rooms now," she told him.

He shook his head. "We don't want anyone wondering why you want to move out in the middle of the night."

"Why the hell does it have to be a secret?" She stared up at his face. "I almost called security to report the break-in. The only reason I didn't was because you said I shouldn't have anything to do with anybody. Stay, you said, as if I was a pet terrier. Then off you went to play 007."

She leaned her head back and looked him in the eye. "Which reminds me. Where were you? I called and called your house but there was no answer."

"I told you I had to look into Anna's death."

"*Where* did you look into it?"

"At the cave. Talking to the staff. Then seeking out other people—" He broke off.

"Informers?"

"Contacts," he amended.

She mulled that over for a while and decided he was probably telling the truth. His hair smelled smoky enough to make her nose twitch, which probably meant he'd been nosing around taverns.

"Why the secrecy?" she demanded again.

He was silent for at least two minutes. Concocting an answer? She couldn't read his expression. He had the ability to mask his thoughts completely, to shut himself off. Why would he do that with her? Because he was about to lie to her?

"I'm not officially a policeman, Jamie. If it were to get out that I was conducting my own investigation without authority, there would be hell to pay."

"Okay," she said with a sigh. "I guess I can understand you wanting to keep your profile low, but it surely wouldn't have hurt anything for me to blow the whistle on my burglar."

"It would have drawn attention to you, Jamie. And I don't want attention drawn to you." Touching her cheek, he smiled wryly. "I'd really like to put you on a plane for Boston tomorrow morning." He put his fingers over her mouth before she could protest. "I'll say it for you, shall I? *No way.*"

He sighed. "The next best thing is to have you check out openly and casually in the morning. Tell the front desk you're going to look into conference possibilities elsewhere. The Southampton Princess. But don't let anyone think you're soured on the Victoria—we don't want word getting out to our intruder that you were awake and watching."

"Why not?" She answered her own question. "He might come back to shut me up?" A shiver ran down her spine. "If you think I should move, I'll move." She looked at him. He still hadn't reported any *facts* about his investigation.

As if reading her mind, something he came close to doing every once in a while, he set her away from him and said, "I've a few things to tell you, Jamie, and I'm quite sure you have a lot of questions for me. We need to talk things out and see where we are. However, we didn't have much sleep last night and it's been quite a day. I don't think either of us is in any condition to make much sense right now."

He really did look exhausted, but Jamie wasn't about to let him go off to his own bed without a fight. "We might as well talk now," she said. "If I have to spend the rest of the night in this room, I'm not going to sleep, anyway."

"Not even if I stay with you?" he asked. "If we sleep together?" One hand touched her cheek again, then slid under her hair to massage her scalp lightly. It felt wonderful.

"I'd certainly feel better with you here," she told him. "But I'm not sure I—" She broke off, wondering how she could tactfully explain that after the events of the day, lovemaking was not high on her list of desired activities.

She didn't have to. "I really did mean sleep together," he said gently.

Within a few minutes he had removed his clothing and draped it neatly over a nearby chair. Then he climbed into her bed. Still wrapped in her robe, she checked the locks, turned off the lights and slid in next to him. With a sigh he took her in his arms, pulled her close in against his warm, naked body and fell asleep all at the same time. It took Jamie a few seconds longer. Just before she drifted off, just as she was realizing that in his arms she felt completely safe, she remembered that she still hadn't asked Turner why he'd arrived at the cave so late. She would ask him first thing in the morning, she decided.

BUT IN THE MORNING, there wasn't any time for questions. Turner roused her at the ungodly hour of 7:00 a.m. and poured coffee into her. While she drank the coffee, he very efficiently repacked her duffel bag, folding skirts, shorts, pants and blouses into flat square shapes and sort of filing them on end—an amazing feat she couldn't hope to duplicate. When he was sure she had her eyes open all the way, he told her to shower, dress and check out, then take a taxi to the Southampton Princess, aiming to arrive there about nine.

"I'll meet you there," he said, giving her a quick kiss on the cheek before signaling her to open her door and make sure the hall was empty. "Don't check in at the Princess," he added as he moved out into the hall.

"Why on earth not?" Jamie demanded, poking her head around the door. But he was already walking swiftly toward the back stairs and didn't answer.

The desk clerk must have rung some silent alarm to alert Charles Hollingsworth to her imminent departure, or else the manager had a sixth sense that told him when someone definitely didn't want to see him. He showed up, immaculate as ever, just as Jamie was turning away from the desk.

"You're leaving us?" he said plaintively.

"I have to look at other hotels, Charles," she said briskly. "My boss expects a choice."

"But you haven't given up on us?"

She managed an airy smile. "No way. I'll be back. You can count on it."

"Where will you be stopping in the meantime?" He gave her tan walking shorts and creamy polo shirt an approving glance that narrowed his dark eyes suggestively. "There's no reason we can't have dinner or drinks, is there?"

"Well, I'm going to be pretty busy...."

Luckily Loretta showed up at that moment. "Understand you're checking out," she said.

There definitely had to be a silent alarm.

Jamie shook hands with her, feeling slightly embarrassed, remembering the way Loretta had treated Charles at Putney's party. Charles hadn't fired her, which meant he really was a nice guy. A nice guy who was looking disappointed at the moment. "Sure we can have dinner," she said to him. His face lit up immediately. "I'll be at the Southampton Princess for a while," she told him. "Give me a call, why don't you?"

"Wonderful," he said, then smiled amiably and wandered off.

"Don't forget my offer," Loretta said. "If you read in the paper that I'm going to be in charge, come ask for that job."

"Are you expecting to be in charge?" Jamie asked.

Loretta seemed to find that excruciatingly funny. "You crack me up," she said, when she got through laughing. Accompanying Jamie through the revolving doors, she offered her hand and said, "Goodbye."

Something in the way she said the simple word gave Jamie the idea she was relieved to see her go. Which of course made it impossible for her to leave without at least attempting to find out the reason. Grasping at the first thought that occurred to her, she said, "About that suitcase..."

Loretta's face closed up immediately, proving to Jamie she was on the right track.

"You must have been in a big hurry when you packed it, things thrown in every which way like that." Jamie thought she'd hit just the right note of casual curiosity.

Loretta hesitated a moment too long, then shrugged. "Didn't think it mattered how it looked. Police wanted it in a hurry, didn't give me time to do much of a job."

A shiver went through Jamie. "Did you ever remember who the police officer was?" she asked.

Again Loretta hesitated. Jamie could almost hear her wondering if it would be best to keep pleading ignorance, or not. "Sorry," the woman said finally, then turned on her heel and went back into the hotel.

Thoughtfully Jamie watched through the glass doors as Loretta strode across the lobby toward her office. She had quite a sturdy build. Was there really any compelling reason to think that last night's burglar had been a man?

Chapter Sixteen

As soon as Jamie stepped out of her taxi at the Southampton Princess, Turner whistled softly to her from another cab. He was still in his Digby getup. Carrying her duffel and purse, Jamie approached and looked at him questioningly through the open window.

"Hop in, honey," he said in his best American accent.

"Where are we going?" Jamie asked.

"It's not far," Turner said ambiguously.

The driver had apparently appointed himself as a tour guide. He provided a detailed commentary on various aspects of Bermuda, from a complete horticultural description of the leathery-leafed sea grape bushes that sprawled along the shoreline to a dissertation on the island's volcanic base.

"I told Charles I'd be staying at the Southampton Princess," Jamie murmured when the driver paused for breath. "He's going to call there and find out I'm not registered."

"I've arranged for messages to be taken," he said.

As a free-lance investigator, he had amazing powers, Jamie thought. He'd found out in a very short time that Derry had no film waiting to be picked up anywhere. Evidently he could also persuade hotel employees to act as a voice mail service.

She was still mulling over his capabilities when the cab drove down a wide avenue of arching trees and stopped outside one of the handsomest houses she had seen in Bermuda. Beyond it the ocean glittered brightly in the morning sun.

"Home," Turner said with pride in his voice.

The house was a classic example of Bermudan architecture, he told her as the taxi drove away. Two-storied, painted a pale coral, topped with the ubiquitous sparkling white terraced roof, it featured an upper verandah and a lower porch, push-out blinds, which he called jalousies, a curved stone "eyebrow" over the front door and "welcoming arms" steps, wide at the base, narrowing as they reached the porch. The house had belonged to his parents, he added. He'd grown up in it, had always loved it, had been happy to move back after his divorce and had bought it from his father when he'd left.

The interior was excruciatingly tidy, which didn't surprise Jamie. It looked comfortable, but sterile. The antique furnishings were attractive but plain. The walls were pale, bare, the uncarpeted cedar floors waxed to a high shine.

Jamie was suddenly aware that they were alone without much possibility of being interrupted. Turner caught her eye and she had the feeling the same thought was traveling through *his* mind. It was difficult to drag her gaze away. The chemistry between them was getting stronger all the time.

"Toss a few magazines on the coffee table, a couple of bright rag rugs on the floor, put a few jars of weeds here and there, nail up some posters, and this place wouldn't be half bad," she said awkwardly.

Turner looked around. "It does look rather like someone's waiting room, doesn't it? My father took the pictures and ornaments with him. I suppose I ought to replace them."

He held up her duffel bag. "I'll just put this away." He disappeared along the hall. Was he putting her bag in a guest room or his own room? Jamie wondered. She decided not to follow him to find out. They had some hard-core talking to do, and judging by the electricity that had started crackling between them they wouldn't get any talking done at all if she turned up in his bedroom.

When he returned, he'd replaced the awful Hawaiian shirt and baggy pants with white shorts and a white-collared, blue and black striped rugby shirt—a combination that showed off his gorgeous body very nicely. Before she could get any ideas, he gestured her to the round table that stood in the kitchen's bow window, overlooking the ocean. The cliffs were high here; she couldn't see the beach, but she could see weathered stone steps going down from the yard, which featured natural ground cover and hedges of the ever-present and beautiful oleander.

Judging by the number of ingredients he was bringing out onto the butcher's block that stood in the center of the kitchen, Turner was going to fix her a substantial breakfast. "We're eating Bermuda-style," he told her.

He smiled at her and she smiled back, and their eyes met and held for a full minute. Then Jamie laughed nervously and averted her eyes. It was necessary to get down to business. "What did you find out last night?" she asked, making her voice businesslike.

He finished peeling a potato before he answered. "I found out that someone went into the cave with Anna."

She stared at him. "What do you mean?"

He put down the potato, picked up another. "The guide who knew her, Troy Winston, noticed her talking to a young man in the lobby. The two of them followed the group that went in ahead of yours. The man didn't seem to be forcing her to go in, but he may have been armed, of course." He paused. "Troy said he was well built, good-looking, white."

"Sounds like the guy who picked up Derry's suitcase. John Doe."

Turner shook his head. "I'm guessing it was Joe Hokins. After the news was released to the media, I spent some time drinking beer in a pub near the cave. The topic for the night was Anna. One of the things I managed to discover was that she had been dating Joe Hokins for several months."

Jamie stared at him. "If Derry was murdered, Hokins was probably the murderer, right? Do you think Anna set Derry up?"

"It's possible."

"Are the police looking for Joe Hokins?" she asked.

"Yes, indeed."

"Why would he take a chance on drowning her in public?"

His mouth was wry. "Well, he's not too bright. He's also an impulsive sort, I understand. And he's conceited enough to think we couldn't prove anything. Which is probably correct. On the surface Anna's death looks like an accident. As Derry's did."

"Anna had a connection to Rex Putney," Jamie remembered out loud.

While he thought that over, he cut the potatoes into quarters and put them into a pot with some chunks of fish—cod? He added water, sprinkled in some seasonings, then put the whole mess on a burner.

"Let's recapitulate," he said. "It's obvious Anna knew something about Derry's death, something she was going to pass on to you. As she was killed before she could meet you, it would seem possible she told someone she was going to talk to you. No one else knew she was going to meet you."

"*You* knew," Jamie said. "So did your reporter friend. Did you tell Superintendent Baldwin?"

He was chopping tomatoes into bite-size chunks. She was willing to bet each one was the same size as its neighbor.

Glancing up, he met her gaze. "I meant that none of the *bad* guys could have known unless Anna told them."

His blue eyes were clear, candid. "Possibly Anna talked to Hokins," he went on. "Possibly she talked to someone else who directed Hokins to act."

"Rex Putney?"

"It's all speculation, Jamie." He resumed chopping.

"Why were you so late getting to the caves?" she asked.

"Didn't I tell you?" He turned his back, ostensibly to get something out of the refrigerator. Bacon. "I was following your bus, of course. But it went over a pedestrian crossing a moment before the light changed. I got caught by the light. A pregnant woman started across the road, stopped in front of me, went deathly pale and fainted on the spot." He checked the pot, which was now simmering. "She was carrying two bags of groceries. Dropped the lot. It took a while to clear the road. I stayed with her until the ambulance arrived."

He frowned as he turned back to the chopping block and began cutting a large onion into precise cubes. "I'd quite forgotten the incident," he said. "I must ring up the hospital and see how she is."

He was apparently giving candid answers to her questions. Yet it was always when she least expected it that suspicion tore through her. Did she *believe* any of this? She only had Turner's word that the guide had said someone else went into the cave with Anna. She only had his word for the incident of the fainting woman. Could she really be sure it hadn't been Turner who accompanied Anna?

The problem was, she thought, it was impossible to convince herself Turner was one of the bad guys because he kept insisting on behaving like a hero. But there was no doubt he was keeping *something* from her. And she was still not sure he'd given her his real motive for working on this case after he'd been suspended. He'd *said* it would look good on his record if he found out who was organizing the drug smuggling. That sounded like a pretty weak motive to her.

"I was worried when you didn't arrive," she said carefully. "I wasn't sure what to do."

"I came in just as your tour group was heading out. I followed along and saw you at the front, but didn't want to push through and draw attention to myself. I thought Anna must be with you, that she had suggested going on the tour."

"Did you check if Rex Putney financed her salon?"

He nodded. "It was a loan, not a gift, but at a very low rate of interest." He swiped at his nose with the back of his hand. Evidently the onion was getting to him. "Nothing illegal about that, of course."

He put several strips of bacon in the microwave, turned down the heat under the potatoes and fish, then began peeling an avocado. Jamie was ravenously hungry; she'd skipped dinner the previous day and hadn't yet broken her fast. At the same time, she wasn't sure this meal was going to be edible.

"I almost forgot," she exclaimed. "When I was checking out of the Victoria, I asked Loretta about Derry's suitcase again. I tricked her. I made some comment about it being a mess. She *agreed* with me. Which means she didn't even *see* the suitcase being packed."

He looked puzzled.

"Derry's stuff looked as neat as if it had come right off the store shelves," she explained. "*You* could have packed it."

The statement hung between them for a moment, then Turner said, "You're saying Loretta *didn't* pack that suitcase? Any idea why she would say she did?"

"As a favor to whoever did pack it, maybe? I told you she was hostile. I thought it was because Charles had told me about her packing the suitcase, but maybe it was because someone else had made her take the responsibility."

She frowned. "You don't suppose Charles could have known...." Before Turner could answer, she shook her head. "He was in England. All he had to go on was what she said."

Turner wiped his hands on a towel and walked out of the room. A moment later she heard his voice in the living room, talking on the telephone. He returned just as the timer beeped on the microwave. "I rang up Dunch Baldwin," he explained as he fiddled again with his back turned. "He hasn't found any record of anyone picking up Derry's suitcase, but he reminded me that Rex Putney did Loretta a good turn a year or so ago. He took up the cudgels for her young brother Sam when he was arrested for shoplifting. Rex arranged for bail and got Sam a job at a restaurant when he was put on probation."

He frowned. "Actually, I was instrumental in putting Loretta in touch with Rex. Sam was a hothead, but I think he was just going through some hormonal changes."

"So Loretta owed Rex Putney a favor," Jamie said slowly. "Just as Anna did. The question is, did Rex try to collect on his favors? Did he persuade Loretta to say she packed the suitcase? Did he get Anna to set Derry up? And if so, what was his motivation?"

"If he had Derry killed, all of that would seem to hang together," Turner said.

"If he had Derry killed because he saw something he shouldn't have seen, then surely Derry *must* have been at the Tudor Tavern when the shooting went down. In which case Rex was afraid Derry could somehow tie him to the shooting."

"Derry would hardly take pictures of whoever was doing the shooting," Turner said.

They were both silent for a while. Then Jamie said, "I had the thought this morning that my intruder might not have been a man. Loretta's pretty solidly built."

He'd picked up a banana and peeled it. Now he put it down and studied her face. "Loretta wasn't on board the *Coral Queen* or present in the cave."

"We didn't ask anyone if she was there," Jamie pointed out. "And she did lie about the suitcase. If she would lie for someone, maybe she'd break into a room for someone."

"Rex, you mean."

"If he's the chief. Or someone else if he's not."

He looked at her with great interest. "Who do you have in mind?"

"I didn't care much for Gordon Stacey."

He laughed shortly and started slicing the banana. "I don't care for him myself, Jamie, but he's a terribly upright citizen. It's a bit of a stretch to imagine he could be involved in running drugs, or arranging for someone to break into your room. I certainly don't know of any connection between him and Loretta Dean."

"He's a part owner of the Victoria Hotel," Jamie said.

His dark eyes blazed. "Where on earth did you hear that?"

"From the horse's mouth," she said smugly. "Otherwise known as Charles Hollingsworth."

"Well, well." He raised an eyebrow. "Gordon Stacey is Rex's attorney, did you know that?"

She shook her head. "All roads lead to Rex, don't they?"

"They do indeed." He was silent again, and then the microwave beeped and he said, "Breakfast's ready."

After serving up the fish and potatoes, he spooned the tomatoes, browned onion and crumbled bacon over them, then arranged sliced banana and avocado decoratively on either side.

Jamie tentatively tried a forkful. To her amazement it tasted delicious. Seeing her eyes widen, Turner smiled, but he was quickly serious again. "So this is where we are then," he said. "Rex is a fairly consistent common denominator.

So far he's popped up in the background of everyone involved either in drug dealing or in Derry's death. Unfortunately he does seem to stay in the background."

He shook his head in apparent frustration, then picked up his knife and fork and started eating. English-style, of course, an elegant manner Jamie had always admired.

"Let's attack this from another perspective, Jamie," he said after a while. "Let's say Derry *was* at the Tudor Tavern during the shooting. Obviously he'd already mailed the letter to you, or he would surely have mentioned such an exciting incident."

"But he did mention the hibiscus."

"And the bartender said he asked for *another* hibiscus. At the time that seemed to indicate he'd had one already. But you told me he wasn't much of a drinker, so it's possible he had the first hibiscus either on an earlier visit, or at some other tavern."

Jamie nodded, frowning.

"Now," he continued. "Someone entered your room last night and stole only the letter Derry wrote you. There wasn't anything incriminating in that letter, but whoever took it didn't know that letter was mailed *before* the shooting. Whatever the burglar's motivation, it seems likely he—or she—*knew* you had the letter. So I want you to think back over all the time you've been in Bermuda. Who knew you had that letter?"

They ate in silence while she thought. "I told Superintendent Baldwin about it," she said at last. Shocked by the implication, she put down her fork. "You don't think—"

He shook his head impatiently.

"Listen now, before you make a final decision here," she said urgently. "How closely have you been in touch with Baldwin through this whole thing?" Remembering he'd avoided one of her earlier questions, she asked it again.

"*Did* you tell Superintendent Baldwin I was going to meet with Anna?"

He stared at her for several seconds. Finally, he sighed. "All right, Jamie. Confession time. I told you Tom Reynolds has been aware of our investigation all along. So has Dunch Baldwin."

"They were the people you met with from time to time? The people you referred to as contacts?"

"Not exactly. I've met with Tom, yes, but Dunch couldn't risk being seen with me."

"But he knew what you were up to?"

He nodded. "I could not have managed without his resources. And yes, I told him you were meeting Anna."

"You could have told me all this at the start."

"I shouldn't even be telling you now. The less you know, the safer you are, Jamie—the safer *we* are."

"You think I'd blab it around town?"

He met her heated gaze squarely. "It's possible you could be persuaded to talk."

About to give him the line about wild horses again, Jamie subsided, suddenly realizing another interpretation could be put on the word *persuaded*. She shivered.

Turner was silent for several minutes before going on. "You need to understand that Dunch and Tom and I have been friends since we were children. We decided early that we were all going to be police officers. We studied the martial arts so our bodies would be prepared for the job. The three musketeers had nothing on us."

Nostalgia had softened his somewhat sharp features. Watching him, Jamie felt a softening of her own. "When we were kids, we even developed a code," he went on. "Part of a very complicated strategy we worked out, dealing with what we would do if we ran into crooks. Using the word *rain* meant *run for it*, anything to do with *attic*, meant *attack*, *skin* meant *hide.*" He laughed. "There were a few others we don't mention in polite company."

"Tom didn't become a police officer after all?"

He shook his head. "He developed a talent for writing in college and changed his goals. But he's still interested in catching crooks. He helps whenever he can." He looked her directly in the eye. "I would stake my life and reputation on the integrity of both men," he said firmly.

"You told me before not to trust anyone. Now you tell me I should trust Reynolds and Baldwin. I don't even know them."

"You must surely trust my word by now, Jamie."

She looked down at the table. "What about the sergeant?" she asked suddenly. "The one who looks like Adonis. What was his name? The sergeant who brought me to your office the first time I came to see you."

"Vance Murdoch? All Vance did was show you in and leave."

She shook her head. "He waited in the hall, just outside your door. He was there the whole time. When I left, he escorted me to the exit."

He looked startled.

"He could probably hear every word we said," she added. "And I believe I told you about Derry's letter at that time."

"You did, but—" He shook his head. "Even if he could hear us, Jamie, that doesn't mean anything. Vance Murdoch is a dedicated police officer. He's a member of my own squad." He frowned. "What *was* my own squad. He's also a personal friend. I hand picked him for his present job. I trust him."

"Are you telling me he's another person *I* have to trust? The police force is above suspicion? What about the officer who wrote the incomplete report on Derry's so-called accident? Cornell Alexander, the guy who headed for the hills right after Derry's death?'' A thought occurred to her. ''Vance Murdoch is white and good-looking and well built. Maybe *he* picked up Derry's suitcase.''

He shook his head, his mouth set in a grim line. He'd given up on his breakfast. ''I don't believe that. In any case, if Loretta lied about packing the suitcase, she could just as easily have lied about who picked it up.''

''Which would again very neatly exonerate your precious police,'' she said flatly. Though to be fair, he did have a point. Exasperated by her own vacillating, she said, ''We're supposed to be having a discussion about *possibilities*. If you're going to shoot down every possibility I mention, I might as well shut up. Aren't you carrying loyalty too far? You trust Baldwin. You trust Reynolds. Both are helping you *unofficially*. Are they really helping you, or steering you in the way they want you to go? Rex Putney's a very wealthy man, right? Are you quite sure neither Baldwin nor Murdoch are susceptible to bribery? How *can* you be sure? What about Reynolds—could he use extra money?''

To her amazement he suddenly shot to his feet, scraping his chair back loudly on the tile floor. Shocked, she watched him throw down his cloth napkin on the floor. A moment later he had kicked his chair aside, almost knocking it over, and stalked from the room, leaving Jamie sitting there stunned, her fork suspended halfway to her mouth.

Chapter Seventeen

Jamie descended the steep flight of ancient stone steps that led down to Turner's small sheltered cove. An hour had passed since Turner stormed out of the kitchen. She'd heard him talking a couple of times on the telephone, but he hadn't returned. From the window she'd watched him go down to the beach. Obviously he'd wanted some time alone, and she'd given it to him, but she could hardly sit around waiting forever.

He was standing in the shallows, his hands stuck in his shorts pockets, apparently watching some terns that were riding thermals. The sky was incredibly blue. The perfumed breeze tousled his dark hair. Gentle waves foamed around his bare feet and blue fish darted like cloud shadows between fingers of coral. It was a peaceful scene, but Turner's tall, lean figure was anything but relaxed.

"This must be the most beautiful place in the whole world," Jamie said softly as she came up alongside him.

"Bermuda?" he asked. "Or my beach? My house?"

"All of the above."

"I've always thought so, too," he said gravely.

"What happened up there?" she asked. "Was it something I said?"

He turned his head to look at her. She'd taken off her shoes and socks. In walking shorts and knit shirt another woman might have looked boyish, but the soft curve of her breasts, the shapeliness of her long legs and the mass of curls glinting in the sun like copper pennies left no doubt of her femininity. He pulled her gently into his arms and kissed her. "I'm sorry I walked out on you," he murmured.

She didn't relax. He kissed her again, not quite so gently, reveling in the feel of her breasts against his chest, the smell of her, the taste of her on his tongue. He felt he could stand there with her in his arms forever, the playful waves washing across his feet, the sun warm on his head and neck. "You may have noticed that sometimes I can be an absolute ass," he murmured.

"True," she said, not giving an inch.

He laughed shortly. "I rang Dunch Baldwin again." She raised an eyebrow. "You hit a nerve," he admitted. "That's what made me storm out of my own kitchen like an outraged guest, the knowledge that you could be right—one of my men might have been willing to accept a bribe." He sighed. "A strong brotherhood exists between police officers, Jamie. It's difficult to face up to the possibility of one of them going bad. However..."

He paused then went on reluctantly. "Vance and his wife are not what you would call thrifty. They like high living— fine clothes, fine wines, fine furniture, vacations in first-class resorts. Vance's wife has a management position with a private investment holding company, so it has always seemed as if the Murdochs could afford to indulge themselves. But your suggestion opened up other possibilities. When I rang Dunch, he promised to check into Vance's current financial situation and call me back, which he did. I didn't like what I heard and charged down to the beach. Watching the waves usually helps to clear my head. But I'm not sure it's working today."

"What did the superintendent find out?"

Letting go of her, he gestured at a natural shelf in the cliffside and they walked over to it and sat down, sinking their toes into the coarse pink sand. "A few weeks ago the Murdochs bought a very expensive sailboat. They paid cash."

She glanced at him sideways. "Looks bad, huh?"

"It looks questionable."

"Is there any connection between Vance and Rex Putney?"

"Vance *knows* Rex. But then so does everybody. We don't have any proof that he accepted a bribe, Jamie. He may have overheard you telling me about Derry's letter, but that doesn't mean he's guilty of breaking into your room to get it."

Jamie reached down and scooped up a handful of sand and began sifting it from one hand to the other, frowning. "Could Vance have picked up Derry's suitcase?"

"It's possible, but again, if Loretta lied, we have no proof." As she dusted off her hands, he reached over and took one of them in his, squeezing it gently. "Don't look so worried," he said soothingly. "We *are* making progress. At least now Dunch knows to guard his tongue in front of Vance until we find out where his money came from. Unfortunately we can't do anything openly where he's concerned without the risk of alerting the chief that we're on his trail. We'll just have to go on looking stupid until we come up with a concrete lead to Rex." He hesitated. "If the chief *is* Rex."

"There must be *something* we can do."

He released her hand and sat back against the cliff face. "Dunch and I have agreed it's time to push Rex a little. Dunch hasn't been able to come up with any leads on the whereabouts of Kenyon or Hokins, so we're at a bit of a dead end there. I told Rex at the party that I'd get in touch with him in a couple of days. When you came down, I'd just decided to go to his house and tell him I'm ready to go to work for him.''

She was silent for a moment, staring out at the glittering turquoise sea. ''Does the superintendent know you're trying to get a job with Putney?''

He nodded.

She bit her lower lip. It worried him when she did that. He'd learned that it meant she was thinking deeply, and whenever she thought deeply, she unraveled another part of the story he'd originally intended keeping from her. There wasn't much left for her to unravel.

''Isn't Baldwin taking a risk, helping you with your admittedly unofficial investigation?''

''No one knows we're working together except Tom Reynolds.''

''Something smells fishy to me here,'' she said abruptly.

''Your imagination's working overtime,'' he said, hoping he sounded convincing. Before she could lodge any more protests, he deliberately changed the subject. ''While I'm gone, I want you to stay in the house. You can take a nap or watch television or read a book. I wouldn't advise coming down to the beach without me, however. I hesitated about bringing you here because it's rather isolated. So no beach when you're alone, all right? I'll lock up the house securely when I leave, so you'll be quite safe.''

He almost groaned aloud, seeing that chin come up in a belligerent way that was becoming familiar to him. ''You are not coming with me, Jamie,'' he said flatly.

She smiled sweetly. He didn't trust that smile at all. ''What's to stop me from calling for a taxi the minute you're out of the house?'' she asked. ''What's to stop me from following you to Stonecrest? Maybe I'll just ask Rex Putney outright if he had anything to do with Derry's death.''

''Jamie, I will not allow you to—''

"Whereas if you take me with you—I take it you can use your car? You'll be going as yourself, of course. So we can have a nice comfortable ride over to Stonecrest, and I'll simply inform Mr. Putney that I came with you because I'm looking for suggestions for my company's conference location and thought he might be able to make one or two."

Jamie was quite capable of carrying out her threat, Turner thought, as they washed their feet under an outside faucet and sat on the steps to put their sneakers and socks back on—and that could be disastrous. He didn't want Rex Putney to know he was under any kind of suspicion. So far he didn't have an iota of proof that Rex Putney was engaged in drug importing, and one couldn't go round accusing a leading citizen of anything without ironclad evidence. He shuddered at the thought. He would just have to take her along, he supposed. Shaking his head, he led her up the steps to the car.

Which wouldn't start.

"I thought you said your car never let you down," Jamie murmured.

Turner winced and tried cautiously to give the engine some gas. A few minutes later he conceded the struggle. "Looks as if we ride the jolly old moped again," he said.

REX PUTNEY wasn't home. Turner hadn't thought to ring him up first. His mental processes were not working as well as they should since Jamie Maxwell had come into his life.

"He's gone out to the States," Putney's pretty young housekeeper explained. "North Carolina. Some sort of benefit. Put together at the last minute. Disabled children." A fond smile lit her face, illuminating clusters of freckles that were more than a match for her auburn hair. "You know how Rex is where children are concerned," she added earnestly.

"Now what?" Jamie asked after the woman closed the door.

Turner shook his head and walked around the house, steering Jamie along with him. After they crossed the lawns to the head of the wooden steps, he looked down at the dock. The yacht was still in place. So Putney hadn't gone on any kind of supply trip—legitimate or felonious.

They walked slowly back to the moped and climbed on. "I could go talk to Loretta," Jamie suggested as they pulled on their safety helmets. "If I tell her I *know* she lied about packing the suitcase, she might be persuaded to tell the truth."

"Not a bad idea," he said, turning to smile approvingly at her. "You make a good partner, Jamie."

"Remember that, next time you want to leave me locked up in a room somewhere," she said tartly.

He laughed, then started the engine.

Riding a moped on narrow roads was a risky business, Jamie decided when one of the ubiquitous pink buses squeezed by, spewing fumes. Every once in a while some unthinking driver edged them too close to the limestone walls that had been left standing when the road was carved out.

One such driver, hidden behind the tinted windows of a small black van, began following them soon after they left Stonecrest, occasionally catching up to hover at Jamie's right heel, which made her very nervous. After a few minutes of this, he would drop back again. Then just as Jamie began to relax, there he'd be again, the van's left front wheel edging too close for comfort.

Turner made a couple of imperious gestures at the driver, trying to get him to pass and get out of the way. Instead the van inched even closer. For a while the two vehicles ran alongside each other, then Turner sped up and shot ahead. The van immediately caught up.

"Hang on," Turner yelled.

Jamie tightened her arms around his waist and leaned into his back, her head craned as she tried to look into the van. She could see only a vague darkness behind the tinted window, like the shadow of a person. Somehow, not being able to see the driver made him more menacing.

He *was* behaving menacingly, Jamie realized.

For some time Turner maneuvered skillfully, slowing down, speeding up, swerving when necessary, but the van stayed inexorably alongside through all the curves. Then the road split in a Y and Turner shot off onto the left fork, which soon became a dirt road. A minute later the van showed up beside them again. Both vehicles were over the speed limit now, doing at least thirty-five, which at any other time, in any other place, would have seemed slow to Jamie, but seemed fast and dangerous on this narrow, winding road. To add to the discomfort, the sun flashed like a searchlight between the casuarina trees that lined the road, dazzling Jamie's eyes and probably Turner's too.

Hanging on to Turner, she felt the moped buck under her as he gave it more gas and the bike shot forward. At the same time the van hit a deep rut and swerved suddenly away from them. Turner shot the bike forward again and turned right in front of the van, bouncing off along another dirt road Jamie hadn't even noticed.

It took a moment for the van driver to recover from the rut, but he was soon nudging them again. If he wanted to kill them, why didn't he just pull across in front of them, Jamie wondered. They wouldn't stand a chance if he did that. Was he just playing with them, she wondered, feeling briefly more hopeful, or was it just that he didn't want any damage to show on his van when their "accidental" death was investigated?

They reached the main South Shore road and turned left, van and moped still neck and neck. Ahead, a limestone wall loomed. "Hang on," Turner yelled again and Jamie braced herself. Without further warning he stopped the bike so suddenly it almost stood on its nose. Only his broad back stopped Jamie from being flung forward. As it was, the bike fell out from beneath them and they rolled together over and over on the rough grass at the side of the road. Jamie's right leg scraped against a rock and she felt it burn.

She was never sure exactly what happened next. Maybe when the van driver realized what Turner had done, he stopped too fast himself. In some way he lost control of the steering wheel, and the van slewed around and crashed into the wall.

As Turner and Jamie, both a little dazed, were scrambling clumsily to their feet, the van driver pushed open his door, climbed out and ran across the street and onto the dunes.

Throwing his helmet to the ground, Turner took off after him. Jamie dropped her own helmet and her purse beside the moped and limped in pursuit. She reached the dunes just in time to see the van driver jump down to the beach. He was a white man, wearing jeans and a short-sleeved khaki shirt. He had straight black hair that was receding at the temples. At first Jamie thought he had a beard, then realized it was just a five-o'clock shadow that was particularly dark. Someone had mentioned that. Lathrop.

The man stumbled a few yards across the soft sand, then stopped abruptly and swung around to face Turner who had just jumped down himself. Turner stopped in his tracks. "Don't be a fool, Bobby," he yelled.

Bobby? Bobby Kenyon? Still limping onward, Jamie saw the sun glint off something silver colored in the man's hand. To her horror she realized it was a gun, and it was pointing directly at Turner.

Quite suddenly, as adrenaline raced through her system, Jamie's mind seemed as crystal clear as the remarkable

Bermuda light. She saw a couple of things at once. One—
Kenyon was standing directly under a limestone archlike
formation, whose steep slope began not two steps in front
of Jamie's feet. Two—he hadn't noticed her yet. Without
hesitation, she scrambled up and over the limestone arch
and launched herself just as Kenyon fired the gun. A split
second later Jamie landed on him, knocking him flat on the
pink coral sand. The gun flew out of his hand.

A few yards away Turner lay still.

Chapter Eighteen

Kenyon heaved himself upward, trying to shake Jamie loose, but she clung to his back, winding her arms and legs around him. Looking frantically around for a rock to crown him with, she saw that there was nothing within reach.

"Best not to move, Kenyon," Turner said in a low, menacing voice close to Jamie's ear. "I have your gun and I do assure you I know how to use it."

Relief exploded inside her like a firecracker. Turner was up and moving and apparently unhurt. Beneath her, Kenyon went flat, like a balloon that had suddenly lost all its air.

"I thought he'd shot you," she murmured weakly as she eased herself off Kenyon's prone body.

"So did I," Turner said grimly. "If it wasn't for his astigmatism he would have. The next shot might have finished me."

As he spoke he tucked the gun in his waistband and reached into the back pocket of his shorts. To Jamie's astonishment he hauled out a pair of handcuffs. Pulling Kenyon's arms roughly behind him, he snapped the handcuffs on his wrists, then yanked the man upright, grabbed him by his shirt collar and shook him like a terrier with a rat. "Why the bloody hell were you trying to run us off the road?" he yelled at him.

All color had left the man's face. "Don't hit me the way you did that old man," he pleaded. "You can't put me in no coma—the woman will tell."

"You're sure of that, are you?"

The man shot Jamie a helpless glance then cringed away from Turner, looking terrified. "Please, Inspector, don't hurt me." He was almost crying.

Jamie stared at Turner's face. His face was tight, his eyes midnight dark. In that moment she was convinced if Kenyon gave him an excuse he would reverse the pistol and bring it down on the defenceless man's head. For a few seconds she was paralyzed by fear. Then she felt sick, as though someone had punched her in the stomach. "Turner," she said urgently.

He had already let go of the man and was telling him his rights, his voice harsh. "You're not obliged to say anything unless you wish to do so. Anything you say will be taken down and used as evidence."

Kenyon had stopped pleading. His mouth was fixed in a one-sided sneer. His dark eyes, one of which was badly turned in, glared pure hatred as Turner swung him around and propelled him toward the road.

A few minutes later Turner flagged down a motorist and asked him to call the police. When two officers responded, he handed Kenyon and his gun over to them. "Don't let him wash his hands," he ordered them tersely. "Deliver him to Superintendent Baldwin at Wallbridge—no one else. Tell Baldwin I'll be in touch."

The officers nodded.

Turner waited while they put Kenyon in the back of their car, then he said, "After you report to the superintendent, I want you to forget you saw me, all right?"

The officers exchanged a glance, then answered with one voice. "Whatever you say, Inspector." They both glanced curiously at Jamie as they climbed into the car.

"Have you been carrying handcuffs around all the time?" Jamie demanded as she and Turner crossed the road to the moped. "Are you *allowed* to arrest somebody while you're suspended?"

"Yes to the first," he said shortly. "As for the last—" he hesitated "—it's done now."

He stopped the moped at the first phone booth they came to, to call Baldwin, he said. His expression was still grim when he returned. Jamie's nausea wasn't going away.

As soon as they arrived back at Turner's house, she faced him squarely. "Would you have hit that man, if I hadn't been there?" she demanded.

He shook his head, suddenly looking weary. "If I may borrow one of your favorite expressions—no way."

"Kenyon thought you were going to hit him."

"I wanted him to think so. Fear is good for the criminal soul." Coming toward her, he glanced down at her leg. "You're hurt."

"It's not important. Turner, I have to know..."

He bent to look at the scrape. "Of course it's important." Taking her arm, he urged her toward the bathroom, sat her on a stool and ran water into the sink. Questions were leaping through her brain, but she was still so nauseated, she wasn't sure she could stand it if he gave the wrong answers.

He squatted in front of her, gently dabbing a warm damp cloth over the scrape on her leg, mopping up the debris that was embedded in the abraded flesh. Then he took a clean cloth from a drawer and sloshed some strong-smelling liquid onto it. "Hang on to your back teeth," he advised her and draped the cloth over her leg. "Sorry," he murmured when she yelled. "It seemed better to just do it and get it over with."

"Is that your philosophy of life?" she asked sarcastically.

"Quite close to it, actually." Standing up, he took her hand and brought her to her feet. About to put his arms around her, he looked at her face. Whatever he saw there caused him to change his mind, and he led her into the living room and sat with her on the long sofa.

"Out with it, Jamie," he ordered. "You didn't like the way I treated Kenyon? Believe me, I surprised myself. I can only plead that I was unnerved, realizing that bloody idiot could have killed you with his stupid stunt driving."

"What unnerved you where Walter Seaton was concerned?" she asked coldly.

He reached to smooth her hair away from her face, gazing at her with affection. She didn't want affection. She wanted truth. "The thought of me battering poor old Walter has worried you all along, hasn't it, Jamie?" he said softly.

She held her body rigid. "Among other things," she said.

"What other things?"

"I don't believe you're pursuing this case in order to make your record look good," she said stiffly. "I think you have a whole secret agenda of your own. You seem to be missing at all the wrong times, late at others. And I still don't understand why Baldwin and Reynolds would help you, when you're in disgrace over Seaton."

"Is that all?" he asked softly.

She shook her head. "Not quite. It seems to me it's entirely possible you want to get Rex Putney or whoever the chief turns out to be and take care of him yourself, because of your wife. That's not going to restore your career, it's going to wipe it out altogether, and possibly you with it."

His dark eyebrows lifted. "Thinking all that, you still made love with me?"

She winced. "I couldn't seem to resist you. I have no excuse for that. I guess I'm weaker than I thought."

Turner shook his head. "There isn't anything weak about you, Jamie." He inclined his head. "You're quite right about the chief. I've planned all along to take care of him."

The nausea was back, twisting her stomach into knots that might never unravel.

"It all depends on how you define *take care,*" he added. "Personally I'd define it as bringing him to justice, hoping the court would have the sense to lock him up for the rest of his natural life."

She stared at him. "That wasn't how you took care of Walter Seaton."

His mouth twisted into a wry smile. "I can see you'll accept nothing less than a full confession this time."

Jamie nodded, her stomach clenching. What exactly was he going to confess?

He leaned back against the sofa cushions and considered for a moment. "Walter went missing after the shooting, so no one had been able to question him. One night, about a week before you arrived in Bermuda, I was working late at the office when Tom Reynolds rang to tell me Walter had shown up at one of his old hangouts—a restaurant that doled out leftover food to the homeless at the end of the day. Tom promised to keep an eye on him until I got there."

"Wait a minute," Jamie said, leaning forward so she could watch his face. "Was Tom Reynolds the reporter who wrote about you beating up Walter?"

"He was indeed."

"But that's...if he's your friend...why would he do that?"

He raised an eyebrow. "Who's telling this story?"

When she subsided, he went on. "There's an alley behind the restaurant. It was dark—probably half past nine or so. I sat with Walter on the back doorstep of the restaurant and talked to him. Which wasn't easy. He was rather the worse for drink. However, I did manage to get out of him that he'd been hiding out with a friend on St. David's Island, and the friend's wife had just kicked him out. He'd slept through the whole shooting at the Tudor Tavern, he insisted, and hadn't woken up until police cars came careening into the parking lot, at which time he deemed it politic to disappear. A likely tale, you might say, but I believed him."

She frowned. "Then why did you hit him?"

"You're getting ahead of the story again," he chided. His fingers had started playing in her hair, exerting pressure, trying to bring her closer. She was very aware of his warm body so near hers on the sofa, but she kept her own body stiff.

He sighed. "When I left Walter I joined Tom, who was waiting round the corner," he went on. "We talked, then I invited him to join me for a drink and we started walking toward my car. That's when we heard the shouting."

"Walter?" she asked, frowning again.

"Walter. Apparently his friend Luke Darwin, another homeless individual, had wandered into the alley with an unopened bottle of black rum, which Walter decided he rather fancied. A fight broke out. Just as Tom and I shot around the corner into the alley, Luke crowned Walter with the bottle, knocking him cold. Then while we were seeing to Walter, Luke did a bunk. I was about to chase after him when I realized I could *use* Walter. So that's when—"

"Wait a minute," Jamie interrupted again. "Are you saying you *didn't* hit Walter?"

"Never laid a hand on him," he said.

Relief contracted her heart as though a giant hand had reached inside her chest and squeezed it. "Why didn't I catch on?" she said disgustedly. "I never did want to believe you could have beaten up that old man. I probably *wouldn't* have believed it if you hadn't told me so yourself.

And then everyone else seemed to think all that mattered was whether he deserved to be beaten or not.''

His gaze met hers. ''That wasn't the issue for you?''

She shook her head. ''I couldn't accept the beating itself.''

''I couldn't have accepted it, either,'' he said. ''There is never any excuse for excess force.''

''But if you didn't hit Walter,'' she said slowly, ''why did your friend Tom write that awful story?''

''Think about it,'' he suggested, sliding his arm around her shoulders.

Her mind raced to assimilate all he had told her. ''It was a put-up job,'' she said faintly. ''Your suspension was a fake.''

''Bright girl,'' he said, and kissed her on the nose. His free hand had slipped around her waist and once again he urged her closer.

She went willingly this time, though she was still pondering the implications. If he would just stop kissing her she might be able to work it out, but... ''I want the details,'' she said sternly, pushing him away.

He sighed and sat up straight. ''All right. Here it is. For some time I'd been looking for a way to go undercover in an attempt to find out the identity of the chief. Baldwin and I had considered two scenarios. One— I would simply assume a disguise to see what I could find out on the street, so to speak. Often people who pretend to be blind, deaf and mute when a policeman comes round will talk to a civilian.

''Two— I would be discredited in a way likely to make me bitter, to lull the chief, who might or might not be Rex Putney, into trying to conscript me for his own purposes. Waiting for an ambulance to pick up Walter, I thought of using the poor old man as a way to get myself kicked off the force. Apparently no one round about had seen or heard anything. It seemed unlikely that Luke would come forward and announce that I was innocent because he was guilty.''

He smiled wryly. ''We were implementing that scenario when you showed up and Baldwin decided it might be a good idea for me to combine both ideas.''

''Using me as cover.''

He looked at her apologetically. ''We had no idea Derry's death had anything to do with the Tudor Tavern shooting, of course. We would not willingly have exposed you to danger.''

She laid her hand against his cheek and he leaned into it, then turned his head so he could gently kiss her palm. ''It was so awful to believe you *had* beaten that old man,'' she murmured. ''It kept getting in the way of...making me not want to...'' She gave up. ''I'm too tired to put a coherent sentence together.''

''It's all right, Jamie, I understand,'' he said. Looking at her earnestly, he went on. ''I couldn't see how exploiting the incident would make any difference to poor Walter's condition. It wasn't totally ethical, of course, but the Tudor Tavern shooting had made it urgent that we do something drastic. That shooting was an indicator of how things would go if we didn't put a stop to them, so we decided the end justified the means. Baldwin, Tom and I all feel very strongly about getting drugs off the island and will do just about anything to achieve it.''

Standing up, he helped her to her feet and drew her against him, then held her in his arms. ''I'm sorry it was necessary to deceive you,'' he said after a while.

''It's okay,'' she said. ''You had to make a convincing case to get Rex to believe you were thoroughly disgruntled. I understand that.'' She looked at him curiously. ''I'm not sure why you're coming clean now, though.''

He kissed her lightly, then tenderly stroked her hair away from her face. ''Because I've learned I can trust you with my life. And because when Kenyon was trying to run us off the road, I thought if I died you'd always believe I was capable of beating an old man into a coma. I didn't want you believing that, I discovered. I cared quite strongly about it."

His dark eyes held hers. "I never did thank you for saving my life, Jamie. You were quite wonderful, you know. I salute your courage." He kissed her again, not lightly this time. Quite suddenly she didn't feel so tired anymore.

"Nothing courageous about it," she said truthfully. "If I'd stopped to think, I'd have been too scared to try it."

Why hadn't she stopped to think, she wondered. She had seen that Turner was in danger and had acted automatically to save him. Something about that seemed very important, but she wasn't sure what it was.

He released her with obvious reluctance. "I have to ring Dunch and find out what's happening with Kenyon," he murmured.

While he was telephoning, Jamie took a few minutes to freshen up and change into jeans. Turner looked grim again when she returned to the living room. She sat down in the armchair opposite him.

"According to Dunch, Kenyon swears we were the ones who were driving recklessly," he told her. "Says he was in fear of his life. Had no idea I was a police officer, that's why he fired the shot. He also swears Derry's death was an accident, and he never heard of Anna Campbell. And of course he knows absolutely nothing about the Tudor Tavern incident or where all the excess cocaine is coming from. Dunch says he probably wouldn't have owned up to shooting at me if the primer residue test hadn't proved he'd fired the gun."

He laughed shortly. "At first he insisted he hadn't seen Hokins since they were in prison together. So Dunch told him we *knew* Hokins was the diver on the *Coral Queen* the day Derry died. Then he said he hadn't seen Hokins since then, but that as far as he knew Hokins had tried to save Derry, not kill him."

He let out a long breath in apparent frustration. "He's lying his head off all the way, of course. An officer did a sweep of the van and found a ski mask and a pair of cotton gloves. Not much need for a ski mask in Bermuda, unless you're going to break into someone's hotel room."

Jamie shuddered.

"The van is registered to Hokins," Turner continued.

Jamie leaned forward. "So what do we do now?"

He raised an eyebrow. "We?" He laughed, his eyes lighting up in the way she loved.

Loved?

Ridiculous. She couldn't think of anything more self-defeating than falling in love with Turner Garrett. She was in Bermuda temporarily. If they ever got this whole mess sorted out, she'd be returning to Boston. Alone. She admired Turner, yes. She was infatuated with him, sexually attracted to him... strongly attracted. But that was all—wasn't it?

"What *can* we do?" she asked.

He mused for a while, then sighed. "I haven't decided yet. I have to take some kind of action, and quickly, too. The two officers who took Kenyon into custody will talk."

"They promised not to."

His smile was wry. "They'll talk. And sooner rather than later, word will get to the chief that I'm still on the job." He leaned back and gazed thoughtfully up at the ceiling.

"Why do you suppose Kenyon suddenly decided to kill us?" Jamie asked. "If he was in my room, he had a perfect opportunity then...." Her voice trailed off. "Unless he wanted to make our deaths look like an accident? But how did he know we were on that road?" Again she answered her own question. "Someone might have seen us at Putney's house, I guess, and worried that we were getting too close.

Or the housekeeper called someone and they dispatched Kenyon."

"You're getting pretty good at this, Jamie," he said with a smile. "I was just thinking myself that it would seem a bit coincidental that Kenyon would go for us right after we'd visited Putney's house." He was silent for a few minutes, then he added, "With that in mind, I keep getting an image of Rex's boat, sitting there at the dock, apparently without anyone on board. And Rex is away...."

"You think there might be drugs stashed on board?"

He laughed. "You watch too much television, Jamie, but yes, I think I'd like to take a look around."

Jamie nodded. "If we happen to run into an inquisitive deckhand we can always tell him you've been offered a job by Rex. You could be checking on how good security is."

"I'm not sure if you'd make a good detective or a good criminal," Turner said with a sigh.

THE YACHT was still moored at the foot of the wooden steps, still unoccupied. Swiftly they went through the ornate salon and several cabins, lifting bench cushions, probing into the storage underneath, checking cabinets. "I've no idea what I'm looking for," Jamie said after a while.

"Well, you won't find any boxes or bags labeled illicit drugs," Turner said. "Watch out for something that doesn't belong, seems out of place or doesn't seem quite right."

They went through the well-appointed galley, a couple of heads and a forward stateroom, searching every niche and cubbyhole, finding nothing. They were back in the salon, rummaging through the well-stocked bar, when Jamie noticed a change in the atmosphere. Glancing up, she saw a man standing in the entry. In his right hand was a matte black gun.

Turner's hand gripped her arm as though warning her not to try to run. He evidently hadn't realized she was paralyzed with fright. The man with the gun was around her own age—extraordinarily good-looking, tall and muscular and tanned. Light brown hair curled over his forehead and the collar of his yellow tank top. Tan Bermuda shorts showed off his sturdy legs to great advantage. She could suddenly hear Jordan Lathrop's voice saying, "He lifts weights and shows it." What else had Lathrop said? "Hair-trigger temper. *Likes* trouble."

"Hokins, isn't it?" Turner queried, sounding very authoritative. "Perhaps you hadn't heard that I'm working for Rex. Security. Thought I'd start looking things over. Miss Maxwell was hoping to consult with Rex about conference facilities, but he's not home, apparently."

The young man smiled. It was not a pleasant smile, and it didn't in any way involve his eyes.

"You are a card, Inspector Garrett," he said flatly. "Perhaps you'd be kind enough to come this way," he added with exaggerated politeness. "And do bring the bird with you."

She, Jamie supposed, was the bird.

Turner took hold of her hand and gripped it tightly. "Don't do anything silly," he murmured.

Keeping her gaze fixed on the menacing gun, Jamie picked up her purse—she'd set it down so it wouldn't hamper her search—and slung the strap over her shoulder. Hokins gestured with the gun for Jamie and Turner to precede him along the companionway. Another man joined them on the dock, a young black man who said "Hi folks" in a very friendly manner as though he'd been appointed their guide. He was an American. Jamie recognized him and his voice immediately. He was the young man who had sat at a nearby table in the Hog Penny, the man who'd mugged her. He was probably also the man who had sat behind her on the bus with his cap pulled down over his eyes. Her blood ran cold as she saw he was holding a black gun that was a twin to Hokins's.

"Up the garden path," Hokins said, then chuckled. "Always did like leading birds up garden paths."

Evidently whatever he intended doing with them he was going to do in the house. Maybe Rex Putney was home after all, had been home all along. Would he have Hokins just shoot them both in cold blood?

"Keep going straight," Hokins said as they hesitated where the path branched to the front entry of the house.

Turner was obviously as surprised as she was when Hokins's gun waved them onward beyond the house, over the grass and into the parking lot, where Turner's moped looked forlorn next to a compact white car. "In the back..." Hokins ordered.

He sat himself in the front passenger seat, skewed around so that he could keep his gun trained on them. The young black man settled himself behind the wheel. "Keep to the speed limit, Kyle," Hokins cautioned.

Kyle. Kyle Hammond. The man who had hosted the party at which Clyde Kane had gotten sick. He shot Hokins a sour glance. "I'm not stupid, Hoke."

"You are if I say you are," Hokins snarled, transferring the gun's aim to his partner's head.

Jamie shuddered at the murderous expression on his face. Kyle stiffened. Turner leaned forward as much as he could in the cramped rear section, his hand slipping free of Jamie's. Hokins waggled the gun at Turner. "Don't get your hopes up, Garrett. I'm not giving you a chance to play hero. One move from you and *she* gets it. *First.* Understood?"

His eyes met Turner's and Jamie felt Turner's body relax deliberately back into his seat. "Understood," he said.

His fingers found hers again and curled warmly around them. "Where are you taking us?" he asked.

Hokins laughed. "For a drive. Just like in the movies." He picked up a car phone and punched numbers with his gun hand. But he kept his gaze fixed on them, eyes flickering from one to the other. "We're bringing them in," he said cryptically after a moment. "Caught them rummaging round the yacht."

Evidently there was some argument on the other end. His face darkened. "Not much else we could do with them. Not when you keep insisting it should look like an accident." He listened, then laughed. "No, I don't know where Bobby is. He was supposed to be following them this morning, me this afternoon. That's all I know." There was another pause, then he said, "We'll be there in forty minutes."

Where? Jamie wondered. And who was expecting them? Rex Putney? It had to be Rex—they'd been plucked right off his boat by two men who worked for him.

"Didn't take you long to get over your boyfriend, did it?" Hokins said, glancing at Jamie and Turner's clasped hands.

It took her a moment to understand he was referring to Derry. Her body went rigid with horror. She stared at him mutely for a second, then said flatly, "You killed Derry."

His eyes widened in assumed innocence. "It was Bobby's fault, if you want to get technical. He panicked because the guy kept staring at him, like he'd seen him before."

"*Had* he seen him before?" Turner asked in a very calm voice. His hand was gripping Jamie's even tighter than before. Warning her to stay in control, no doubt.

Kyle snorted. "Stupid bloke was taking pictures outside the Tudor Tavern the day the shooting went down. Can you imagine that for bad luck?"

Jamie shivered, remembering that Derry had asked at the Tudor Tavern for picture postcards. There weren't any, so he had evidently returned later and taken pictures himself, and for that he had died.

"Me and Bobby had got out of the van before we saw him," Kyle was explaining. "We'd already started for the pub. Luckily we didn't have our masks on yet. We ducked back into the van soon as he turned that damn camera our way. Didn't occur to us he might have a picture of the van. Occurred to the chief, though. That's why he's the chief. Thinks things through."

"The chief?" Turner asked casually.

Hokins laughed. "The man I work for. We call him that so no one gets to know who he is. That includes you, Inspector. You'll find out who he is soon as we've got you where you can't get away."

"The man you work for," Turner repeated in a thoughtful way. "I understand you've done a lot of work for Rex Putney."

Hokins eyes glinted, but he didn't speak. It was obvious he wasn't going to agree or disagree.

Evidently Turner recognized the same fact. "How did you track Derry down?" he asked.

"Asked around. We knew he had red hair and wore a 'Cheers' cap. When he turned up at the ducking ceremony, I volunteered Anna to get to know him, get him on board the *Coral Queen*."

"She *knew* you were going to kill him?" Jamie blurted out before she could stop herself.

He shook his head. "You kidding? Anna Campbell wouldn't hurt a fly. Sweetest bird I ever—" He broke off, looking briefly sad. "Nah. Anna was supposed to try to get the pictures off him without him knowing. If she failed, we were going to bop him on the head and take them ourselves. If we'd known where he was staying, we would have gone in and taken them and your friend would still be alive. But as it was, your bloke remembered seeing Bobby. My guess is that started him thinking back. He had to have heard about the shooting, but hadn't realized he knew anything about it. But then it hit him, looking at Bobby. You could see it happen. In his eyes."

Jamie shivered and Turner gripped her hand more tightly.

Hokins kept his gun aimed directly at Jamie. "Like I said, it was Bobby's fault. Soon as he saw the bloke recognize him he chucked him overboard and told me to finish him off. Wasn't much I could do about it then. So I followed him in. He'd bounced off the coral and was acting a little winded, so I just bounced his head on the coral a couple more times and let him go down. Then I pretended I was saving him. Made damn sure he was dead before we pulled him out though." He looked directly at Jamie. "He never knew what hit him, sweetheart."

Jamie swallowed a spasm of revulsion, sure she was going to be sick. Her eyes stung, too. Surely she wasn't going to cry, not in front of this monster.

She looked out the window, blinking rapidly. They were passing through a small community's main street. The sun was shining brightly and people were going in and out of shops, waiting for buses. One man was putting a letter in a mail box, schoolchildren were ambling home along the sidewalk, boys in shirts and ties, navy caps and khaki shorts, girls in white blouses and navy jumpers. It all looked unreal; as though she had ceased to be a part of everyday life.

"You removed the film from Derry's camera?" Turner asked. The expression on his face was cold and tight.

"Took all the film he had, used or unused, didn't want to take any chances. Got it while everyone else was watching 'hero' Bobby supposedly trying to breathe the guy back to life." He laughed. "Turned out the chief was right, as usual. Had me develop the film and there it was, front end of the van just showing in the edge of one photograph—license plate dead center."

Jamie rubbed her eyes with her fingertips, which was a mistake—it made them sting more. What on earth was wrong with them? "Did Anna know you'd killed Derry?" she asked.

"Not right away. I told her the bloke got dizzy, stumbled and fell. He'd told her he wasn't feeling too good, and she saw Bobby helping with CPR so she believed me." Without warning, he poked the gun forward almost into Jamie's face. "You hadn't said you thought the bloke's death wasn't an accident, she never would have questioned it. But you had to stick your nose in, shake her up. She got herself convinced I killed the guy. Threatened to tell you. Said she was going to meet you at the cave."

"She told you that?" Jamie said.

He shook his head. "Nah, she wasn't that stupid. She told one of the other girls, Tammi. Tammi told me." His expression changed to a cocky grin. "She rather fancies me, Tammi does." He shook his head. "Even then, I might have talked Anna into keeping quiet, but the chief said to finish her."

"Hoke, maybe you shouldn't—" his partner interrupted.

"Don't you ever watch telly?" Hokins asked him. "Bad guys catch the good guys, they always tell them what happened. Fair play, that is. Tradition." He seemed to find that excruciatingly funny. But even while he laughed his eyes remained cold.

"Who broke into my room?" Jamie asked, more to distract herself from dwelling on her own responsibility for Anna's death than out of curiosity. If she hadn't questioned Anna...

He was still smirking. "That was me, sweetheart. I can move like a cat in the dark. In and out, nobody knows I'm there." Hokins's grin faded as he looked at her. "How'd you know I was there?" He frowned briefly, then his face cleared. "I had to leave the door unlocked, was that it?"

A hair-trigger temper, Lathrop had said. She couldn't risk setting him off by letting him know she *had* been aware of his presence. She grimaced briefly as though agreeing in spite of herself, and he let the subject drop.

"We've been watching you two all along," Hokins volunteered. "Me, Kenyon, Kyle here, Stan—another bloke who works with us. Stan was on you early," he added, looking at Jamie. "Got a report of you asking about Derry Riley."

"A report?" Turner echoed.

This time his offhand tone didn't fool Hokins. He grinned and shook his head. "No names, no pack drill," he said.

"Vance Murdoch?" Turner asked and an amused glint appeared in Hokins's eyes.

"He a police officer?" He shook his head. "Never heard of him. Alexander's the only copper I know about on our side. Stan was standing by at the hotel," he told Jamie. "He saw the inspector here meeting you. He didn't know it was the inspector, though. We never did know that. Thought it was some Yank interfering. Fooled us, you did." Admiration showed in his glance at Turner.

Jamie had been keeping an eye on the route the car was taking. Now they were coming into Hamilton. Trying to read street signs, she became aware that the discomfort around her eyes was increasing. No doubt about it now. The culprit was her old familiar allergy to tobacco. No one was smoking, but someone had, in this car, regularly and heavily.

A thought entered her mind, making it reel. It seemed ludicrous at first, impossible, but the more she examined it, the more it began to make sense. There was one other person she knew who had access to a boat, the person who had known all along that she was asking questions about Derry's death. And Hokins had said someone named Stan was standing by in the hotel lobby!

She exclaimed softly and Turner looked questioningly at her. She shook her head. The car slowed. "You're taking us to Jamie's hotel?" Turner asked, peering out of the window.

"Not quite," Hokins said.

Kyle parked some distance from the dock. Looking toward the hotel, Jamie saw that a gate had been fastened across the footpath between the hibiscus hedges, obviously to discourage wandering guests. It hadn't been closed when Charles had brought her to the *Kiskadee.*

"All right," Hokins said. "Here's what happens now. Kyle here takes the inspector on board. Once he's got him there, I'll follow with the bird. If our heroic policeman causes any trouble, his lady love gets shot. And vice versa. Clear?"

Jamie took a steadying breath as she let go of Turner's hand. She didn't know if she would ever see him again. He looked at her steadily while Kyle came around the car and opened the door. Then he touched her face lightly.

She watched as he walked toward the *Kiskadee,* closely followed by Kyle. His head was up, his lean figure militarily straight, eyes straight ahead. She was quite sure that he was thinking through all possible plans for them to escape, but at the moment, with Kyle walking almost on his heels, his hand alertly tucked over the gun he'd stuck in his jeans pocket, Turner Garrett looked very helpless indeed. So helpless that Jamie's heart seemed to swell as she watched him.

In the middle of her anxiety, there was suddenly and unexpectedly a moment of happiness so intense her veins seemed to sing with it. There was no longer any doubt. She had fallen in love with Turner Garrett.

Almost at once she sobered, knowing that if anything happened to Turner, she would never know happiness again.

If she happened to survive herself. Which seemed doubtful.

"Our turn," Hokins said, getting out of the car. Instantly dismissing from her mind the bizarre escape plans that clamored in her mind, knowing any attempt would endanger Turner, Jamie settled her purse strap on her shoulder, carefully opened her door and stepped out, also. Hokins put an arm around her shoulders, keeping his free hand, with his gun, in his shorts pocket. She shuddered away from his touch. This man had killed Derry. And Anna. His grip tightened.

"What are you planning to do with us?" Jamie asked, keeping her voice even.

He laughed. "We're going to kill you, sweetheart," he said.

Chapter Nineteen

Charles Hollingsworth was leaning on the rail of the *Kiskadee's* flying bridge. He watched Jamie in his usual good-natured but slightly vacuous manner as Hokins prodded her aboard. Jamie abruptly recalled him sitting in her hotel room, watching in just that way, as she set Derry's letter on the coffee table. No doubt he had recognized the stationery and had read Derry's name above the return address. Of course he had wanted the letter. He'd needed to know what Derry had said to her. It was ironic that Derry had been staying at his hotel, and he hadn't known how easy it would be to get the photos from him. Ironic and sickening.

He was smoking his pipe, looking as attractive as usual, his golden hair shining in the sun. Unfortunately evil people did not always wear evil faces. Behind him at the wheel stood a large, young white man with a brown beard and a mass of brown fuzzy hair. Stan? She had seen him before, too.

Kyle was nearby, his gun in his pocket, still aimed at Turner. Turner took hold of her hand.

"How touching," Charles murmured.

"I can't believe you fooled me so completely," Turner said, his face tight and hard.

Charles bent his amused gaze on him. "Didn't think I had the spine for it, old boy? That was the idea."

"What possible excuse could you give yourself for getting involved in this filthy business?" Turner demanded.

"Money," Jamie answered. "Loretta said his family owns a mansion in England. Charles told me he was supporting his family. Besides which," she added, "our Charles is a snob. I think I told you that. He's impressed by anyone with money. So I guess it follows he had to have plenty of his own."

Charles chuckled, not at all offended. "Perhaps money had something to do with my getting started in—the trade, but it didn't take long to restore the family fortunes, Jamie. One can quickly become filthy rich, trafficking in drugs. But it's not just the money—it's the thrill of it all that keeps you going. Living on the edge." He smiled slyly at Turner. "Fooling people."

Abruptly he glanced around, perhaps realizing it wasn't too wise to keep them out in the open, even though no one was nearby. As Hokins pushed Jamie forward, he spoke again. "This really shouldn't have been necessary, Jamie," he said. "I held off as long as I could, thinking you'd eventually give up questioning your friend's death and go home. I do hope you won't judge me too harshly. I certainly didn't intend to be directly involved—Bobby Kenyon was supposed to arrange an accident for both of you. He rang me up on his car telephone, told me you'd been to Putney's house. Seemed an excellent time for you to have an accident. If it didn't work, you were almost bound to blame Putney." He frowned. "Evidently something did go wrong. Bobby's gone missing, which leaves me no choice but to handle this myself."

"Kenyon's under arrest," Turner said. "At this moment, he's spilling all he knows."

Charles smiled. "You don't know Bobby well, do you, Inspector? He's a coward. He's far more afraid of me than he is of going to prison. He won't talk." He looked at Jamie very earnestly. "Derry's death was a bungled affair. It should never have happened. As for Anna, she brought it on herself, as you have. I'm sorry. I *do* abhor wasting lives."

"What about the lives you ruin with your damn drugs?" Turner said harshly.

Charles raised skeptical eyebrows. "The people who use them make the choice." Jamie felt Turner's hand tighten painfully on hers. She could sense energy pulsing through him. For a moment she was afraid he was going to lunge forward and tackle Charles, but he evidently thought better of it. Taking a deep breath, he remained still.

A moment later Hokins ushered them below decks and into a small cabin. A movement of Hokins's gun sent them to sit side by side on a bunk. Turner instantly put his arm around Jamie. She clutched her purse in both arms as though it was a shield.

After a low-voiced conversation with Kyle, Hokins left. Kyle stood against the closed door, his gun hand steady. Jamie felt despair wash over her. They were going to die, she and Turner, they weren't going to get out of this situation alive.

"You knew it was Hollingsworth before you saw him, didn't you?" Turner said, obviously trying to distract her.

Jamie nodded. "I guessed in the car." She let out a breath. "I wish I could claim great powers of deduction," she added. "But it was my nose that told me." She explained and Turner gave a short sharp laugh.

"Glad you're having such a good time," Kyle said.

"We still have hanging on the books here," Turner commented.

Kyle's grin was without mirth. "I'm already in deep enough to get the rope. Bobby and me, we did the Tudor

Tavern job together." He chuckled. "Chief let Bobby do it, he wanted to so bad, but he was only allowed to aim at the walls. Chief figured that was safer for all concerned. Me, I got to do the two guys." He seemed proud of the fact.

He cocked an eyebrow at Turner. "Don't think you can con me into helping you out of this mess. Those two guys at the Tudor Tavern thought they could get away with disobeying orders. Got greedy. Held on to a lot more money than they were supposed to. Chief didn't take kindly to that. Wouldn't take kindly to me letting you two go even if I wanted to. Which I don't." He squinted at Turner suddenly. "Heard you questioned my lady—Linda. Didn't talk, did she? She's a good kid. Wasn't even supposed to be working—I'd made sure of that, but the stupid bartender got sick and she had to go in."

"Mr. Hollingsworth's the chief, is he?" Turner said casually.

"He is. Got him some higher-ups in Florida, I've heard tell. But out here he's the dude in charge."

They were underway. Jamie could feel the throb of powerful engines vibrating under her feet. She looked worriedly at Turner, who tightened his grip around her shoulders. "I really did believe Rex Putney was the chief," he said.

Kyle snorted. "You were supposed to," he said.

Turner ignored him. Still looking at Jamie, he said, "It was very clever of Hollingsworth, don't you think, employing only men who worked for Rex. The man topside with him, Stan Craymer, is another ex-con Rex employed. Hollingsworth had his pick of criminals, all nicely to hand. If anything went wrong, all indications would point to Rex rather than himself." He shook his head. "Pretty stupid of me," he said bitterly. "I believed exactly what Hollingsworth wanted me to believe."

"You had reason to," Jamie pointed out. "Do you think Charles will get away with killing us?" she added, trying to sound calm, but only halfway succeeding. The boat was speeding up now, heading out of the harbor toward the open sea.

"No way," he said, copying her favorite expression one more time. He smiled at her. "Those words make me feel nostalgic. Remember when I got nostalgic about my old friends and the games we used to play?"

His gaze held hers, his eyes darker than ever. She was pretty sure he was referring to the boyhood code he and Baldwin and Reynolds had used. "Does it rain in Spain?" she asked to demonstrate her understanding.

"Definitely not," Turner said very firmly. Okay, they couldn't make a run for it, she hadn't thought they could.

"Won't matter to you if it does rain," Kyle said, with another of his habitual snorts.

Jamie kept her gaze fixed on Turner's face. "I keep thinking how nice it was in the attic," he said.

Adrenaline shot through her body, alerting it to action. Turner was telling her he planned to attack their captors, which should have made her very nervous, considering it was the bad guys who held the guns. It was probably the prospect of action that made her feel better. Anything was preferable to going to her death without a fight.

He leaned over and kissed her. "When?" she breathed.

"Soon," he said against her mouth.

Hokins returned a moment later carrying a bottle of black rum. And his gun. "Here's the plan then," he said cheerfully. "The story will be you took out one of the hotel's motorboats." He glanced at Kyle. "Rupert's gone ahead with one."

"That would be Rupert Westerhope," Turner said.

Hokins ignored him. "Mr. Hollingsworth will explain that Miss Maxwell asked to borrow the boat for her and the inspector to take a little pleasure cruise," he went on. "Terribly sad and all that. Something wrong with the engine. Got it out to sea and it blew up." He beamed at Turner and Jamie. "Our Rupert's good at stuff like that." He gave Jamie a sympathetic smile that was patently phony. "No need to be scared, ducks, you'll be unconscious, won't feel a thing."

"Going to be a little hard to get away with, if anything goes wrong," Turner suggested. "If the postmortem shows we were knocked out, the pathologist's going to—"

"Oh, we're not going to *knock* you out," Hokins said. "That's what the rum's for." He held the bottle up for them to look at. "Good quality stuff, this is." Uncapping the bottle, he held it toward Turner. "Gents first?" he suggested.

Turner got off the bunk and took a couple of steps forward, accepting the bottle without comment.

"Don't hold back, now," Hokins said. "There's plenty more where that came from. If one bottle doesn't do the job we'll pour another one down you."

Turner frowned. "You surely don't expect us to drink out of the bottle, do you?" he said coolly.

Hokins laughed. "You've got style, Garrett, I'll give you that." He grinned at Kyle and gestured at the bureau. "You heard the gent. Get him a glass."

Turner took the glass, when Kyle proffered it, and poured a generous amount into it. Then he hesitated, his whole body suddenly slumping in an attitude of defeat. Jamie's heart sank. He couldn't mean to give up, surely? He glanced at Hokins. His whole posture had changed in some subtle way. As if he were about to plead with the man. "May I give my lady a last kiss?" he asked.

Hokins nodded, grinning.

Jamie slid off the bunk and went to stand with Turner, both hands still clutching her purse.

"This is better than the movies," Kyle said as Turner leaned to her and kissed her gently on the mouth.

"It's more like being in the attic," Turner said clearly.

"What is this attic you keep talking about?" Kyle asked as Turner raised the glass in a mock toast to him and Hokins. "You two been up to some hanky-panky? I *knew* I should have watched through your bedroom window."

Hokins turned his head to grin at his colleague. For one second his attention was distracted.

Stepping forward, Turner flung the contents of the glass in Kyle's face, then reversed the bottle in his right hand, bringing it down smartly on Hokins's gun hand. Rum spewed all over. The gun clattered to the floor. As Turner closed with Kyle, Jamie swung her heavy purse in a full circle, delivering a hard blow to the most vulnerable area of Hokins's anatomy. Hokins turned slightly green and bent double. Before he could begin to recover, Turner's foot came up and connected with his chin. Hokins crumpled to the floor. Kyle was already down there, victim of a right hook to the jaw that Jamie had barely caught from the corner of her eye.

"Get the other gun," Turner said, picking up Kyle's.

Jamie didn't hesitate. Within seconds they were heading aft. But before they reached the stern ladder, they heard footsteps coming down. Next to them was a large wooden locker. Turner lifted the lid. Jamie boosted herself up and dropped in on a large pile of life jackets. Turner was right behind her, pulling the lid closed after him.

The heavy footsteps hit bottom and started forward. Neither of them moved. The smell of rum was very strong; it had splashed both of them.

The footsteps stopped. A door opened. A minute later they heard a flushing sound. Someone was using the head. Jamie bit her lower lip hard, praying that whoever it was didn't check to see how Hokins and Kyle were making out....

The door opened and closed. The footsteps receded. Stan, Jamie thought, judging by the heaviness of the footsteps.

Turner and Jamie pulled themselves upright on the shifting mass of life jackets. "What now?" she whispered.

He raised the lid of the locker and peered out. "Now we replay *Mutiny on the Bounty*." His hand found Jamie's face and caressed it. "You were marvelous," he said.

"So were you."

The brilliance of his smile enveloped her like a blessing. "I've never met a woman quite like you, Jamie Maxwell," he said. "I'm going to do my damnedest to get us out of this alive, but before we start, I want you to know I love you."

Her breath stopped in her throat. "Likewise," was all she could manage to say.

He shook his head. "Not good enough."

"I love you," she said.

He kissed her hard, then vaulted lightly out of the locker. "Let's have a chat with our friend Charles," he said, reaching up to help her out.

Gingerly thrusting the gun into the waistband of her jeans, Jamie took hold of the edge of the locker. But just as she got one leg over the side, she heard a sound to her right. She swung her head in time to see Kyle coming straight for Turner, about to jump him. Letting go of Jamie, Turner swung around and let loose one of his very effective kicks. This one sent Kyle flying. He landed some distance down the companionway. But then as Turner swung back to Jamie, Kyle came at him again. This time Turner almost fell, knocked off balance by his own momentum. Reaching for the first thing that came to hand, Jamie grabbed one of the life jackets and socked Kyle on the side of the head with it, putting every ounce of strength she possessed into the blow.

It was just enough to knock Kyle off balance and turn him around. One of the seams couldn't take the strain. It burst open, showering dozens of Ziploc bags all over. One of the bags also burst, letting loose a cloud of white powder.

Easy to see why cocaine was called snow, Jamie thought.

Turner reversed the gun as neatly as he had the bottle and tapped Kyle behind the ear. The man went down with only a slight whimpering sound. "Well, well," Turner said. "I've heard of the stuff being packed in frozen broccoli and hollow fence posts, but life preservers seem a bit ironic."

A second later, Jamie was out of the locker and running behind Turner to the companionway steps. At the top, after securing the door with a key that was conveniently in the lock, they paused. No one was in sight. "I didn't see anyone except Hokins, Kyle, Stan and Charles, did you?" Turner murmured.

Jamie shook her head. "The only other person mentioned was Rupert, and he's supposedly gone ahead with the motorboat."

Turner took a deep breath. "There's only one way to find out if Charles has any reinforcements within reach," he said softly, taking Kyle's pistol from his pocket.

Still leaning on the rail, with Stan at the helm, Charles wasn't aware of Turner until he came up behind him and pressed the gun against his spine. His right hand immediately went inside his jacket, but Turner was there before him. Swinging the man around he pulled a gun from his inside pocket and passed it back to Jamie for safekeeping. He then frisked Stan and came up with another.

"Considering this is a country that doesn't allow guns, we seem to have more than our share," he commented, adding to Stan, "Let's head back to Hamilton, shall we? Without trying even the smallest of tricks. I'm not used to handling a gun. Your boss just might have an accident if you're not careful."

Jamie looked at him, alarmed. He was pointing the gun steadily at Charles, who had gone very pale. The expression on Turner's face was stone-hard, his eyes cold. He was gripping the pistol so tightly his knuckles were blue white.

For one long minute, Turner continued to stare coldly at Charles, then he drew in a breath and seemed to shake himself slightly. Jamie let out a long breath of relief.

"You might keep an eye on the door back there," Turner told her. "If the others manage to get it open and show their heads, beat them down with your handbag."

"I left it in the cabin," Jamie told him.

"Then I suppose you'll have to shoot them. Which is probably more humane at that." Obviously she was going to be in for considerable teasing about using her purse as a weapon.

There wasn't much conversation on the way back into the harbor. Jamie imagined Turner was as exhausted as she was. Adrenaline had been rushing around in their bodies for some time; now that the danger was over they were due for a slump.

She couldn't resist asking Charles one question though, just as they were coming into the Victoria's dock. "Who did pack Derry's suitcase?" she asked.

His smile was as charming as ever, though irritable around the edges. "I did," he said. "I even posted it to Riley's mother. There never was a police officer involved. That was just a spontaneous invention, intended to cause some confusion in the ranks." He laughed shortly. "I had to threaten Loretta with the sack to get her to say *she* did the packing. Damn woman's made my life hell ever since."

"But you were in England," she protested. His blue eyes gleamed. He'd *said* he was in England when Derry drowned. But no one had checked. No one had suspected the easygoing hotel manager with the charming smile. Why should they?

Chapter Twenty

Superintendent Baldwin leaned his arms on his desk and beamed at Turner and Jamie. "Well, I suppose that is everything then," he said in his lilting West Indian accent.

They were in the superintendent's office at Wallbridge—Turner and Jamie, the superintendent, and Tom Reynolds, Turner's reporter friend, a fair-haired man with a friendly smile and merry gray eyes. Tom had been scribbling continuously as Turner and Jamie recounted their adventures, looking up to grin at one or the other when they described the hairiest parts.

"Not quite everything," Turner objected. "I think we're entitled to some reciprocity. We'd already spent half the night dictating our formal statements before you decided you wanted to hear details in person. We were happy to oblige. But early on while we were changing our rum-soaked togs and taking a criminally short nap, you and your minions questioned our erstwhile captors. What did you find out?"

Baldwin glanced at Jamie, a frown on his round face.

"Jamie has earned the right to hear the rest of the story," Turner insisted. "You should have seen her swinging that lethal purse of hers."

"Point taken." Baldwin's smile split his dark face, showing all his even white teeth. "I am most happy to report

Charles has chirped like an English sparrow. Hoping to make a deal, he has named names from all over Europe and the U.S."

"There isn't going to be a deal, is there?" Turner demanded, looking alarmed.

Baldwin shook his head. "Not for this man." He leaned over his desk and looked solemnly at Jamie. "Charles Hollingsworth is only the tip of the iceberg, Jamie. He is part of a drug organization that has headquarters in London and Milan and Florida." He glanced at Tom who was still scribbling industriously. "This last is not for publication, Tom. Not until every last person on Hollingsworth's list is in custody."

Tom grinned. "Have I ever let the cat out of the bag too early, Dunch?" He looked down at his notes. "How did they get the stuff into Bermuda?" he asked.

Baldwin's face took on a wry expression. "Ah, that was the interesting part, don't you see? The drugs came out of South America by boat and were transferred well beyond Bermuda's limits. The Kiskadee has some ingenious waterproof pods under the hull, held in place with nets. Divers, including Hokins and Kenyon, lashed the pods into place, then later unloaded the contents into the life preservers. All involved are being exhaustively questioned of course, including Linda Belant, the waitress you talked to. And we are negotiating to bring Cornell Alexander back to Bermuda."

He glanced at Jamie. "We are all as happy as sandboys, Miss Maxwell, yet you are looking sad. What troubles you?"

"I feel responsible for Anna's death," she told him. "If I hadn't come storming in here to ask about Derry's death, Anna would still be alive."

Turner took hold of her hand. "And Charles Hollingsworth might have gone merrily on importing drugs and condemning countless numbers of people to a living death,'' he pointed out.

She shook her head, though she did feel better, looking at it that way. ''You would have caught him eventually,'' she said.

They smiled at each other. Jamie caught her breath at the love that glowed in Turner's dark eyes. Then she realized Tom Reynolds and the superintendent were exchanging grins. She sat back in her chair, feeling herself flush idiotically.

Tom Reynolds stood up and looked at Turner. ''I need to get this story filed if we're to have you exonerated in the evening news. I'd best hop to it.'' He smiled at Jamie and shook hands with her. ''I look forward to seeing you again, Jamie. I'm glad our boyhood code proved useful.'' He darted a sly glance Turner's way. ''I'm also delighted to see our Inspector Garrett brought low.''

''Brought low?'' Jamie inquired after Tom had left.

Turner gave her a sheepish grin. ''I imagine he's referring to my fairly obvious . . . affection for you. He and his wife have been trying to match me up for a long time. Without success.''

She smiled at him, wishing she knew what word he'd substituted affection for. ''He's going to publish the truth about your so-called suspension?''

Turner nodded and began to speak, but the superintendent interrupted. ''While you were making your statement, Jamie, I informed Turner that Walter Seaton emerged from his coma yesterday. Tom will inform the public of that truth also.''

They all stood. Baldwin shook hands with Turner, then with Jamie. ''Bermuda owes you both a debt beyond measure,'' he said, then added to Turner, ''I expect you're as relieved as I am to know Murdoch's in the clear.''

''He is?'' Jamie queried as Turner nodded.

Turner smiled at her. "Vance's wife got an enormous bonus from her company. Hence the sailboat. Vance may never be thrifty, but he's not a criminal."

"What now?" Jamie asked as they walked along the hall.

He grinned at her and put an arm around her. She wanted to lean into it but was aware that someone could appear at any moment. "I know you're tired," Turner said, "but I'd really like to look in on Walter, just to be sure he's all right."

Jamie nodded agreement, a little reluctantly. Were they never going to be alone? When Turner looked at her, his eyes were full of promises. She wanted to know what those promises were. All the same, she was anxious to meet Walter Seaton, the unwitting reason for most of her earlier suspicions of Turner.

THE MAN IN THE hospital bed seemed extrememly old and sick. His dark skin had a gray cast. His eyelids seemed translucent. Now that he was out of the coma, however, his doctor expected him to recover.

"How are you feeling, Walter?" Turner asked him.

"Cool-cool," the old man said. "Thought I'd had my chocklits for a while though." His brow furrowed in thought. "You happen to know what made me so sick, Inspector Garrett? Isn't arrybody wants to tell me."

"Your old friend Luke Darwin crowned you with a bottle of rum," Turner told him.

Walter squinted. "Now why'd he want to do that?" His eyes gleamed. "Did arrybody save the bottle?"

Turner laughed. "The bottle broke, Walter, you've a hard head."

Walter sighed, then looked fretful. "Hope nobody's going to ax me to pay the bills. I didn't ax to be brought here."

"Don't worry about it," Turner said, getting up to go. "The police department's going to take care of it. And when you're well, we're going to find you a place to stay."

"Why would you do that?"

"To thank you for your help," Turner said.

Walter still looked puzzled when they left the room.

Jamie glanced at Turner as they headed for the stairs. She was wearing clean jeans and her favorite green blouse but Turner was elegant in his Bermuda gentleman's outfit. He looked as exhilarated as she felt. Even though they had been up most of the night after a horrendous day, they were both on a high that wouldn't quit. Success was a powerful stimulant.

"Are we finally free?" she asked as they started down the hospital's main stairway.

About to answer, Turner stepped aside for a man coming up. The man stopped and Turner did a double take.

"Mr. Stacey," Jamie exclaimed.

Gordon Stacey nodded gravely at her then looked directly at Turner, an expression on his lean weathered face that Turner could only characterize as sheepish. "Dropped in at Wallbridge this morning," Stacey said. "Had to consult with Superintendent Baldwin about a client of mine."

Turner waited.

"Superintendent told me the whole story. Importation, conspiracy to import. Trafficking. Millions of dollars worth of cocaine. Murder. Hollingsworth, who'd have believed it?"

"Who indeed," Turner said.

"Superintendent told me I might find you here. Owe you an apology. Acting above and beyond the call of duty. Undercover work. Drug busting. Admirable. Going to ring the commissioner and tell him so." He held out his hand tentatively. "Don't suppose you'd want to shake? Reprehensible, way I behaved."

"No problem," Turner said, shaking the man's hand firmly.

Stacey actually beamed, an expression that didn't quite fit his old soldier's face. Then he gave a short laugh that was more like a bark. "Going to talk to Rex later," he said. "Advise him to rethink his whole employment policy. No more ex-cons. I expect he'll give it serious consideration."

They all laughed. Then Jamie looked at Stacey. "Now that Mr. Hollingsworth's going to be out of circulation, who'll run the Victoria?" she asked.

"We'll bring in a new manager." Something that was almost a dry smile flickered across Stacey's face. "Have to check his references a little more carefully, wouldn't you say?"

Jamie gave the man the full benefit of her green-eyed, thousand-watt smile. Turner came alert. "Have you considered putting Loretta in charge?" she asked.

Stacey frowned. "Miss Dean?"

"She's been running the hotel all along while Charles indulged his...extra-curricular activities. He was mostly window dressing anyway. Seems to me it might be fair to let her continue as before, but as the official manager."

Stacey looked bemused. "She was running things?"

"Very efficiently. I'm sure the rest of the staff would confirm that, if you were to ask them."

"I shall do so," Stacey said, sketching her a salute.

"Can't resist interfering, can you?" Turner teased as they continued downstairs.

She smiled sweetly, innocently, then became serious. "Sometime soon, I want to go out in a boat to the place where Derry drowned," she said slowly. "I'd like to lay some flowers in the water."

"I'll arrange it, of course," Turner said promptly. "Perhaps Jordan Lathrop would take up out."

She nodded. "I'd like to thank him before I leave."

The words echoed in the stairwell. Now that they knew what had happened to Derry, now that all the people involved had been rounded up, there was no reason for her to stay. To add to the despair this thought brought, her ruthless brain picked this moment to remember what Turner had said about his former marriage. "It taught me not to get married."

She felt as if someone had socked her right in the middle of her abdomen. Turner had said he loved her, but that had been in the heat of the battle. It didn't commit him to anything.

She tried to ignore the hollow feeling that was growing inside her. If she didn't want to be wounded too badly, she'd better keep everything between them good and light. "As I was saying," she said, forcing a smile. "Are we free now?"

"Why don't we go to my place and talk about it?" Turner murmured, with a suggestive lift of one aristocratic eyebrow.

Her smile became demure. "I would like that," she said.

Turner took a large tartan blanket from the hall linen closet and added it to the things he'd already arranged on the floor—a picnic basket with an ice bucket, champagne, glasses, a couple of papayas cut in two, a honeydew melon sliced and ready to eat, a pair of bran and raisin muffins, cutlery.

Just as he picked up the basket, Jamie appeared in the bedroom doorway, wearing a loose shirt over a couple of strips of green flowered cotton that left nothing to his imagination. "Maybe the picnic can wait," he said huskily.

Jamie shook her head. "Something always interferes with me getting into the water. This time I'm going to do it."

"Stubborn wench." He said it lovingly. How could he speak in any other way to this incredible woman who had faced death beside him and had fought back and come out smiling?

Handing Jamie the blanket, he led the way out of the house and across the garden to the stone steps that went down to the beach. When they reached the bottom, Jamie spread the blanket on the sand and sat down on it, while he carefully placed the basket in the shade of the limestone cliff.

"Aren't we going to eat?" she asked.

He shook his head. "You wanted to swim. We'll swim."

"But you didn't bring a swimsuit down."

He didn't bother to answer. He had a point to prove here and he wasn't going to allow any distractions. Looking at her, he slowly and deliberately took off his blazer and dropped it carelessly on the sand. Without haste, he did the same with his shirt, tie, shoes, socks, Bermuda shorts and underpants, letting the clothes fall wherever they wanted to.

She caught her breath when he stood naked before her, but almost at once mischief showed in her green eyes. "You aren't going to fold your clothes?" she asked.

He shook his head. "I'm a reformed character."

She nodded, then stood up herself. With dramatic ceremony, she shrugged out of her shirt, folded it with exaggerated care and placed it precisely on the edge of the blanket. She did the same with the two pieces of her bikini. "Never let it be said I'm not willing to meet a man half way," she said solemnly.

He raised an eyebrow. "What about all the way?"

She took a step forward into his arms and he kissed her gently, then set her away as passion threatened to send his senses reeling. "Not yet," he said. "Dunch has given me a week off. I don't want to burn out in the first five minutes."

She laughed. "Then I guess we'd better go swimming."

Lifting her easily he carried her into the water, wading out until he was waist-deep, and kissed her again.

They played for some time, touching each other, kissing. Then they floated on their backs with their toes up, holding hands, letting the sun shine on them. Until at last Turner's patience left him and he reached for her and pulled her to him and moved his hands urgently over her.

Her mouth closed on his and blood surged through him as he recognized a passion equal to his own. Swinging her into his arms again, half running, half stumbling, he carried her back to the tartan blanket waiting on the pink coral sand. And there he made love to her, gently at first, then more roughly as she quickened to him.

Afterward, they lay for a long time in the sunshine, drained but happy, sleeping a little, kissing lazily when they awakened, moving together again, then finally separating and sitting up to look around, slightly dazzled by the sunlight.

"Where did my bikini go?" Jamie asked.

Turner grinned. "Haven't the foggiest."

She made a face at him, then got up and went to fetch the picnic basket from its rocky shelf. They ate in contented silence and with good appetite, then Jamie expertly opened the champagne, popping the cork with abandon, poured a healthy-size portion into each of the flutes he'd brought along and handed him one. "What shall we drink to?" she asked.

"The merger," he said promptly.

She raised her eyebrows. "What kind of merger did you have in mind, Inspector?"

He was suddenly afraid. He had intended keeping this whole thing light so he wouldn't frighten her off. Now he felt solemn, serious, and he was afraid she'd make jokes. "What kind of merger do you want it to be?" he asked as lightly as he could manage. "I do remember that you were against marriage. As I recall you felt marriage restricted a woman. You said something about wanting to stop for latté with the girls after work, going to conferences whenever you wanted to."

She nodded. "I did say all of that, didn't I?"

He stroked her fine cheekbone with his thumb. "I want you to know that I will never try to stop you from doing anything you want to do, or make you do anything you don't want to do."

She did so love him when he sounded stuffy. She cupped his face with both hands, looking directly into his eyes. "I love you, Turner Digby Garrett. But you may have realized that patience isn't one my virtues. If this is supposed to be a marriage proposal, will you please say so?"

"There's still the matter of my job," he said. "It's not easy for a woman to be married to a police officer."

Her face came alive with mischief again. "I just might become a police officer myself. I wasn't bad at the job."

"True."

"At the very least," she continued, "I have a unique understanding of some of the stuff you get involved in."

"That's true too."

"Your job is what makes you the person you are, Turner Garrett," she said. "I can see that anyone who loved you would worry every time you might be in danger, but I would never want you to change what you do. You're very good at it."

He still looked worried. "What about *your* job?" he said.

She frowned. "That is a problem," she said with mock solemnity. "You wouldn't want to move to Boston, not when you're dedicated to keeping all the serpents out of this Eden of yours. So..." She paused. "I guess I'll just have to relocate." She gave an exaggerated sigh. "It's going to be a disaster. My brothers will love this place. They'll arrive en masse, with all their wives and children."

If she lived to be a hundred, she would never tire of watching his smile make its appearance. "You'd give up your job, just like that?" he asked.

She nodded. "I've always wanted to start my own meeting planning company," she said. "The Victoria might be my first customer. I've got Stacey considering Loretta for the manager's job, remember. She told me she'd be happy to work with me if she ever got to be in charge of the world." She looked him in the eye. "However, before I apply for a business loan, and send invitations to my brothers, maybe we should pin down what kind of merger you have in mind."

"Marital, of course," he said.

"You said your first marriage taught you not to get married."

"I told you, I'm a reformed character. Besides, Digby and Rose are very conservative people. You can tell that by the way they dress. They would never agree to anything less than marriage."

"I've become very fond of Digby and Rose," she murmured. "I miss them already."

"We could keep them around for our more private moments."

"Like now?"

"Exactly." He looked deeply into her unearthly green eyes. "What do you say to my proposal, Rosie?"

She smiled. "I say yes, Digby."

Not a minute later, they were lying on the blanket again, holding each other close, kissing as enthusiastically as though they'd invented new ways to do it. The Bermuda sun shone down on them from a clear blue sky, glinting on their golden skin. The breeze, fresh with the perfume of flowers

nd salt-scrubbed air, touched them and ruffled their hair,
nd the turquoise sea, splashing over ridges of coral, crept
lose to their blanket, then backed away, leaving them
lone. . . .

HARLEQUIN®

I N T R I G U E®

HARLEQUIN INTRIGUE INVITES YOU TO

A HALLOWEEN QUARTET

1993 Keepsake

CHRISTMAS

Stories

Capture the spirit and romance of Christmas with KEEPSAKE CHRISTMAS STORIES, a collection of three stories by favorite historical authors. The perfect Christmas gift!

Don't miss these heartwarming stories, available in November wherever Harlequin books are sold:

ONCE UPON A CHRISTMAS by Curtiss Ann Matlock
A FAIRYTALE SEASON by Marianne Willman
TIDINGS OF JOY by Victoria Pade

ADD A TOUCH OF ROMANCE TO YOUR HOLIDAY SEASON WITH KEEPSAKE CHRISTMAS STORIES!

HX93

HARLEQUIN®
INTRIGUE®

"I AM BETRAYED"

In the still of the night, those were the words spoken to
Emma Devlin by her husband, Frank . . . from beyond the
grave. She'd given him no cause to doubt her devotion, yet he
haunted her waking hours and disturbed her dreams.

Harlequin Intrigue brings you a chilling tale of love and
disloyalty . . .

#241 FLESH AND BLOOD
by Caroline Burnes
September 1993

In an antebellum mansion, Emma finds help from the oddest of
sources: in the aura of a benevolent ghost—and in the arms of
a gallant Confederate colonel.

For a spine-tingling story about a love that transcends time,
don't miss #241 FLESH AND BLOOD, available now from
Harlequin Intrigue.

FAD2

Calloway Corners

In September, Harlequin is proud to bring readers four
involving, romantic stories about the Calloway sisters,
set in Calloway Corners, Louisiana. Written by four of
Harlequin's most popular and award-winning authors,
you'll be enchanted by these sisters and the men
they love!

MARIAH by Sandra Canfield
JO by Tracy Hughes
TESS by Katherine Burton
EDEN by Penny Richards

As an added bonus, you can enter a sweepstakes contest
to win a trip to Calloway Corners, and meet all four
authors. Watch for details in all Calloway Corners books
in September.

HARLEQUIN CELEBRATES
THE SEASON OF SHARING
AND FAMILY WITH

Friends, Families, Lovers

Harlequin introduces the latest member in its family of
seasonal collections. Following in the footsteps of the popular
My Valentine, Just Married and *Harlequin Historical Christmas
Stories*, we are proud to present FRIENDS, FAMILIES,
LOVERS. A collection of three new contemporary romance
stories about America at its best, about welcoming others into
the circle of love.... Stories to warm your heart...

By three leading romance authors:

**KATHLEEN EAGLE
SANDRA KITT
RUTH JEAN DALE**

Available in October, wherever
Harlequin books are sold.